Acclaim for *Schroder*

"4 stars! Like Nabokov's Humbert Humbert, Schroder is charming and deceptive, likable and flawed, a conman who has a clever way with words. Schroder's tale is deeply engaging, and Gaige's writing is surprising and original, but the real pull of this magnetic novel is the moral ambiguity the reader feels."
                                                                —*People*

"Gaige writes beautifully...The novel's climactic chapter is also its best conceived: the item that brings about Schroder's downfall is perfect, both dramatic and mundane. The reader will realize that he or she has been given every detail necessary to see what was coming, yet didn't, which is plot-making of the highest order."   —*New York Times Book Review*

"With Schroder, Gaige has achieved a remarkable feat. How impressive to have created a protagonist who's brilliant, narcissistic, creepy and unhinged, yet somehow sympathetic... Gaige is such a masterful writer that she makes Schroder seem more pitiful than hateful...As unlikely as it sounds, you'll be half-rooting for this lost soul to prevail."   —*USA Today*

"It is to the credit of Amity Gaige, that her third novel, SCHRODER, transforms this thriller plot into a deeply moving tale...What distinguishes SCHRODER is its insight and language...Ms. Gaige excels at landscapes; her writing has the still, clear beauty of a mountain lake."   —*Economist*

"Brilliantly eliciting sympathy where, theoretically, none is deserved, this is a tense, ambitious, bravura exploration of the physical and psychological limits of identity—how we are seen by others, and what we make of ourselves."
                                                        —*Sunday Times* (UK)

"The measure of Gaige's great gifts as a storyteller is that she persuades you to believe in a situation that shouldn't be believable, and to love a narrator who shouldn't be lovable. Seldom has such a daring concept for a novel been grounded in such an appealing character."

—Jonathan Franzen, author of
Freedom and *The Corrections*

"[A] superb novel...Gaige makes fraudulent, kidnapping Eric utterly sympathetic—heartbreakingly so—which is part of this book's intelligence and depth. We have so little distance from him that we become myopic in our desire to have his outrageous escapade work, even though we know it cannot."

—*San Francisco Chronicle*

"Urgent and concise...Gaige's storytelling [is] effortlessly spontaneous."
—*Guardian* (UK)

"Daring...a clean, suspenseful, economical story that is also a clever act of social commentary...As a case study of the unreliable narrator, SCHRODER is beautifully managed... [Gaige] is an accomplished writer, and the novel elegantly navigates its ethical razor's edge, bringing the reader along on a kind of joyride gone wrong...half sympathy-inducing mea culpa, half a bristling act of bravado and self-ignorance... Novelists like Gaige remind us that we live not in the age of the nineteenth-century marriage plot but in the era of the twenty-first century divorce plot...Gaige writes with a cool strangeness, a strong sense of style...Schroder is by turns dry, peculiar, expansive, and visionary."
—*Bookforum*

"Heartbreaking...could be *O My Darling* author Amity Gaige's breakout work. Starring a doggedly compelling lead character and Gaige's signature smooth prose, this novel wows with its exacting, subtle grace...She mixes warmth, lovely tenderness, and wit with fear and loathing, nakedness and shame, moving her narrative swiftly to an end that hits like a punch in the gut...An engrossing paradox. And Gaige is a talent who deserves attention."   —*BookPage*

"[A] fascinating psychological portrait of love, longing, and self-loathing...Written as a jailhouse confession to his ex-wife, SCHRODER's closest literary relative is probably *Lolita* (minus the pedophilia): The compellingly unreliable narrator of European background, the East Coast road trip with the precocious child, the narcissism, the unsavory motels, the whiff of danger. SCHRODER easily stands up to the comparison...And yet the book, at its heart, is a love story. Schroder may be deluded—and a woefully irresponsible parent—but his touching, sincere adoration of his daughter and ex-wife is his great redemption."   —*Los Angeles Times*

"You will not want to put this book down. You will want to read it in one big gulp. This is a bullet of a novel, aimed at our pieties about parenthood and familial love. You won't soon forget Schroder or his daughter or the sentences that bring them to life. To those who know Gaige's first two novels, it's no surprise she's produced another stunner. To those who don't, you're in for a treat."

—Adam Haslett, author of *Union Atlantic*,
and the *New York Times* bestselling short story
collection *You Are Not a Stranger Here*

"Terrific...SCHRODER grabs you early on, holds you with its lyrical prose and surprising insights and lingers in the mind long afterward." —*Pittsburgh Post-Gazette*

"SCHRODER is a beautifully told story about how a father's undeniable love for his young child can be distorted by the pressure he experiences at the thought of being cut off from her...we all are destined to fall short of our expectations, to fail to match our lovingly painted self-portraits, some of us more dramatically and tragically than others. It's but one of many penetrating insights that transport Amity Gaige's novel from the realm of mere artifice to the status of real art."
—BookReporter.com

"To say that the piece of fiction Gaige has produced is successful is a serious understatement...SCHRODER is refreshingly bereft of the formal wizardry that characterizes much of the postmodern fiction that attracted academic interest in the second half of the twentieth century. This is good and this is nice. Instead, Gaige turns to the ineluctable parts of life that go by big-sounding names: love and fear, for instance.... Not to mention the fact that this book is great fun to read. It is relentlessly compelling in the way that mystery stories can sometimes be." —*Artvoice*

Schroder

Schroder

a novel

AMITY GAIGE

NEW YORK **12** BOSTON
TWELVE

Twelve
Hachette Book Group
237 Park Avenue
New York, NY 10017

www.HachetteBookGroup.com

Printed in the United States of America

RRD-C

First trade edition: October 2013
10 9 8 7 6 5 4 3 2 1

Twelve is an imprint of Grand Central Publishing.
The Twelve name and logo are trademarks of Hachette Book Group, Inc.

The Hachette Speakers Bureau provides a wide range of authors for speaking
events. To find out more, go to www.hachettespeakersbureau.com or call
(866) 376-6591.

The publisher is not responsible for websites (or their content)
that are not owned by the publisher.

The Library of Congress has cataloged the hardcover as follows:
Gaige, Amity, 1972–
Schroder / Amity Gaige. — 1st ed.
p. cm.
ISBN 978-1-4555-1213-3
1. Fathers and daughters—Fiction. I. Title.
PS3557.A3518S37 2013
813'.54—dc23
2012013882

ISBN 978-1-4555-1212-6 (pbk.)

For my father
Frederick H. Gaige
1937–2009

Schroder

here is the deepest secret nobody knows
(here is the root of the root and the bud of the bud
and the sky of the sky of a tree called life;which grows
higher than soul can hope or mind can hide)
and this is the wonder that's keeping the stars apart

i carry your heart(i carry it in my heart)
                                    —E. E. Cummings

What follows is a record of where Meadow and I have been since our disappearance.

My lawyer says I should tell the whole story. Where we went, what we did, who we met, etc. As you know, Laura, I'm not a reticent person. I'm talkative—you could even say chatty—for a man. But I haven't spoken a word for days. It's a vow I've taken. My mouth tastes old and damp, like a cave. It turns out I'm not very good at being silent. There are castles of things I want to tell you. Which might explain the enthusiasm of this document, despite what you could call its sad story.

My lawyer also says that this document could someday help me in court. So it's hard not to also think of this as a sort of plea, not just for your mercy, but also for that of a theoretical jury, should we go to trial. And in case the word *jury* sounds exciting to you (it did to me, for a second), I've since learned that a jury gets all kinds of things wrong, cleaving as it does to initial impressions, and in the end rarely offers the ringing exonerations or punishments that we deserve, but mostly functions as a bellwether for how the case is going to skew in the papers. It's hard not to think about them anyway, my potential listeners. Lawyers. Juries. Fairy-tale mobs. Historians. But most of all you. You—my whip, my nation, my wife.

Dear Laura. If it were just the two of us again, sitting together at the kitchen table late at night, I would probably just call this document an apology.

APOLOGIA PRO VITA SUA

Once upon a time, in 1984, I created another fateful document. On the surface, it was an application to a boys' camp on Ossipee Lake in New Hampshire. I was fourteen and had been living in the United States for only five years. During those five years, my father and I had occupied the same top-floor apartment of a tenement in Dorchester, Mass., which if you've never been there is a crowded multiracial neighborhood in Boston's southern hinterlands. Even though I had quieted my accent and cloaked myself in a Bruins hockey shirt, and tried to appear as tough and sulky as my Irish American counterparts who formed Dorchester's racial minority, I was still mentally fresh off the boat and was still discovering, on a daily basis, the phenomena of my new homeland. I remember the electronic swallowing sound of a quarter by the slot of my first video-game machine, as well as the sight of a vibrating electronic toothbrush, and how, one day while I was waiting for the bus, a boy not much older than me drove up to the curb in a Corvette convertible and hopped out without use of the door. I remember seeing many sights like this and more, because the feelings they brought up

were confusing. At first I'd feel a pop of childish wonder, but this wonder was followed by the urge to stuff it back, because if I were a real American I would not have been in the least impressed with any of it. Self-consciousness was my escort, a certain doubleness of mind that I relied upon to keep myself from asking stupid questions, such as when Dad and I drove across the border of Rhode Island one day on an errand, and I resisted asking why there was no checkpoint between state lines, for I had—if you can believe it—brought my German passport with me.

I first saw the brochure for Camp Ossipee in my pediatrician's office. I studied it every time I was sick until I slipped it in my jacket and took it home. I stared at this brochure for weeks—in bed, in the bath, hanging from my pull-up bar— until its pages started to stick together. The American boys in the photographs hung suspended in the air between cliffside and lake water. They walked in threes portaging canoes. I started to envision myself swimming with them. I imagined myself crawling through the wheat or whatever, learning to track and to mushroom. I would be the go-to man, the boy out in front, not so much the hero but an outrider. I was particularly interested in the Ossipeean rite of passage available only to the oldest boys in their final year—a solo overnight camping trip on a remote island in the middle of the lake. And here is where my future self was really born to me, in this image: myself, Erik Schroder, man alive, stoking a fire in the night, *solo*, self-sufficient, freed from the astrictions of society. I would fall asleep as one boy and wake up the next day a totally different one.

All I had to do to apply to the camp was to fill out a form and write a personal statement. What sort of statement were

they looking for? I wondered. What sort of boy? I sat at my father's card table, gazing out the window at the corner of Sagamore and Savin Hill Ave., where two classmates of mine were fighting over a broken hockey stick. I slipped a piece of paper into my father's typewriter. I began to write.

Mine was a tale that, by certain lights, was the truest thing I had ever written. It involved the burdens of history, an early loss of the mother, a baseless sense of personal responsibility, and dauntless hope for the future. Of course, by other lights—the lights that everyone else uses, including courts of law—my story was pure canard. A fraudulent, distorted, spurious, crooked, desperate fiction, which, when I met you, I lay bound at your feet. But this was 1984. I hadn't met you yet. I wasn't lying *to you*—I was just a child, sitting at my father's typewriter, my legs trussed to the knee in white athletic socks, my hair still rabbit blond, not dark at the roots like it is now. I addressed the envelope. I filched a stamp. When it came time to sign the bottom of that crowded page, it was with some flair that I first signed the name by which you came to know me. The surname wasn't hard to choose. I wanted a hero's name, and there was only one man I'd ever heard called a hero in Dorchester. A local boy, a persecuted Irishman, a demigod. He was also a man who'd spoken to cheering throngs of depressed West Berliners circa 1963, leaving them with a shimmering feeling of self-regard that lasted long beyond his assassination, his hero status still in place when my father and I finally got there much later. In fact, you might say John F. Kennedy is the reason we showed up in this country at all.

I spent months intercepting the mail looking for my acceptance letter from Ossipee. The letter would offer me full acceptance to camp on scholarship, as well as sympathies for

my troubles. I dreamt of this letter so often that I had a hard time believing it when it actually arrived. *We at Ossipee believe that every boy deserves a summertime . . . We are dedicated to supporting boys from all circumstances . . . Come join us by the shores of our beloved lake . . . Ossipee, where good boys become better men.* Yes, yes, I thought. I accept! I've got plenty of circumstances! My excitement was tempered only by the sound of Dad's key in the downstairs foyer, and I realized I wasn't going to be able to show him the letter itself, which was addressed to a different boy. Instead, I showed him the disintegrated brochure. I told him of the man-to-man phone call from the camp director. I even made the scholarship merit based, rounding out the fantasy for both of us. We trotted around the apartment all evening. It was as close as my father ever got to joyful abandon.

No one ever checked my story. When the time came, I took a bus two hours north from Boston to a bus stop called Moultonville, where a camp representative was to greet me and another scholarship boy we picked up in Nashua. When we got off the bus, a stout woman in canvas pants came toward us. This was Ida, the camp cook and its only female. The other boy mumbled an introduction. Ida looked at me. "Then *you* must be Eric Kennedy."

Why did they believe me? God knows. All I can say is it was 1984. You could apply for a social security number *through the mail.* There were no databases. You had to be rich to get a credit card. You kept your will in a safety deposit box and your money in a big wad. There were no technologies for omniscience. Nobody *wanted* them. You were whoever you said you were. And I was Eric Kennedy.

For the next three summers, that's who I was. Steady-handed Eric Kennedy. Iron Forge Eric Kennedy. Eric

Kennedy of the surprisingly tuneful singing voice. My trans-
formation was amazing. The first summer I spoke in a qua-
vering voice that only I knew was meant to prevent any trace
of an accent. I harbored a fear that some real German would
come up to me and ask me, *"Wo geht's zum Bahnhof Zoo?"* and
I would answer. But this never happened, and besides, nobody
distrusted me or scrutinized me or seemed to wish me harm;
at Ossipee, the boys were taught that trusting other people
was something you did for yourself, for your own ennoble-
ment, and this old-fashioned lesson, however perversely I
received it, is a debt I still hold to the place. Over time, I left
the periphery of the group and moved toward the center of
things. I took off my shirt and joined in dances around the
campfire. I led the chanting for food in the dining hall. By the
end of my first summer, they couldn't shut me up. After that, I
never really stopped talking.

The time eventually came for my solo camping trip. It was
my third and final summer at Ossipee, a strikingly clement
one. A steady wind swabbed the surface of the lake, forming
darkly iridescent wavelets that tapped the bottom of the camp
Chris-Craft. All the boys I'd lionized in previous summers
were gone. The younger arrivals, their hair still bearing the
ruts of combing, hung around on the dock watching me set
off, and I realized that I had become the older boy, the one
they'd remember once I was gone. The boathouse counselor
motored me toward distant coordinates and left me there on
a hard beach wearing a crown of gnats. The night was endless, but that isn't the point of my story. The part I want to
tell you about is the morning, how when I heard the sound
of the Chris-Craft approaching through the fog, I zipped out
of my nylon tent as from a skin and knew that I had achieved

something truly monumental: I had chosen my own childhood. I had found a past that matched my present. And so, with the help of enthusiastic recommendations from the folks at Ossipee, as well as a series of forgeries I hesitate to detail here despite the fact that Xeroxes of them have been pushed across tables at me quite recently, I was accepted—as Eric Kennedy—to Mune College in Troy, New York. I was a work-study student at Mune, operating the tollbooth at a multistory parking garage, and the rest of my tuition was furnished via Pell Grant (which I paid back, by the way). I majored in communications. I was a B student. Smart in class, you know, but inconsistent when actual work on my own was required. My secret bilingualism led me to excel in the study of other languages—Spanish, even conversational Japanese. When I graduated, I got a job nearby as a medical translator at Albany's Center for Medical Research, and there I stayed for six uneventful years, as free as a bird.

Of course, birds aren't free. Birds do almost nothing freely. Birds are some of nature's most industrious creatures, spending every available hour searching and hoarding and avoiding competitive disadvantage, busy just having to be birds. Like a bird, I was constantly at work being Eric Kennedy, and like a bird, I did not think of it as work. I thought of it as *being*. The earliest and cruelest deceptions had already happened— meaning, my deceptions of my father. Whenever I was Eric Kennedy, I'd made myself hard for Dad to contact. Even at Ossipee, I had told him there were no telephones in the wilderness of New Hampshire, but that if he wanted me to call him, I would happily set out on foot to the nearest town, and of course he said *Nein, nein, Erik.* Then, in measured English, *I will see you when I see you.*

Right. He would see me when he saw me, which was seldom. During college, I was like any other young man, busy trying to appear more interesting than I was—you know, amassing a music collection, composing mental manifestos, once or twice appearing in a piece of student theater. I drove down to Dorchester only when absolutely necessary. I commenced alone, in my black gown and mortarboard, and then waited until July to bring Dad up for a campus tour, when the place was desolate except for the students at an adult tennis camp. I had befriended a childless professor during my time at Mune, and it was this man, not my father, who cosigned my lease on my first apartment, a sunny one-bedroom kitty-corner from Washington Park.

I was happy in Albany and rarely left it. I liked its protected horizons, its belligerent small-time politicians. And there was always a girl—some girl or another—and laughing, and making fun of tourists in the South Mall. These relationships were easy and promise-free. I had a talent for choosing women who were already temperamentally predisposed toward happiness and therefore wouldn't use me as a catchall for their disappointments. In my free time, I worked erratically on my research (see page 15) and played soccer with a bunch of foreign transplants on a hill we borrowed from the College of Saint Rose. And the thing after that, I supposed, would be the thing after that.

I did not know the thing after that would be you.

You. The first time I saw you, you were strapping a splint onto a child who had just fallen out of a tree. About a dozen other children were standing in a loose circle watching you. By

then the boy was screaming so loud that no one but you could get near him. It was my lunch hour, and the noise annoyed me, and so I stood to leave. But my gaze caught on you, and I paused.[1] What caused this snag? What was it about you, or about the moment in which you came to my attention? Was it the way you continued to wrap the boy's wrist so coolly, despite the fact that he was hysterical, kicking and screaming? It was August. Late, hot, rotten summer. I would later learn that you had been charged with leading twenty of Albany's neglected children through the poison ivy since July. You looked in need of a shower. But my attention snagged on you. My mind cleaned you off and put you in a sundress and placed a glass of Chardonnay in your hand and turned your face to mine. So I stood up and walked toward you, offering my help, wondering if the feeling would last, wondering if I could string together two or three more moments of this rapturous attention that was commanding me. Who knows why, Laura? Who knows why so-and-so falls in love with you-know-who

---

1. What is a pause? For the purposes of this document I will restrict my answer to conversational interaction only, in which a pause is a cessation of speech between two or more participants (not, for example, a moment of counterargument during one's solitary existential inner monologue in the bathtub). Compared to a silence, a pause is briefer, a kind of baby silence—the sort of hesitation that occurs while one is fishing for the proper way to put a thing, for example. Or when one is reflecting upon what one just said with a measure of criticism or regret. Or when one is distracted by a second subject or a loud noise but wants to appear thoughtful. Nobody asked me, but I would personally time a pause at two to three seconds in duration. It may be true that pauses are, at least historically, second-rate silences, whereas silences—those yawning spans of time in which the heart sinks, the mouth dries, the truth dawns—are infinitely more consequential and worthy of study. However, this writer maintains that both pauses and silences may be what the theorist and mother of pausology Zofia Dudek calls *functionally deficient* (i.e., a nothing that is a something). Both are worthy of study and attention.

instead of what's-his-name? Reams of poetry have languished in the guessing. I mean, I'm sorry for you, that I chose you. But I guess part of my motivation here, with this document, is to remind you that it wasn't entirely a waste. Listen:

Were we compatible? I believe yes, we were, very compatible, for a while. Although you made a pretty brittle first impression, you turned into one big marshmallow as soon as you decided I was a decent guy. You couldn't stop yourself. Soon you were bringing me books, loose tea, candied apricots. Your flirtations were sweet, a little fussy. It was as if you'd been sequestered from men your entire life and therefore could only seduce me as if I myself were a young girl.

Although you were the real American, I was by far more American*ish*. I was more spontaneous. I was more relaxed. I was still, in many ways, Eric Kennedy of Camp Ossipee, a persona for which I'd been richly rewarded at Mune College, but who, as I climbed toward thirty, was in need of an update. With you, Eric Kennedy matured. You were four years his junior, but no one would have guessed. You were prompt. You were responsible. You were deliberate. You were health conscious. You often traveled with your own baggies of gorp. You were easily offended. There was a whole list of social issues over which you took quick offense (e.g., the lack of handicap accessibility in public buildings). The mere mention of such issues made your cheeks red. You were always ready for polite but tense debate. It was as if throughout the course of your life, you had been traumatized by chronic misunderstandings.

How quickly I dropped all other commitments, all other friendships, clubs, and interests. I had a sense of loving you, despite your youth, as if I were your student, and therefore whatever you did—however obscure, however specific—was,

to me, the right thing. You had such a careful way with the truth. You wanted everything you said to be true on several different levels. It took you a long time to fill out simple forms in a doctor's office, tapping the pen to your lips. Did you exercise daily or weekly? Well, you exercised several days a week but not *daily*. I leaned over your shoulder to help you scrutinize whatever bit of inconsequentia was capturing your attention. I was happy to study bar codes and ingredients and all genres of fine print with you. The grocery store, the DMV. In America, the opportunities to be accurate are endless. And nothing escaped your eye. Nothing, of course, except me.

Marriage. The clashing of expectations produces a new chord. We had a small civil ceremony. A honeymoon in Virginia Beach. And after these rituals, there was the renting of the apartment, and the rearranging of furniture, and then an idleness descended upon us, and we were like any newly married pair, nervously wondering, OK, what next? How should we go forward? For a while, there seemed to be someone missing—someone *else*, like a leader, or a chief. An urgently needed third party whose role it was to direct traffic between us, to negotiate conflicting plans, forge compromises, translate cultural or religious differences. Or were we really supposed to go it alone? *Us?* The bride—you—struggling to outstretch her parochial upbringing, born as she was to slightly ignorant but good-hearted Catholics from Delmar, New York. And the groom—me—raised in a (completely fictional) town on Cape Cod he called Twelve Hills, a "stone's throw from Hyannis Port," a treasured only child, endowed with a last name that could only be uttered in rapture.

ERRATUM

For the record: The groom *never* told the bride that he was related to the Kennedys of presidential fame. This has been reported in the papers, and the groom categorically denies it. No, it was simply the word "Kennedy" plus the words "near Hyannis Port," and everyone started rushing to conclusions. The groom will admit that once or twice late at night with his female peers at Mune College, he *did not sufficiently debunk the rumor of himself as a second cousin twice removed* to the Hyannis Port Kennedys. And he does not deny that the name often greased the gears of bureaucracy, making what would otherwise have been dull encounters with bank loan officers, traffic cops, etc., slightly *charged*, even when he denied any family connection.

The bride, however, never seemed much interested in the groom as a "Kennedy." If the bride was impressed by the name, that day they met in Washington Park and all the days thereafter, she never talked about it. The bride was a serious and moral woman, not easily wowed. She was also a woman who acquired (by the way), in the period of years in which the groom loved her, an incredible, inflationary beauty, and

the groom just wants to mention that here and to put it here in words in case either of them forgets it. The truth is, she stunned the groom whenever he saw her. I mean *whenever* he saw her. Just the simple fact of her. Whenever she came into one room from another room. For example, stepping out of the kitchenette in Pine Hills with a plate of scrambled eggs. The groom was in love with her. That was no lie. And when he was in love with her, a minute no longer seemed like the means to an hour. Rather, each minute was an end in itself, a stillness with vague circularity, a gently suggested territory in which to be alive. This trick that love did with minutes endowed hours and days with a kind of transcendent wishy-washiness that encouraged an utter lack of ambition in the groom and was the closest thing he had ever felt to true joy, to true relief, and he still wonders what would have happened if they could have kept up with it, if they could have stayed in love like that, if maybe they could have crawled through a wormhole to a place where their love could find permanence. Because in the end, the great warring forces of our existence are not *life* versus *death* (the groom has come to believe), but rather *love* versus *time*. In the majority, love does not survive time's passage. But sometimes it does. It must, sometimes.

APOLOGIA CONT'D.

Anyway. Soon after his wedding, the groom became a real estate agent, but not by his own choice. It wasn't a bad choice. It just wasn't his. The bride's father had started to bug the couple about the groom's future plans. He suspected that the groom made little money as a medical translator and even less on his "independent research" (see page 49). The bride resented this intrusion on the part of her father. She did not think the groom needed to *conventionalize* his lifestyle. She liked the idea of him at home, deep in thought, and she liked finding him sitting in the same place she'd left him when she returned from her teacher training. In fact, the bride maintained that if the groom abandoned his research, he would be *selling out*. He would be selling out his dreams, which deserved a chance. In retrospect, it seems that the groom was an exemplar of the kind of suicidal integrity toward which the bride liked to encourage her middle schoolers.

So the bride told her father to *back off*. She told her father that the groom's independent research would come together. The bride told her father that her groom was working very hard, that he might even be a *visionary*, a term that must

have alarmed her father, *visions* sounding an awful lot like *hallucinations*.

Still, the man was her father. He remained concerned. Soon after the pair returned from their honeymoon, the father-in-law came over for a tête-à-tête. The groom remembers this interview very well. The father-in-law—let's call him Hank, because that's his name—sat across from the groom on their used sofa in Pine Hills, knees cracking arthritically, and the two of them spoke at length about the number of automotive accidents occurring on a low salt stretch of Hackett Boulevard, before they fell into an awkward and loaded silence.[2]

"Eric," Hank finally said. "I'm not sure how to say what I want to say, so instead I'm going to tell you a story."

The story was about Hank as a young man of twenty. The story was about how, back in Troy, New York, when Hank

---

2. How comfortable one is with conversational pauses depends largely on cultural norms, and which his society values more, taciturnity or volubility. Take the Finns, for example. A notoriously silent and somewhat depressing people. Contrast the Finn to the archetypal American and suddenly the Finn appears to be suffering from selective mutism. The American goes to the other extreme. For him, no matter his socioeconomic background, talking for the sake of talking is viewed as an evolved social skill. An American who can banter for a reasonable length of time is seen as a social savior, a dispeller of tensions, the person who might tell a joke to other persons trapped in the same darkened elevator, for example. An extra beat of silence—what we might call an *awkward pause*—is, in many cultures, a thing to be avoided. Often such pauses divulge feelings that much of our speech has been attempting to suppress. Dudek, in her seminal work *Pausologies* (1972), would call this *communicative silence*.

Let's take an example from the Brits. Pause #33: Margaret Thatcher's when asked if her successor, John Major, had yet become a great prime minister. The question was followed by resounding communicative silence. "I think he has carried out his duties," Thatcher replied, but not before her awkward pause had already lodged itself in the annals of British politics.

first married his then-slender wife, he had been lectured by his own father-in-law in an apartment not unlike this one. In the story, Hank had to sit and listen to *his* father-in-law drone on about responsibility and the future and savings and the importance of being heavily insured, adding such stress into the mind of young Hank that he almost wanted to take the whole thing back, the whole marriage. He swore to God that he would *never* be like that. He would never pressure his own future son-in-law. Because a newly married man, Hank said, was like the captain of a rudderless ship. Out there, at sea, with no compass, no stars, no crew, no sight of land. But in the end—and this was the story's moral—young Hank had followed his father-in-law's instructions, albeit with a lot of resentment, and only after the old man passed away did Hank understand that he had been right about things, and that maybe he'd even loved Hank. Hank missed him sometimes, this unasked-for father, on certain bracing winter mornings.

The groom had listened, laughing gratefully, wincing with sympathy, his bride blending ice angrily in the kitchen, but all the while the groom kept thinking: What stress? What rudderless ship? The groom had never felt happier in his life. Never more carefree. In that modest hotel on Virginia Beach, both of them hilariously pale with northern winter, they had honeymooned for five days. Every night, they ate mounds of food garnished with pineapple, and every morning, they arrived at the beach early, when the tide was still out, and they placed their two chairs straight on the sandbars, which they called the *cheap seats*. Those honeymoon mornings seemed to be suggesting something to the groom. The suggestion was this: Be happy. *Decide* to be happy. If you want to be happy, be happy! No one cares if you're happy or not, so

why wait for permission? And did it really matter if you had been deeply unhappy in your past? Who but you remembered that? It was really one of the groom's most standout moments, and it liberated him. After realizing that he could be happy, that he could thrive, it seemed to him that there was no one powerful enough to make him unhappy again, and thereafter his happiness would always belong to him, even if he lost everything else. His body braced, his heart roused, he finally got it—the American secret—that the only person who could obstruct a man was himself.

So there is no other reason for why he would continue his elaborate and ultimately disastrous deceit re: his bogus identity except that he was just firmly and sentimentally committed to it. His decision to be happy seemed only to invite him to rededicate himself to his made-up past. On the final morning of their honeymoon, he watched the children on the beach, and he watched his bride watch the children, and he thought, No, I will not tell you. I will never tell you. I'll cut out my tongue first.

Then he pointed into the distance. "Hey, Laura," he said. "Look over there, at that old lighthouse. There was one just like that outside of Twelve Hills. Total déjà vu. Huhn."

The bride smiled. "Tell me about it."

"About the lighthouse?" He lifted his sunglasses and smiled. "Well, you could climb all the way to the top of it. Up these old stone steps. No rail. All very spooky and dangerous. Once you got to the top, you could see for miles. And there were those viewfinders that open up when you put a quarter inside. You could see all the way to Boston. Tiny Boston. Tiny mother, waiting below in the shade. Huhn. It's funny what you remember."

The bride closed her eyes. "That's beautiful, Eric," she said. "You're lucky. You're lucky to have memories like that. What a sweet childhood."

"It was," the groom said. "I am."

Her eyes widened. "We should go there sometime," she said. "To your lighthouse on the Cape. Do you think it's still open? Could we go? I want to see what you saw. I want to see where you grew up. Twelve Hills, and everything."

The groom's eyes lit up, he was so touched.

"Let's!" he agreed.

Her smile was so loving, and the beach so breezy, his happiness so incontrovertible, that for a moment the groom believed that he actually *would* take the bride to the lighthouse, and that he actually *had* climbed it as a boy, and that there actually *was* such a place as Twelve Hills, and his mother really *did* stand waiting in the shade. Closing his eyes, he even saw distant Boston as if through two little portals of memory, sitting in petticoats of mist.

By the time the groom had returned from his daydream and back to his father-in-law on the sofa, the moment to make objections had passed. In fact, explicit plans had been laid for his future. Plans had been made, and the groom took no objection. *Good.* His father-in-law was nodding at him. *Then I'll have a talk with Chip Clebus, and he'll show you the ropes. I'm glad we understand each other.* By sheer coincidence, the men did understand each other. Apart from his research, and loving his wife, the groom had few ideas for how to organize his time on earth. And so within days he was sitting in a classroom with a bunch of other unfocused extroverts, preparing for his

real estate certification by studying the contractual nuances of sale-leasebacks.

Turns out the groom had a talent for making money in real estate, and for the three or four years in which his larger dreams were totally and effectively repressed, the groom made a shiny pile of commissions. These commissions took the young couple through the birthing and infancy of their daughter, Meadow. The money bought the baby a cradle that swung via a mechanical arm, and it bought calendula oil for her bottom and pretty music and as many spins on the carousel as someone who would never remember any of it could wish for. And they were happy years. Seriously. If the groom could have wrung all the necks of his lies and eccentricities, he would have done it. There is no explaining—and it pains me to think he will never be believed now—how much the groom loved his life then. How grateful he was. Once, looking out over Poestenkill Gorge in winter, the baby asleep in her sling against her mother's chest, he watched the new-fallen snow glitter at the base of the trees, and he watched the naked branches form an overlapping lace through which he could see down onto the church spires and chimney smoke of the valley, and he felt as if he'd been walking for a long time—years—and had finally arrived at his intended destination.

Oh, Laura. If I had lived my life as one man, one consolidated man, would I have been able to see what was coming? Would I have guessed that it was all bound to fail, and that within five years, we would separate? Would I have been able to

prevent it—I mean that night when, your face streaked with tears, you asked me to get out? You'd had it with me. You'd felt for years—you'd explain this later—like you were living in a house with tilted floors. We'd gone wrong.

Pine Hills. We were in the kitchenette. You were facing away from me, leaning with both hands against the sink basin. We'd been arguing for some time. Arguing and washing dishes. Meadow was asleep. She was four by then, old enough to hear raised voices, and so we tried to keep disagreements strictly late night. What were we fighting about? You name it: your increasingly fervent Catholicism, my laziness, your need for order and structure, my lack of discipline, your martyred reticence, my tendency to talk too much. We had a mouse infestation. I'd caught one of the rodents and, without the heart to kill it, had given it to Meadow for a pet. As we argued, I watched this mouse tunnel in the infinite corner of its plastic box.

"Is this about school?" I was saying. "Fine. I'll be better about school. I'll get her there on time, and it's a negative on the spontaneous field trips, OK? Effective immediately. I don't love the school—you know all this, hon—the bloody Jesuses hanging all over the place. It's just not my idea of a place for children. You know, 'sweet childish days, as long as twenty are now'?"

You said nothing.

"But OK, OK," I said. "I'll be better. I'll work on my attitude. You know, you told me you were Catholic when we got married, but I didn't think you were *serious*."

Finally, you turned around. I could see now you'd been crying. This astonished me. I'd been trying for a joke.

"Oh, Eric," you said, crying. "We're so far apart."

My hands were still poised to dry the dish you'd been washing. Palms up, a damp cloth draped over one forearm.

One thing I'm sure of is that despite the late-night arguments, despite our differences, despite the way the light in our marriage had dimmed, even to my blind eyes, I never thought of leaving you. Not once. But there was a gap between how bad I thought things were and how bad you thought things were, and our life fell into that gap.

"We are?" I said.

TENDER YEARS

We may no longer remember that until the mid-nineteenth century, children and their mothers were viewed as a man's property. When marital strife led to that carnival we now call *divorce*, the child was whisked away to the father's arms, leaving the mother sobbing in the street, without recourse. We have all read, or been told abridged versions of, *Anna Karenina*, yes? But it did not take long, you see, for the custody pendulum to swing in the other direction. By the late 1800s, a *maternal preference* in divorce cases was supported by the "tender years" doctrine. This doctrine held that children of "tender years"—that is, younger than eight—should be raised by their mothers. Therefore, men who wanted custody of their children appeared not only misled, but also slightly skeevy. But the issue of custody did not arise much, because divorce itself was fairly rare.

Well, time passed and for reasons I will not go into here, divorce lost its edge. Somewhere in the bowels of the 1970s and '80s, some people started to see divorce as an act of empowerment, for stifled men and women alike. Marriage became the problem, and divorce, the solution. Soon, everybody wanted

one. Divorces became much easier to obtain. They might as well have passed them out on street corners. You could get divorced on a boat, or on a train, or in a mall, or in a box with a fox.

Coterminously—and I'll be done with this soon—those decades lent the field of divorce litigation some new and exciting ideas. For example, the *no-fault* divorce, in which a marriage was alleged to have malfunctioned somehow on its own, independent of its participants. And even though the concept of a divorce with no fault is oxymoronic, and a better term might have been fault-fault divorce, as a legal category, it caught fire. The upshot to no-fault divorces and my point at present is that they presumed *neither maternal nor paternal preference* in matters of custody. What's more, when parents were encouraged to settle custody disputes prior to a hearing, via the quieter process of mediation, divorce lost its inherent staginess. Gone were the exciting, perjured testimonies of one family member against another. This enabled a legal preference (in twelve states) for the concept of *joint custody*.

You and I picked a hairy little folknik as our mediator, an MSW from Cornell who wore shorts and huaraches even in cold weather. You sat across from me at his table, your eyes downcast, your shyness on display, the lonely, bookish girl beneath your righteous exterior, as you struggled to defend your desire to deep-six our union.

Is it damaging to my case to say that I looked forward to seeing you at divorce mediation? I shaved, I aftershaved, I picked out shirts you had once bought for me. The mediator worked out of a cottage near the thruway. In the back-

yard he'd created a pleasure garden full of autumnal dahlias, and two chairs tilted hopefully toward one another on a slate patio. Our separation was still very fresh. I still didn't understand why we were separating, and I'm fairly sure you didn't either. We'd been living separately for a couple of weeks, and this apartness gave our meetings an air of courtship. I missed you, OK? Even though you had been granted temporary custody of Meadow, you always let her come to see me at my whim or hers. It felt like we were still on the same team. She would arrive to my new place in North Albany in the backseat of your father's immense black Chevy Tahoe, looking rather glamorous through the tinted window. Your father's friendliness contributed to my sense that the situation was, like the custody arrangement, *temporary*. If I handled it well, you would come to your senses.

If ever there was a man who deluded himself with dreams of reconciliation, I was that man. How much legal leverage I lost in the effort to win you back! I chronicled your talents as a mother, as well as the faithful way Meadow loved you back. When allegations were cast my way—that I was insensitive, that I had ignored numerous warning signs, that my behavior was occasionally "erratic" and my parenting style "unpredictable," that my research interests were "esoteric" and finally just tedious and maybe even make-believe—I accepted these criticisms and heaped a couple of fresh ones atop the pile. *You're right*, I said. *You're so right.* I wanted to persuade you that I was flawed on purpose. Because if I was flawed on purpose, then I was just as capable of being perfect as I was of being flawed. I was in total control of who I was. I was capable of change.

You blushed and barely looked at me. I see now that you

were embarrassed for me. You were embarrassed for me that I knew so little of the cold nature of the law. Only after I found myself the *noncustodial parent* did I realize my error, my wasted sacrifice.

In one of our final meetings, when I finally sensed the sour turn my fate had taken, the mediator assured me that if I had objections in the future—if I were to change my mind—I could do so within the court of law, during a hearing. In the meantime, it seemed to him that there was a lot of good in giving one parent sole physical custody and that this arrangement would still provide me with a bounty of visitation rights. For some children, especially young ones like Meadow (our hippie said), it was better to live in one home. *My* new place could be Meadow's sleepaway home. An exciting change of scene.

With this parental "agreement" in place, thereafter you and I worked through the mail. Without the hit of seeing you, our correspondence took on a chill. The fact that I was getting screwed dawned on me slowly. The many visitations I was initially promised were scratched down to every other weekend. These impersonal negotiations unsettled me and began to absorb restless nights.

I took a stand and arbitrarily demanded that in addition to my weekends, I'd get Meadow every Wednesday. After this request was received, Meadow was curiously unable to make it over to my place for an entire two weeks. I called many times; no one answered. I visited our hippie; he was powerless. And then I returned to my new home—the water-damaged ranch I was renting off New Scotland Ave.—and sat paralyzed, listening to the sump pump labor away in the basement. It was the sort of week in which the clock's ticking seems recriminatory (*Look how you've been imprisoned by your unwillingness to*

kill yourself!). I drank, but that failed to bring about world-wide revolution. So I sat at my kitchen table to think, and I thought until my mind became raw from thinking, and for the first time in years I became aware of my essential conundrum. I was Eric Kennedy. I knew it, and I had decided it, and it was true. It had been true for too long. But whenever I ventured out into emotional and physical joint space—that is, society—my identity became predicated on some sort of collective agreement. In other words, I was Eric Kennedy only inasmuch as I could secure a consensus that I was. And suddenly I saw that achieving a total consensus, a unanimity, was a campaign for which my life was too short. For example, I had no legal recourse. I couldn't get mixed up in a custody battle! It would be only a matter of days before someone went digging for old records, looking for someone who knew me in high school—hell, looking for Twelve Hills on the map. After all, I had written my life story at the tender age of fourteen. It wasn't a very sophisticated one.

You may be surprised to hear that until then, I rarely worried about being found out. Maybe I didn't worry about it because I am insane (as most people who've read about my case now assume). But I'll *tell* you: I think that I didn't worry about it because I had become Eric Kennedy so long ago and with such appreciation that I was, years later, truly and squarely *him*, more than I had ever been anyone else. More than most people are themselves. Because where other people are accidentally good or bad or upbeat or pessimistic, I got to shoot for a deliberate self, a considered, researched self. And that self was a good guy—I really thought so, and *a lot* of other people did too. And I assumed he would be granted the rewards and allowances given to good guys (e.g.,

Clebus & Co. Realtor of the Month, February 2007). But during that stretch of days, denied access to my daughter, sleepless, unshaven, dehydrated, the true flammability of my life became clear to me.

I saw that my love for Meadow would be the last thing to burn.

Just as I started to dream about throwing myself off a cliff in Thatcher Park, I received, in the mail, your act of kindness. You had granted me my Wednesdays.

Of course, there were limitations. I would be allowed only to pick her up from school (that Catholic academy we used to fight about), returning her to your home by six p.m. sharp. Net time of togetherness: three hours and twenty-three minutes.

Giddy, exhausted, I signed.

Our parental agreement floated through the courts of Albany to be stamped into officialdom.

Meadow arrived that very afternoon, bearing oatmeal cookies the two of you had made together. I can't quite describe my happiness at seeing her step from her grandfather's SUV. It was as good as all the best moments. As good as when I first held her as a newborn. As good as the moment I discovered she'd defaced all of my professional stationery with her newly mastered alphabet. I hugged her and let myself believe there were better times ahead. Times of healing and beginning again. She seemed happy to see me too. We ate the cookies in one sitting.

Restored to insanity, I once again harbored notions that you still loved me.

After that, well, I suppose I was my one remaining enemy.

*   *   *

Winter came. The first winter of our separation. There was a horrendous slowdown of real estate sales, the first baby step of what would become the Great Recession. I tried again to further my research. Instead, I ended up catching a virus that left me delirious in bed, clinging to your old body pillow. I watched Animal Planet on mute and tried to think of what the animals were really saying. I tried to remember the folk remedies of my primitive childhood. I tried to forget it was almost Christmas. It was at this juncture that I began having difficulty making child support payments.

The tender years.

No kidding they were tender.

What do I remember of my own tender years, long ago? The wheezing of the kettle. My mother and myself deep in parallel silence. The pleasure of a banana. The friendship of a dog. A song about Lenin's forehead. Flurries of pollen in springtime, steam tents, a cream-colored Trabant that suffered frequent mechanical breakdowns, searchlights, salted caramels in wax paper, the unique humiliation of being dressed in a bow tie. That's it. So little, and so much.

FEBRUARY

B ut let's move along. You want to know how I arrived at what is universally regarded as my catastrophic decision regarding our daughter. There's been some embarrassing and poorly researched news coverage, and I know that this is exactly the sort of easily misunderstood intrigue that could find its way into the tabloids or the lesser glossies, so I will hurry up and try to address several of the most common questions about my case.

#1. *Were the actions of the accused premeditated?*

In order to answer this question, I really have to start with a description of North Albany in February:

In North Albany in February, the flora and fauna are dead, the traffic turns the snow the color of tobacco juice, the children are shuttered away in their schools, and the long days are silent. The cats grow wet and skinny, and the rain grows hard and bitter, as if it is not rain but the liquid redistribution of collective conflict; it's a frigid rain, a rain that pricks the skin of any upturned face, a damning rain that makes

men eke corks from bottles. O February, you turn our hearts
to stone.

Now, at every other time of year, Albany is a delightful city.
With its magnificent state capitol, cribbed from some Parisian
design, and its city hall based on that of our sister city, Ypres,
Belgium, and the thirty-six marble pillars along the colonnade
of the education building, Albany *surprises* the casual tourist.
How, the tourist wonders, in the middle of upstate New York,
did he stumble across this European metropolis? He walks out
into the wide open of the Empire State Plaza and is awed by
the scale, the towering buildings—even the one that resem-
bles an immense egg—doubled in the reflecting pool, which is
itself end to end the length of three football fields.

I took to walking this plaza in February, looking for a
way out of my situation. I could not get a good critical angle
on my life. Since our separation that fall, I'd hosted Meadow
every other weekend at my ranch, and these visits seemed to
be meeting expectations. Two days of puzzles, glitter, screaming, and contraband Hostess products. Two days of soaking up
her prattle, of being her stooge in games of house or school.
And Wednesdays were sweet, when we snatched them. But
Meadow's entrance into kindergarten was a passage into a
new life for her as a distinct person, and occasionally I only
sat ignored, watching her play with a friend we'd run into
at Washington Park. Or worse, I'd receive news that prep-
arations for a competing event meant there would be no
Wednesday visit at all.

Besides, there was the underlying problem of days.
Between every allotted weekend visitation sprawled the weeks
themselves. Worm-eaten, heartsick, exaggerated days book-
ended by conciliatory Saturdays and Sundays in her presence.

Then, every other weekend *without* her. Grief made those weekends drag. I sat like a teenage girl by the telephone hoping that some scheduling conflict would necessitate my services as a babysitter. As the cycle went on relentlessly, I found myself getting tired from it. Anticipating her arrivals, I would pace the marshy carpeting of my ranch for hours, but when she'd finally pull up in the back of her grandfather's Tahoe, fatigue would hit me. I had exhausted myself waiting. In the end, the hardest thing about having once been screamingly happy is that after your life takes a turn for the worse, you wish you'd never known anything different. Watching her emerge from the car, I'd wonder if it was all worth it, worth these few days. Meadow herself wore the same optimistic smile she always wore walking up to my stoop. She would not have approved of my self-pity; no soul of a shop girl had she; she was always the best of the two of us, Laura. I knew that the moment she was born.

And yet you and I were still not divorced. You had not filed for divorce. I began to wonder why. Was it on religious grounds? Or did you want *me* to pull the trigger? Or were you genuinely considering coming back to me? I'll never know. I rarely saw you. I rarely spoke to you. You were protected by your parents and your diplomatic child. You sent your father as emissary. He and I waved to one another through the window of his terrifying car. Polite to a fault, having borrowed some notion of chivalry, I tried to give you space. Time to think.

This patience was an act—my hardest, hands down.

March brought a spate of sunshine. I sold two houses. I began having sex with a fellow Realtor at Clebus, a woman you knew and never liked much.

When I told her you and I had separated, she seemed disappointed and instinctively took your side.

AFFORDABLE, ACCESSIBLE, DIGNIFIED

When I first walked into the law offices of Rick Thron, I did not look my best. I was in need of a haircut, and I was freezing cold. I'd left my winter coat behind while showing a house in Delmar and, inexplicably, never went back to get it. Thron's office was on the upper floors of a building that overlooked Quackenbush Square, where, in the summertime, amphibious trolleys collected Albany's tourists to carry them back and forth across the Hudson. But it was not yet spring. The world utterly lacked an upshot. March was almost over, but a late winter snowstorm had covered the streets of Albany with slush. My boots squeaked all the way down the hallway to Thron's office door. When I entered the office, I was dulcified by the pretty secretary, who must have been installed precisely for men like me, desperate men, men who had come at last (too late, way too late) for help.

"Here's what I hear you saying," said Thron after listening to my sad tale. "I hear you saying that you love your daughter. I hear you saying that you were a coequal parent, if not a genuine Mr. Mom, before the separation. I mean you were, in fact, a stay-at-home dad for a year—the primary

caretaker—when your daughter was three. Am I hearing that correctly?"

"Yes, you are," I said.

"And I hear you saying that in a gesture of goodwill toward your estranged wife, you got your nuts crunched in mediation, and now you're left with this sense that—the sense that you feel—"

"Spiritually squandered," I said. "Without meaning. Void."

"Bad," said Thron. "You feel really bad. Your feeling bad is made more bad by the sense that you—out of the goodness of your heart—forfeited your paternal rights—out of—of—"

"Love," I said.

"Love." Thron sat back. "Right."

"I still love my wife," I said. "My estranged wife."

Thron, a broad-shouldered man whose generic office lacked a single plant or photograph, made an axing motion with his arm. "Forget. About. That. Your estranged wife does *not* love you. Someone who is trying to estrange you from her and from your child does *not* love you. Don't be like the battered wife, Eric, stabbed fifty-seven times by her own husband. How does a person hang around long enough to get stabbed fifty-seven times by somebody? Because they're still waiting around for *love*. Don't get distracted, Eric. Don't let your estranged wife stab you fifty-seven times. She stabs you once, that's it. You stab right back."

"OK," I said.

"Do you know, Eric, that spouses who initiate divorce often think of the divorce as a 'growth experience'? They even show better immune function. But you—the spouse who stuck around, the loyal one, the one who *meant* his vows—what do

you get? You get left holding the bag. Your divorce could make you sick."

"It has!" I cried. "I've had bronchitis for months."

"If I've seen it once, I've seen it a thousand times, Eric. You should have come to see me a long time ago." Pertly, Thron stacked some papers. "Now, who filed the petition?"

"Petition?"

"The petition for divorce."

"We haven't filed. It's—we're separated. It's a trial separation."

"Then we're filing today." Thron licked his thumb and peeled a form off a thick pad. "We're going to file today, so we can start litigation. You can't litigate with no divorce. Otherwise, it's just a friendly disagreement. And you tried that already, right? You need to sue."

"I can't," I said.

"You can. File first, Eric. Be the plaintiff. Don't be the defendant. Don't spend your life counterpunching."

"I need a day," I said.

"One day. One day. Tomorrow you come in and file. Then ASAP we'll also file a petition in family court for a modification of the custody agreement. If your estranged wife does not agree to it, *bam*—we go to court."

"OK," I said.

"We're also going to hire—granted, at some expense—a topflight, independent child custody evaluator. This individual will observe you alone, and also you with your daughter— you know, playing checkers, sharing a soda—and he or she will write what I'm sure will be an A-plus report on your skills as a father. This report will be on file to aid the judge's decision should we go to trial. OK?"

"OK."

"Because you know what, Eric? You are a good father."

"Thank you."

"I can *tell* you are a good father. I can see it in your eyes."

They could not help it; those eyes filled with tears. My heart let its ragged doves to the sky. I hadn't realized how much I'd wanted someone to say just that to me. *You are a good father.* I was sweating everywhere, my underarms, my forehead, my back, secretions that seemed born of relief.

At the same time, a different voice inside me said, Don't. Don't do this. *Trottel. Idiot.* Don't you know a *thing*?

"Now, Eric," said Thron. "Let's go over some basic information. Let's start with your date of birth."

"March 12, 1970."

"Place of birth?"

I looked out Thron's window. The clouds were easing down the Hudson, as they often did in the afternoons, leaving the sun canting down into the valley in shattered-looking rays.

I came very close to telling Thron the truth in that moment. *I am not who I say I am*, I almost said. *When I was five, I crossed the East German border holding nothing but my father's hand* (I almost said). *I spent my shitty adolescence in an immigrants' ghetto in Dorchester, Mass. And that's just the beginning* (I almost said).

Out Thron's window, between the buildings on Quackenbush, I stared at the Hudson. How pitiable is a river. Nothing belongs to it, neither its water nor its sediment. This will never be over, I reminded myself. You created it to have no end.

"I was born," I began, "in Twelve Hills, Massachusetts, not far from Hyannis Port."

"Sounds nice," said Thron, taking notes. "A small town?"

"Very small."

"And you lived in town?"

"Right in the middle of town," I said. "Our house was a modest saltbox. Sixteen hundred square feet, not counting the finished basement. We weren't rich, although both of my parents came from money. My paternal grandparents lost their entire fortune when they were betrayed by a trusted business partner in the late fifties. They moved into the Cape house, and my father grew up there. And I grew up there. The property itself was a gem. Oceanfront. Landscaped with beach heather, wild roses—"

"Fine," said Thron. "And your parents? Alive or deceased?"

"My mother passed away when I was nine. She's buried right there in the village cemetery. My father, an entrepreneur, now lives overseas. I rarely see him."

Thron squinted at the page, and his eyes took on a greasy iridescence. "Hey. You're not related to the *Kennedy* Kennedys. Are you?"

I smiled, shrugging.

"The connection," I said, "is distant."

DADDY

I had been bullied in Dorchester. Habitually. The black kids were decent to me on the whole, if only by turning away from my vulnerable stare as if I wasn't even present, but the Irish American princes who looked like me and lived, like me, in sagging three-story tenements were looking for a fall guy. They tricked me, shoved me, and suckered me, while never being so cruel that I could easily recognize any one of them as the enemy. They made fun of my German accent long after I could have sworn that I no longer had one. On one occasion, a boy no bigger or stronger than me confronted me in the concrete drainage ditch we used as a shortcut home from school. I had never considered this boy an enemy. In fact, we often compared homework on the school steps in the morning—and so I was surprised when he put up his fists and began hopping from one foot to the other.

"Come on, Schroder," he said anxiously.

I was confused. "Come on and what?"

"Come on and fight. Fight!"

"Why?"

"Because! That's why!"

I could have fought him. I probably would've won. I knew that a victory would bring some relief from the teasing and unchecked xenophobia that surrounded me every day. But I didn't fight him. I had been taught only to escape. I spied a swinging gate in someone's chain-link fence and I ran through it and slammed the gate back toward my pursuer.

I ran. I ran for a long, long time. I ran in a hysterical pattern that was random enough to lose anybody sane. Tearing my way through the weeds and broken tricycles and dirt yards of Dorchester, I didn't even turn around to see if the boy was still behind me. I ran crazily, crisscrossedly, as some sort of artistic expression, now that I look back at it, of what it felt like to be me.

Later that evening, against my will, I began to cry in front of my father. I was ashamed. I told my father what had happened, that a boy had tried to fight me, but that I had not stood and fought him, but instead I'd run away.

My father put down his fork and looked thoughtful. I stared at his beard, cranberry red at its thickest, and hoped that whatever he'd say would relieve me. He was a man of very few words, and the longer we lived in Boston, the fewer of them there seemed to be. After a moment, he picked up his fork.

"*Natürlich hast Du nicht gekämpft,*" he said. "*Es ist nicht natürlich, zu kämpfen. In Wahrheit ist es natürlich, wegzulaufen.*"[3]

---

3. Of course you did not fight. It is not natural to stand and fight. The truth is, it's natural to run.

EVALUATION

I will not rehash here the series of contortions, gambits, and hurt surprises that took our custody battle onward to its next, more acute stage. Of course, any shred of hope for marital reconciliation was lost as soon as I enlisted Thron's services, but I guess I expected that. And although my time with Thron would turn out to be short, for several months that spring he was something of a friend, and I trusted him. So when he proposed we go ahead with the child custody evaluation, I agreed. I would have several long, probing conversations with the evaluator, in the privacy of his or her own office, but first I would meet him or her in public, with Meadow, during a regular visitation.

I picked my site—the playground at Washington Park. This was the playground on which Meadow had virtually grown up. When she was a tot, she had feasted on its wood chips, and when she was old enough to grip the handlebars, she had sagged back and forth on the metal spring horses. In recent years she had learned to kite on the adjacent hill. Whenever I wanted to spoil her, I'd buy her some huge, delta-winged kite made out of brightly colored ripstop, and we'd wait for a good

day to try it out. So I pictured us there on our hillside, tethered to the broad blue belly of the sky via one taut string, looking favored, looking somehow worthy of endorsement.

The first stumbling block came with the news that Thron's pick for our evaluator had been nixed, and soon we were forced to accept a last-minute substitution of a different expert by The Opposition. Also, there was no wind. Awaiting our rendezvous, Meadow and I tried to force the kite into the sky. Several attempts left it flightless in the grass. We tried again, and a rogue gust tacked the kite sharply sideways, where it looped itself around the low branch of a large beech tree. This augured poorly. And I—maybe I was making Meadow nervous?—because the whole goddamned thing was making me nervous, but *still*—I proposed we rescue the kite. I figured Meadow could easily reach it if she stood on my shoulders.

Usually, it's easy to get Meadow excited about things like that. All you have to do is add a dash of intrigue, a little pretending, in which our small task becomes a principled affair. (*If we don't retrieve the kite, the Stalinist zealots will swarm the city by nightfall!*) But that day, I couldn't get Meadow to play along. She seemed put out, suspicious of me. I could tell she'd been talking about me with her mother. I didn't really blame them. I think I speak for a lot of divorcing parents here when I say that there's so much bad shit coming at you during a divorce that a child's emotional distress takes its place in a whole constellation of problems, and these problems are so numerous that one starts to pin one's hopes on a legal resolution as some kind of final, almost atomic solution, something obliterative, and until then, well, it's almost a *personnel* problem; you don't have the staff; there aren't enough *yous*.

"What's the matter, Butterscotch?" I asked her.

"Nothing," she said.

"You sure?"

"Yeah," she said. "I guess I'm just not feeling partyish."

"Well, you don't have to feel *party*ish. But if nothing's wrong, maybe could you put a little pep in your step? A little zip in your skip? You look like someone just killed your puppy."

"I don't have a puppy."

"Exactly. Come on. Crack a smile. Please? For me?"

She wandered across the old playground, making a half-hearted sally across the monkey bars. She wore an old purple jumper and white stockings, dingy at the knees. Her hair was lank and flat, slipping out of her headband. Here was one of many moments in which I might have walked away, called the whole thing off, gotten used to being powerless, learned to be patient and conciliatory, and spared us all of what was to follow.

But a car door slammed nearby, and here she came—our potential savior.

I had never seen anyone who looked quite like her. The woman's face was as round and white as a potato, but her hair was black and coarse. Across her puffy cheeks was a spray of pigmentation, dots too big to be freckles. On each wrist she wore a black splint. She walked from her beat-up Toyota with a slightly neuralgic gait. Although she was one of the homeliest women I'd ever met, I remember thinking, Good. Here is a woman who can sympathize with me. Why else had she entered the field of psychology, but because of her own rich ache?

"Thank you so much for coming," I said, shaking only the fingers of her hand. "Your expertise means so much to me and Meadow. We just want to resolve this dispute and get

our lives back to normal. We've been kiting—" I gestured to the snagged object in the beech tree. "Too bad you missed it. Meadow is an excellent kiter. She has excellent motor skills for a child her age. Please…" I gestured toward a picnic table on which I'd set up some supporting materials. "I've got some things to show you."

The evaluator, a Ms. Sonja Vang, followed me. I whistled for Meadow. She peered around the tree and pleadingly shook her head no.

Please? I mouthed.

No. No.

For me?

No.

I turned to Ms. Vang, who was gazing at me evenly, and said, "Meadow can be shy at first. She'll come around."

The woman shrugged and rested her splints against the edge of the picnic table.

"To me," I began, "fatherhood is no onus. It's not a burden. Some men, I know, take a kind of martyred pleasure in feeling trapped by the family? They like to believe—and this is just my armchair analysis—that were they not trapped by the family, they would be, what, disabling bombs somewhere, breaking a world record, what have you. This belief enables them to a) come up with an explanation for their lack of personal success and b) get out of the more tedious aspects of child rearing—you know what I mean, the bottom wiping, the shushing, the nagging, in general, the relentless being aware of the child—by suggesting that they have been *dragooned* into the role, away from a higher purpose. Do you know what I mean?"

I smiled, waiting for encouragement. Sonja Vang made

no movement except to adjust her bottom against the picnic bench. She was panting slightly. I had my first flash of doubt. Had The Opposition planted a mole?

"From the moment Meadow was born," I continued, "I was involved with her care. Not because I thought I should be. It was because I wanted to be. When the recession hit, I spent a year at home with her, as her primary caretaker—a stay-at-home dad—which in any court of law would qualify me for custody, though I don't have to tell *you* that, right? And so—right—it was my close attention during that year which yielded what I have come to see as a unique understanding of her needs, and the way her mind works. Children aren't mysteries. We don't have to teach them sign language, like gorillas. No. We only have to pay attention to what they're *already saying*. Do you know what I mean?" I checked to see if Ms. Vang knew what I meant; she was rubbing her eyes with the back of her splint. Helplessly, I continued, "Fathers don't have to be 'like mothers.' Men aren't *soft*. Men don't smell good. You know, floral. But a good father can take a kind of abstract, human interest in the child that a mother is incapable of taking. A good father can help a child develop her aptitudes vis-à-vis a broader social backdrop. I have located a study"—and here I pushed forward several pages, printed off the Internet—"that has proved that children of both genders show better psychological health when living with the father as the custodial parent, due to—well, you can read it yourself."

The woman removed a case from her battered handbag and withdrew reading glasses. She peered down at the report.

"Your splints," I said, finally unable to bear her silence. "Did you fall?"

She did not look up. "Repeated stress."

I pushed forth my next bit of evidence. "Now, I'm just plain old bragging here, but I wanted to show you this piece of paper. Given to me when Meadow was three. The results of an IQ test, done over at the medical center, by old colleagues of mine, on a lark."

A shadow of irritation crossed the woman's face. I had the sense I should wrap it up.

"This material is significant only in that I feel, as a scholar myself—and I won't bore you with the details of my own research here—I feel more than ever required as Meadow's father. This gifted child needs two parents to—jointly, and with all the resources they can muster—lead her through—"

"Excuse me," Ms. Vang said. "Where *is* the child?"

I blinked back at her. "Meadow? She's here somewhere."

"Because I'm here to observe the two of you. Together. You know, playing and stuff. Being together."

"Of course."

"I'm not a jury, Mr. Kennedy."

"No, no you aren't."

"And I'm not *inner*ested in theories about parenthood."

"No, of course not."

I turned and scanned the playground desperately for Meadow.

"And with the divorce rate in the United States at about fifty percent," she continued, picking up steam, "higher than any industrialized nation, I do brisk business. And mostly what I see in these custody battles are people who think too much. People who could easily sort out their differences if they weren't so full of *ideas*. People who'd rather be right than happy."

I stood, panicking now, the woman close at my side.

Meadow was nowhere to be seen. She was not on the play structure, the rock climber, the swings. A stampede of young men with their shirts off blew through the playground, the Saint Rose cross-country team.

"This is awful," I said, walking briskly downhill toward the water fountain, where I was sure I'd find Meadow petting the dogs. "Sorry to make you walk so much."

Unsurprisingly, Ms. Vang withheld reassurance.

"Meadow is always wandering off. Just ask her mother. She's always petting someone's dog. Admiring someone's bicycle."

"Should watch out," grumbled the woman, loping beside me. "What I've seen done to children would give you nightmares."

"So how did you get into the business?" I asked.

"I started out in law enforcement."

"Aha."

"And then I was managing my father's seafood business, but then he died."

"Oh."

"So I made lemonade. Went back to school. Found my calling."

Several dogs nosed around in the fountain, their owners milling nearby. No Meadow. Finally, abandoning all pretense of composure, I cupped my hands around my mouth and shouted her name. People stared. A park attendant pruning rosebushes reached for his walkie-talkie. The barbarous woman who held my fate in her hands settled her buttocks down upon the granite rim of the fountain—built by some magnate in honor of his dead father—and looked at me with flat eyes, and I thought, Screw you, screw you, I never had a chance with you anyway.

And that's when I saw my daughter. She had been very close to us all along, right over our heads, having climbed the large beech in which our kite was stranded. I could see her now clearly, now that I was so far away, at a distance that seemed to increase exponentially with my own dawning regrets. As she inched out on the branch, her hand seeking the kite string, her eyeglasses flashed in the sun. The lenses were like mirrors flashing code: *Am completely confused. Will try this.* She was a child in the sky. I had put her there. And although seeing her totter on the branch was a blow to me, I saw, as I never had, how much worse things could get.

CAROUSEL

The rest of the story can be told summarily.

Meadow did not fall. The kite was not retrieved. The independent evaluation was not favorable to me. Sensing a window, The Opposition regrouped, and meanwhile my weekend visitation came and went Meadowless, and there was nothing I could do about it, nothing whatsoever. Despite the fact that Thron told me the threat was ridiculous, that losing visitation altogether was impossible, I fell into a depression worse than the one that had brought me to him. For two weeks, I did not leave the house. Unless you count going to the liquor store and Dunkin' Donuts. After a couple of angry calls, my last active client—a yogic master looking for commercial space—moved on to someone else.

May came. One morning I left the house and just started walking. I walked all the way down New Scotland, right into town, and several hours later found myself standing in front of the

7

New York State Museum. With its top-heavy modern design, and hundreds of joggable stairs rising to a monumental balcony, the building is hard to miss. From the museum balcony, you can get a clear view of all four mountain ranges that surround the capital region: Adirondack, Green, White, and Berkshire. Everywhere up here, you're surrounded by mountains.

I had not come to look at the mountains. This was more like a pilgrimage. My own personal Lourdes. Because this was the place where Meadow and I had spent so many days during my year at home with her. The year she was three. The year in which she learned to read. The year she learned to play the recorder, waltz, read the periodic table, and speak passable German. During that long northern winter, we'd gone to the library almost every day. I'd bring my research (sorry, as it turns out, I still don't feel like talking about my research), and she would settle on the carpet nearby with crayons or a fan of books, and we'd spend companionable hours like that. At some point she would tug my pant leg and I would know it was time for a visit to the carousel.

What carousel? The one made a gift to the people of Albany by the people of our sister city, Ypres, in 1935. All its mirrors still intact, as well as the original, somewhat deafening organ, the carousel found its way into the New York State Museum in the 1970s. Boasting thirty-six horses, two deer, two donkeys, and one monkey, it's worth a visit, if you're in town.

The day I went to see the carousel alone, I noticed that the assortment of people waiting in line was the same as when Meadow and I had been among them—young parents absentmindedly bouncing babies, toddlers with their foreheads wedged between the railings. I thought about how the children were too young to understand the value of what

was happening to them, which was that their minds were being imprinted by every scent, every touch, every sound, and that it was from this template they would draw for the rest of their lives. This is how the world would forever hit their nerves.

"How old?" I asked the young mother standing beside me.

The mother looked up from her baby. "Eight months," she said.

"Very cute." I pointed. "Is that a tooth?"

The young woman put her finger in the child's mouth and swiped it. The baby's eyes widened. "Nah. I don't know *what* that is." She fixed his tiny sweater.

"Well," I said. "He's a cute little guy."

"I know he is." She beamed, looking unaccountably beautiful.

Meadow's favorite horse on the carousel was a black one with a golden saddle—the outside horse. I had stood beside it countless times. When she had first ridden the carousel, her waist was thick, a baby's bubble of milk. But each time we returned to the carousel, her body was different. Her waist thinned, seemingly in my hands, and her legs lengthened and her shoes began to scrape me as they rose and fell, shod with hard plastic flats and ruffled socks. When she was little, she barely noticed me, so entranced was she by the lights and mirrors of the carousel. But as she grew older, even after she could safely ride the carousel by herself, she would ask me to stand beside her anyway, and I would whistle, and compliment her stallion, and she would look down at me, and I don't think I ever felt gladder of anything, that a daughter of mine might be in the midst of a happy childhood—that elusive gold standard, a goddamned miracle.

The carousel. Who doesn't have one in his childhood, that universal symbol around which all cravings, fulfilled and unfulfilled, seem to circle magnetically forever? They even had one, if you can believe it, in the middle of Treptower Park in East Berlin, circa 1974. And even though life in Berlin was unique, the children weren't. That is, a child in Berlin tallied the same pleasures as you did: how many rides he was permitted, who was watching and with what expressions, what to call this feeling of going up and down and around simultaneously and whether or not to enjoy it, what the child beside him was doing or not doing, who was crying and how sincerely, how the music sounded, sad or happy, or too tightly wound, maniacal; he tallied it all, especially what was done post-carousel, everything made special and weird by the motion, by a sense of having traveled. Like any child, the child in East Berlin thought about the carousel late that night in bed. His musings were double-edged; by remembering the carousel he felt he "kept" or "possessed" the carousel, and yet he understood that the carousel was not a thing, like a balloon or a toy, and could not be possessed. He noted preciously that the next time he rode the carousel—if he was so lucky, if his *Mutter* would take him there again—would not be like the time he rode it today. Also, he was starting to see that there was a difference between secrets and mysteries, and life was—unluckily for him—a mystery, not a secret, which meant nobody owned it, and therefore nobody could make it transparent for him, and nobody's death would yield the answer to it, and maybe he even understood that from there on in, whenever he looked at a carousel, no matter how old he'd grown, no matter how gray, he would never be able to comprehend the riddle of how it made him feel.

Around and around the carousel went, the frozen horses jumping.

Grief is a carousel.

Guilt is a carousel.

Life is a carousel.

No—history is a carousel.

No, no. Memory.

Memory is a carousel.

FORGETTING

One of the pieces of advice offered to parents in extremely contentious custody cases is confiscation of the children's passports. If there is any worry on the part of one spouse that the other spouse is at risk for flight with a child—that is, kidnapping (there, I said it)—the concerned spouse should request that the courts hold that child's passport. However, parents should understand a) that the United States has no exit controls—in other words, any of us can shamble in or out at any time we take a fit, and b) that there is no way to track or revoke a passport once it has been issued.

This is where things get murky.

I mean, where the unconscious mind enters. Mine.

Emboldened, I guess, by the damning child custody evaluation, your side appealed the custody arrangement with new allegations that I was a danger to my own daughter, stipulating that these charges would not be dropped until I submitted to psychological testing. In the meantime, your lawyer informed Thron that she was making a motion to restructure the custody agreement to be less, not more, collaborative. Their proposal, The Opposition warned us, was that I

be forbidden under any circumstance to spend unsupervised time with Meadow. Visits between us would be monitored by a state-appointed chaperone. Never again, the lawyer vowed, would I be allowed to endanger the girl with my bizarre, neglectful parenting. Nor would I be allowed to speak with her privately. If I wanted to be with Meadow, I would have to do so under the supervision of someone from Child Services.

I responded to this development by imbibing such a quantity of Canadian Club that I woke up the following morning shirtless on the carpet, my face hot with midday sun. I looked around the bedroom in which I lay. Everything that was not nailed into the floor had been pushed over—I could only assume by me—the secondhand bedside table, the bookshelf, and even the old, gothic wardrobe that I had taken from our Pine Hills apartment, claiming it as a Kennedy heirloom. As I tried to lift this wardrobe back onto its feet, something slipped out from between the wardrobe and its pasteboard backing and fell to the floor at my feet.

Now, even though I had erased any sort of paper trail of my life *before* I became a Kennedy, I had not, by necessity, destroyed my German passport. I was not an American citizen, so the German passport would have to do in the event of emergency international travel, which I'd easily avoided. I'd hidden the booklet inside this wardrobe who knows how many years ago. Now it lay open suggestively on the floor. I rubbed my eyes and leaned down to peer at it. There I was, a decade younger, an unmarried man of twenty-eight. My skin was taut, my stare a little icy. I barely recognized the face.

The name?

Well, everyone knows it by now.

Schroder.

Erik Schroder.

No, no. *Schroder.* Try to pronounce the *r* as a guttural. Really get in there.

Schgroder. That's it.

Where's the umlaut? Relinquished. Before we left Germany, Dad had been forewarned by somebody or other that Americans didn't believe in umlauts, and that no one in the United States used surnames anyway, but rather greeted each other by saying, Halloo, Guy! And since my father barely assimilated in the eight years in which I lived with him in Boston, I would count the umlaut as Dad's single concession to America, a change he noted to each of his auditors in 1979 as we processed from queue to queue at Logan International.

He had planned to naturalize us, my father. But he never did. We remained resident aliens. Therefore, we lived with the low-level paranoia of people vulnerable to deportation. We drove slow, never jaywalked, carried no debt, and avoided the giving and getting of favors, basically alienating ourselves from the rites of Boston brotherhood. A stickler for rules, however much he resented them, Dad even made me carry my permanent resident card with me at all times, as he carried his.

I didn't get it. My father spoke venomously about Germany. He said he didn't care what people said against him or against Germans because nobody hated Germany or Germans more than he did. No greater country had ever *ficked* itself so thoroughly as Germany. He had surrendered our umlaut. Didn't that just about sum it up? One day when I was in high school, I actually went and got naturalization forms for both of us and brought them home. I had been astonished to learn that on Part 1 (D) on Form N-400, the applicant is asked if he

would like to legally *change his name* upon naturalization. The possibility of this made my heart race, for I *had* a new name by then, and here was a chance to legitimize it. If I could just say it aloud. To him. To say, *This is who I am now. This is what I call myself. I* like *who I've become.* Standing beside the card table I used as a desk, my father reviewed the documents. He studied them for a long time. During that same interval, I realized that my quest for legitimacy was ridiculous. The difference between summer-me and Dorchester-me was so stark, the space between them so great, no mortal boy could oonch them closer. I would never be able to say my new name to my father. I couldn't be both men to anyone. By the time my father replaced the applications on the card table, crossed his arms, and shook his head slowly, I was relieved.

"*Nein, Erik. Ich will das nicht.*"

"You're probably right," I said.

"*Das Problem hat nichts damit zu tun, deutsch zu sein. Das Problem liegt mit den Staaten. Und daß es Staaten gibt.*"[4]

We remained there for another moment, him standing there beside the card table.

"*Außerdem,*" he said, shrugging. "Don't you know it yet, Erik? There is no such thing as forgetting."

---

4. The problem has nothing to do with being German. The problem has to do with countries. And that countries exist.

ERSTER TAG *OR*
DAY ONE

Curious weather. A thunderstorm gathering down in the valley. The sky dark and roiling, even though it was morning, with patches of crucified daylight dazzling between. Leaves twisted in the wind. Weather vanes whined. The birds were silent. My skin felt different. My scalp, tight. I was sick with some kind of charge—a surge, a change in my fate, a redirection. Some kind of breaking up that I needed.

Despite the fact that you had secured yourself an excellent lawyer, a young, Cornell-minted go-getter, and all I had was Rick Thron and a damning child custody evaluation, somehow we got your side on the run. Due to the skipped visitations, a judge held you in contempt of court. I don't know how he did it, but Thron somehow suppressed the child custody report, and without this key piece of evidence, your team panicked. A hasty move to appeal was thwarted when the judge reminded us that we already had an arrangement on the books—a hard-won parental agreement that had functioned well for Meadow for an entire year. We could still negotiate the conditions and limitations, but you *had* to let her visit me.

By then, I'd stopped caring about the legalities. I knew

it was only a matter of time before I'd be found out. I was reckless, illogical, maybe even lacking moral character, but I was *not* crazy. I could tell how much better your lawyer was than mine. Mine hadn't even checked out my bogus documents. The only thing I knew for certain was that I could not bear it anymore, the suspense of the way things were. I could imagine that someday, maybe, I would feel better, I would get accustomed to my new life, but today—*this* day—I couldn't take it anymore, the way the wind went out of the world whenever my daughter left. When she left, the yards, the parks, the streets of Albany all seemed abandoned. The life went out of things. And until my life returned to its cycle of baked beans and sporadic couch sleep, I would experience a spasm of grief, a kind of spiritual lockjaw, that I stopped wanting to bear. No, I thought. Not today. I can't do it. If you had told me I was going to die at the end of today, I would have said, *Good.*

The familiar black Chevy Tahoe pulled up to the curb.

I came out to the stoop, hands in pockets, and waited. My father-in-law gave me his trademark surprised smile, like *Hey, you're still you,* and waved to me as if I were not actually locked in mortal conflict with his daughter. I waited for Meadow as she jogged across the spring grass carrying her backpack.

To the first question:

Did the accused premeditate the abduction?

The answer is no.

Or, not really.

Besides, the word *abduction* is all wrong. It was more like an adventure we both embarked upon in varying levels of ignorance and denial.

"Good morning, Butterscotch," I said.

She looked up at me, her red-framed eyeglasses reflecting the several large willows that loomed over the ranch house from the backyard. The wind rose, lifting the ends of her long brown hair. She hoisted the backpack onto her shoulder.

"Morning, Daddy."

THE ROAD

After lunch, I told Meadow to wash up and get her backpack.

"We're hitting the road!" I said.

She tilted her head. "We're *hitting* the road? With what?"

"No, no, no," I laughed. "We're going driving. We're going on a trip. A spontaneous trip. You and me. How does that sound?"

She slid off her stool, leaving the crusts of her peanut butter and jelly sandwich on the Mickey Mouse plate I kept around for her.

"OK," she said. "Where're we going?"

"Well. How'd you like to spend the day at Lake George?"

She clutched her hands in front of her chest. "Yes yes yes!"

"Who wants to sit around *here* all day? I think it's plenty warm to swim, don't you?"

"Yes!"

"Did you happen to pack a swimsuit?"

"No!"

"Not a problem!" I shouted back. "We'll buy you a new one when we get up there."

That morning, before her arrival, I had packed myself a small bag (swimming trunks, a toothbrush, some reading material), letting this small bag flirt with my own desire to flee, but not with the *clarity* of premeditation. It was more with a desperate flourish that the last thing to go into the bag—after a slight hesitation—was my passport. Just in case! You never know! We climbed into my Saturn and rolled down all the windows. Meadow sat in the backseat in an age-appropriate booster. The car was clean and impersonal, with CLEBUS & CO stenciled cheerfully on either side, for anyone to see.

We were mostly through the suburban bottleneck of Albany when I became aware of something in my rearview mirror. A big black shadow of a car that had been lurking along several lengths behind. I took a gratuitous left. The car followed. I took a random right. Again the car followed. I sped up. So did my counterpart. I stopped at a Stewart's and idled in the parking lot. My counterpart moseyed past only to pull over to a roadside asparagus stand about fifty yards ahead. I shook my head heavily.

"What is it?" Meadow asked.

"Pop-Pop's following us," I said.

She craned her head forward to gawk.

I stilled her with my hand. "No. Don't look."

"Why's Pop-Pop following us?"

"I don't know. I'd better think."

"Are we still going to Lake George?"

"Hush," I said. "Let me think."

Meadow sighed, folding her hands on her lap, muttering, "You *said* we were going to Lake George. You *said* we could go. You already *said*."

I watched the Tahoe idling just ahead down the road. I

could almost picture the poor man gripping the wheel, trying to retract his head into his torso. Did he really think I couldn't see him?

"It's so *boring* sitting at home."

"Please, Meadow. Let Daddy think."

"That's all Mommy and Glen ever do. Sit around and talk talk talk."

I raised my eyes to the rearview mirror. "Mommy and who?"

"Glen. Daddy, Glen talks *forever*. He's boring. He's a lawyer."

"But Mommy's lawyer is a woman, right? Or has she changed lawyers? Or is Glen just a friend who's a lawyer? Oh, who cares. Right? Who cares? I don't care. Do you care? I don't."

I looked back out at the passing traffic. I thought of my estranged wife confabulating with Glen, whoever the hell he was, toasting another legal victory over a homemade meal. And I almost laughed—a shrill, shattered laugh—thinking of the poor Papa Bear in the story who says, *Who's been eating my porridge? Who's been sitting in my chair?* I reached back and made sure Meadow's seat belt was snug across her lap and gave her an inscrutable tap on the leg. Then I accelerated so quickly the tires shrieked. I nearly clipped the Pepsi deliveryman as I swerved around the side of the building and pulled out onto the two-lane road going the opposite direction, right in front of a huge Sysco truck. In my driver's-side mirror, the Tahoe jerked forward, circling the asparagus stand and leaving the roadside pullover in a cloud of dust. This was just the goosing I needed; Grandpa was giving chase. Behind me, he kept trying and failing to pass the Sysco truck across the double yellow lines, the oncoming traffic wailing past. His willingness

to drive at such risk was a thrill and made me want to see how far he'd go. At a congested intersection, I led him into the right-turn-only lane, toward the highway, only to cross two lanes at the last second before the light turned green to go left. I was heading north again, on Van Rensselaer Boulevard, and had lost sight of Pop-Pop in the bottleneck he created as he tried to avoid being shunted west onto the Thruway. A can-tata of horn blowing. My jaw tingled. I suppressed a whoop of victory.

Who had we been kidding anyway, me and Hank? He was justifiably suspicious of me since the day he met me, and he'd been generous to wait this long to hate me openly. I felt something like gratitude for that. He had always been, to my mind, the kind of upbeat, clannish father I assumed every American was awarded at birth. I stepped on it. We were now going sixty miles an hour through stop-and-go traffic on Van Rensselaer.

I was hesitant to glance back at my passenger. I wasn't used to spending long periods of time with Meadow anymore. In the intervening year since we'd ceased sharing the same roof, she'd conquered kindergarten, and was a big girl for six, taller and smarter than any of her classmates, and I hoped I'd come out OK as she sat in moral judgment of me back there in her zebra-print booster seat. I reminded myself that even as a toddler, she'd been unsentimental. She didn't like drippy speeches or ardent kisses, and so I decided to skip the emotional appeals, the flimsy self-justifications for what I was doing. They barely sufficed anyway.

"Traffic is terrible," I said.

"Yeah," she said.

"You doing all right back there?"

"Actually, I'm thirsty," she replied, her voice slightly strained.

"Well, let's get you something to drink. What would you like? Jelly-bean juice? Hm? Monkey milk?"

"Actually, could I have a Mountain Dew? Mariah drinks Mountain Dew. Her mother lets her."

"Sure," I said. "No problem. I'll stop just down the road a bit and we'll find you a Mountain Dew. We'll do the dew. Can't be that bad for you if it's *dew*, right?"

"Yeah. And can I watch *Star Wars*?"

"Maybe. Listen. One thing at a time."

"OK."

"You sure you're all right?"

"Yes."

"I've got this under control. All right?"

That's when Grandpa reappeared, like a zombie who staggers forward with his head blown off. The fender of the Tahoe was rumpled—I could see this from far away—and he was now driving with fresh desperation, flashing his headlights. Did he really think I would stop? Did he think I would heed him *now*, both of us with our gloves off? I was not in violation of the terms of my allotted visitation period. There was nothing in our parental agreement that said I couldn't drive around the outskirts of Albany at high speeds. No, I thought, looking into the rearview mirror. Not today. You're going to have to kill me.

Somewhere early on in my post-divorce social suicide, I had represented a client in the purchase of a foreclosed bungalow in Loudonville. After the transaction, we became friends, this client and I. He was also single and gave off a whiff, as I must have, of redundant abandonment. When he decided to

go away for the summer, whom else did he call to watch over his property, and occasionally run the engine of his new Mini Cooper to keep the battery from dying, but me? I had already visited this friend's house once and had sat in the garage with the Mini Cooper running, noticing with dispassion that it wasn't just a Hollywood plot device; you really *couldn't* smell carbon monoxide. And it was this Mini Cooper that came to mind—with wonderfully changed function, as an Escape Car—as I headed west on 378, the wounded undercarriage of my father-in-law's Tahoe throwing sparks in the increasing distance behind me.

MOST BEAUTIFUL WATER

The first white men who ever came across Lake George were handily captured, on account of them standing there gawking at its beauty. It's still an oceanic, slate-blue tableau when you come across it a half hour's drive north of Saratoga Springs, propped there in the Adirondacks 320 feet above sea level. Its basin stretches from the town of Lake George all the way north to Ticonderoga, its western border a series of goofy little pleasure towns filled with motels, waterslides, and pancake houses.

Driving northward, full of anticipation, Meadow and I sang. We sang our favorites, like "Yellow Submarine" and "Kentucky Woman." She'd been amused by the Mini Cooper we'd switched for my Saturn in Loudonville and did not ask any questions about why we were driving it or whether or not we were still being pursued by Pop-Pop. We were together again. It was easy. For the first time in a year, I felt some hope. I felt like I had finally taken back some control. No more rope-a-dope in divorce mediation. I knew that we were going to make it to Lake George. I knew that, and I didn't give a shit about what happened after that. Frankly.

It was unseasonably warm for June. We rolled the windows down and sailed our hands in the air. We didn't stop, and we didn't stop. We didn't stop in Saratoga Springs; we didn't stop at Lake Luzerne, or Glens Falls, or anywhere. We didn't even slow down until we'd entered the Lake George strip and Meadow started shouting Popcorn! Candied apples! Frozen lemonade! The water parks and go-cart tracks had opened early, and tourists like ourselves were walking around half-dressed and jaundiced from winter. We had been here the summer before, Meadow and I and you-know-who-you-are, I mean our family, in what we might term Year Zero (to be followed by the post-divorce epoch, or *Annum Repudium*), but neither of us mentioned the fact.

We parked on the street and ran down past a band shell and a playground and straight onto the small, hard-packed public beach near the dockside. Meadow wound her way through the sunbathers right out onto the sand and to my surprise waded into the water with her clothes on. She stopped only when the water soaked the hem of her tangerine-colored shorts.

"Daddy!" she cried, turning back to me. "It's *cold*."

"Of course it's cold, silly," I said, rolling my khakis up to my knees. "It's two hundred feet deep. Come on. Let's buy you a suit?"

"No, Daddy! Not yet."

I smiled, secretly pleased, remembering how impossible it always was to tear her away from whatever her attention had seized upon: a bottle cap, a ladybug, the removal of sticker-backing goo from a glass bottle.

I put my hands on my hips and looked around at the crowd of bodies. Some were inching their way into the icy water; others were spreading out picnics, parcels of tinfoil, coolers of

ice, everyone trying to save a buck, bringing bologna sandwiches from home or smoking generic cigarettes like Basics
or Viceroys, because we were all into it by then, the recession,
we were all inside it or knew that we were about to be. An
attractive young family was lounging close to the waterline
near Meadow. I smiled at them, all four of them, that ideal-
ized American square—a large, good-looking father rapt by
the movements of the distant steamboats, a strawberry blond
mother in a sturdy bikini, a sarong wrapped around her waist,
and two focused children digging in the sand.

I said aloud, in their direction, "A day like this just melts
away the stress."

The petite mother glanced my way. "It's *too* pretty today,
isn't it? My problem is, when it's this pretty, I just want to keep
it. I just want to box it up and keep it and have it last forever."

"Oh, don't think like that," I said, taking a step or two in
her direction. "That'll just make you sad."

She smiled, tilting her head slightly.

"Anyway," I said, "you know where you keep a day like
this? You keep it in your heart. That's the box you keep it in."

My eye on Meadow, now almost up to her waist in Lake
George, I grinned down at the woman's children. "Hey, you
two. Strike gold yet?" Below us, her children ignored me, just
as her husband ignored me. The woman's cheeks reddened. I
probably could have kissed her on the mouth and he would
have kept on muttering about the steamboats. I felt a rush of
fellow feeling. My pity for her and for me and for her kids and
for my kid and even for you, Laura, came over me in a wave
so sudden and so felt that I almost lost my balance. I closed my
eyes. I *feel*, I thought to myself. I clenched my hands open and
shut. I *feel*. I'm *alive*.

When I opened my eyes, the woman was staring at me.

"Are you all right?" she asked.

"I'm great," I said. "Never better, in fact."

Along the weathered dockside people strolled quietly. But for the creaking of the dock boards and oars in their oarlocks and the chanting of vendors and the distant churning of the steamboats, the crowd seemed hushed, awed. The world was softening, opening up.

"Spring always feels like such a victory," I said. "Like you did something good to deserve it."

"That is *so* true," said the woman. "Plus, it was such an icy winter. Icy and slushy and eewy."

"One of the worst. At least in my personal history. But"— I looked at her—"I guarantee you, it's going to be an extraordinary summer."

She smiled again, displaying two pearlescent front teeth with a pretty little gap.

"Really? How do *you* know?"

"I just do. Butterscotch!" I called to Meadow. "Come back a bit toward shore, OK? The sign says, 'no swimming.' There's no lifeguard yet."

"I'm not swimming, Daddy," she called without turning. "I'm *fishing*."

My friend and I exchanged a pair of knowing looks whose covert purpose was legitimate eye contact with one another.

"Are you and your daughter staying on the lake?" the woman asked. "It's going to be a beautiful weekend, they say. Unseasonably warm."

"No," I sighed. "We've got to head home. We've got a long drive ahead of us."

"Where's home?"

"Canada."

"Oh. You're Canadian?" The woman blushed again, and I detected a faint note of disappointment, as if she'd already become attached to me. "I always expect Canadians to look different. But they never do."

"It's how we speak," I said. "You have to wait until we start talking about how sooory we are."

The woman laughed, sweeping her foot in the water. "And your girl's mother? She's back at home?"

"Yes." I turned to face her. "My wife's back at home. Waiting for us." In the background, my friend's husband dimly became aware of me. "She keeps calling us. 'How many miles left now? How many more hours?' She misses us."

"Of course she does," the woman said. I watched her face, slightly rosy with the thought of it, whatever *it* is, the universal dream, the dreamed us. The wind played with the beaded hem of her sarong. She pulled one delicate foot out of the sand and the sand made a crude suctioning sound and the steamboat tooted in the distance and I finally looked away from her and across the lake at the hills.

"Isn't that something," I said, overwhelmed. "The way the light is growing long on the hills across the lake. Look at that. The way the hills seem in a different dimension over there. What an afternoon. You're right, you know. This day should not be allowed to end. We *should* be allowed to keep it. You know what? This is the first time this year that I haven't felt like jumping off a bridge." I looked at my companion. A breeze blew her apricot-colored hair off her brow, which was pinched sympathetically. "I know you don't even know me, but I'm glad you're here. I mean, I'm glad you're here with your family. Your family makes me happy."

"Oh," she said.

"It's good, don't you think? It's the point, don't you think? Togetherness. Like this. In families."

She gazed back at me, her expression uncertain.

"Hey, Tex," the husband bellowed. "Your kid is swimming in her clothes."

We all looked. In the near distance, but with commitment, Meadow was indeed swimming, her head held stiffly just above the water, a big grin on her face. Just then the sun reemerged from the sky's lone cloud, spilling outrageous light across the surface of the lake, which now seemed to be filled with boiling gold. I shielded my eyes and watched Meadow swim.

"Will you look at that," I said. "I didn't even know she could swim."

"You didn't—" The woman stepped forward. "Is she all right?"

"Oh, very," I said. "Look at her. Solid. She must have learned last year."

"But is that safe? I mean, no one else is in the water, it's so cold."

"You're right, I should join her. Excuse me."

I was wearing tan khakis, rolled to the knee, and a short-sleeve blue-checkered dress shirt from Eddie Bauer. I flipped my wallet and keys backwards onto the beach and waded out into the frigid water until my shirt belled around me. When the water was at my chest, I pushed off. Leaning my ear into the water, I swam a lazy sidestroke past my daughter. "Hello," I said. "Fancy meeting you here." She treaded in my vision, her glasses speckled with water. "This water is heart-stoppingly cold," I said. "I mean, I think my heart just

stopped." Our laughter rang out over the water. From the beach, people stared. I could see my redhead looking beautiful and puzzled. Some things you can't explain, you just can't, no matter how sympathetic nor how moving in her own right is the listener.

STEAMBOATS

She wanted to ride the steamboats. We chose the *Minne-Ha-Ha*.

"Ha-ha-ha," we said. "Ha! Ha! Ha!"

We ran up the gangplank, dodging the crowd, because we wanted the best view of the paddlewheels. We hung as far over the rails on the upper deck as we safely could, and after a toot from the calliope, the boat left the dock, and we were showered with a chilly mist from the paddles. Meadow screamed, drawing other children to us, several of whom stuck their heads through the rail bars until their parents called them back. We didn't care. I mean, we were wet already. Behind us, the shoreline fell away, and a chaos of seagulls hung over our wake like bridesmaids holding a veil. The wind picked up, soft and clean.

She said, "Here's a joke. Where does a dog do his grocery shopping?"

"I don't know. Where?"

"The Stop 'n' Smell."

"That's brilliant."

"I made it up. I can roller-skate, you know."

"You can swim, you can roller-skate. What else can you do?"

"I can fly."

"Of that I am skeptical."

"Knock-knock," she said. "Orange."

"Wait. You forgot to let me ask who's there."

"Who's there?"

"Ha! No, *I* ask *you*."

The steamboat chugged up the eastern bank of Lake George. Dusk was falling as the boat came about, and we saw the yellow ball of sun disappear in a glint through the keyhole of the northernmost mountains.

"Poof," she said. "Good night!"

"Yeeeeer outta here, sun," I said.

"Yeeeeer out, sun!"

"You're goin' *down*, sun."

"Way down," she said. "All the way downtown."

"You're goin' down*state*."

Grinning, she climbed a metal bench on the deck. "But I *can* fly," she said. "Watch." Stretching her arms out for balance, she placed both sneakers on the armrest, and started wheeling her arms, looking ungainly.

"Careful," I said although she was well clear of the railings. Her shorts were bunched up over either thigh accordion-style, and her T-shirt rode up over her belly as she seesawed above the bench. When she jumped, her wind-knotted hair trailed like streamers.

"I'll eat my hat," I said. "You *can* fly."

"I told you."

"Come on, you crazy kid. Your lips are purple."

We entered the warm inner cabin, where most of the families had fled from the afternoon bluster. An infant given free range was crawling across the tacky linoleum floor, batting an empty soda can in front of her.

"I'm hungry, Daddy."

I looked around the cabin. "We should get you some dinner."

She pointed. "How about something from that venting machine?"

"Brilliant," I said. "It can vent us some dinner."

Famous Amos cookies and a Yoo-hoo for her. Grainy hot coffee for me.

"Voilà," I said, choosing a bench. "Dinner."

Underneath us hummed a powerful motor. The vibration was loud and emptied my mind. I watched the green wall of mountain pass on the starboard side, near enough to see the play of songbirds in the branches.

Meadow said, "Daddy, am I allowed to marry you when I grow up?"

Involuntarily, I winced and looked at my shoes. "Nah," I said, warming my hands on my paper cup. "You can't. Besides, you don't want to marry me anyway. But that's sweet of you to ask. Truth is, you really ought to find someone closer to your own age."

"Mariah's my age. Am I allowed to marry Mariah?"

"In certain states."

"I'd like to marry you. That's my choice. Knock-knock. Daddy? Knock-knock."

I looked at her, trying not to look as sad as I felt. "I love you, you know."

"I know. Knock-knock."

"I love you with my whole soul," I said. "I wish I could explain it."

"I know it already."

"Good." I smiled. "So you know what a soul is?"

"Sure," she said, straightening. "The soul keeps the body up."

I watched the vast sky absorb the darkness, my head buzzing, my heart too full.

"You have a wonderful way of putting things," I said. "You have a wonderful way of seeing things. You have a wonderful mind."

"I know," she said, shrugging. "You say that all the time." She fished in her bag for another cookie.

A blur of happy sensations and half-glimpsed intentions, and we were back inside the Mini Cooper, Meadow strapped into the booster seat, tucked under a large new beach towel that read "Queen of American Lakes." We were driving again. North. The moon doggedly following us through the gaps in the trees. I turned on the radio. Al Green. *I'm so tired of being alone. I'm so tired of on-my-own.* In the rearview mirror, I watched Meadow surreptitiously stick her thumb in her mouth. Immediately her eyelids grew heavy.

"Doesn't the dentist want you to stop sucking your thumb, sweetheart?" I said, remembering some injunction delivered via Pop-Pop. "So your teeth don't get bent out of shape?"

"I'm not sucking my thumb," she mumbled, mouth full.

"You sleepy?"

"Nope. I'm wide-awake. I'm going to stay awake all night."

"Good. Then you can keep me company." I smiled at her

in the rearview mirror. "Turns out, I don't like the quiet. G.K. Chesterton called it 'the unbearable repartee.' Silence, that is."[5] I was driving—just driving—Lake George constant alongside, the moon skipping through the branches.

"And it's too quiet without you around," I said. "No knock-knock jokes. No songs. I feel like I missed a year of your life, really. It's not your fault. But you can swim and I didn't even know it. It's like my life's been on pause, but yours—yours kept going." I laughed at myself. "God. Your mom used to hate this about me, how I would just talk and talk—"

Predictably, there was no response from the backseat. Her thumb was suspended in front of her mouth, but her head had fallen to one shoulder, her glasses resting on the bulb at the end of her nose.

---

5. I tend to agree with Chesterton. In early days, before parenthood, when nothing at all was wrong yet, I still didn't feel comfortable being silent with you. There was a sunny corner of the apartment on the top floor—we called it our Florida room—where the light blazed in for several hours in the late morning. I remember the starfish of your hand through the thin, illuminated newspaper, the uncombed crest of your hair above the front page, and the shameless gap in your robe. I've never been able to pay attention to anything for very long. I can't even really pay attention to the newspaper. So you would read, and I would chat, or fix breakfast, or run my hand down the back of the cat we fostered for a single winter. I used to mimic her voice—nasal, complaining—and you would laugh, half listening. Once you'd dressed and tamed your hair, we'd go outside, blinded by the daylight. I can remember our twin shadows against the brick buildings, and kissing on rigid benches, and how you warmed your hands between your thighs, and pints of stout, and sports bars, and the small hit of vindication I got whenever I glanced at your profile, how you made me want to brag, how you made me feel large, and how I wanted to be seen with you. Sometimes, alone together, what I felt for you was too much. But the noise of the street and the bars relieved it. You looked dreamily out of windows. Games went into overtime. I could just brush you with a hand or leg, and you were there.

People say that I've found a way
To make you say that you love me
Hey baby, you didn't go for that it's a natural fact
That I wanna come back show me where's at, baby

We lost the radio signal somewhere north of Ticonderoga.

WELL-WORN DREAMS

L et me tell you more about that scenic byway north alongside Lake George, about my state of mind. Dusk had
fallen, leaving only the outline of the Adirondack foothills
on the east side of the lake, black behemoths in the purple
dark. Stars were clustered above the neon signs of innumerable roadside motels. The motels themselves were indistin-
guishable, their names infinite recombinations of the words
cove, *lake*, and *cozy*. The air through the gap in the driver's-
side window tasted clean and atmospheric, as if siphoned from
virgin space.

When I had driven through this thicket of life, into the
northern darkness, a truly keen sense of longing had washed
over me. I realized that my situation was irreparable. I was
like a dead man, appealing my death. It made me too sad, to
realize how late and how insufficient such an appeal would
be. But why couldn't this have been mine? *This* world, this
world of togetherness. These towel-dried families trekking
under the streetlights barefoot like migrating turtles, four or
five to a room, sleeping below a ceiling fan, dreams leaping
from head to head, the baby curling now against his sister, the

dad—suddenly awakened—lazily counting his brood, one two three kids and a wife, the wife (old friend, how could you still be so pretty?) in the midst of some well-worn dream. Walking to the ice machine in his boxer shorts with a bucket. Moths swarming the spotlight. Midnight, a touch of Canadian Club in a plastic cup. Why couldn't I be him? Even the boredom, the functional alcoholism—I would have taken it. I would have been grateful for it, every day.

But the dead man, his soul in ascension, goes north. I drove a little farther than I had planned. (There's a lot of road up there.) I knew only that to go further from one thing is also to come closer to something else.

Closer, but to what exactly?

Further, but from what?

The guilty mind accelerates, its pedal stuck. Thoughts come with too much velocity. This is its own punishment. Whenever headlights appeared in my rearview mirror, or I saw a car catching up with me from some distance, this velocity took effect. As the lights came closer, filling my rearview mirror, I could not help but drive faster. To speed, like my mind. Only once the cars passed me would I feel myself reeling from the sudden deceleration of my mind. The red glow of the taillights left me nauseous. I knew I was doing something wrong. But many wrong things had been done to me. And sometimes wrong things are done in the service of rightness.

I passed a sign that read, PARADOX, 2 MILES, and laughed bitterly.

Meadow stirred in the backseat.

"Daddy?" she said sleepily. "Are you OK, Daddy?"

"God yes, I'm great. I mean, it's great to be with you. Go back to sleep."

And that's when we lost Al Green, and all I could raise on the radio were a couple of angry men talking about Manny Ramirez. I spied the black smear of Lake Champlain to the east.

There is no such thing as forgetting.

Unsettled by the sight of Lake Champlain's dark expanse, I fled the back roads for the thruway. I searched the contents of my friend's glove compartment and to my relief found a flask with a crusted nozzle and took a swallow. The dashboard glowed spaceship green. The radio signal, as I said, had been lost. It was close to midnight by then anyway. No one seemed awake with me. No one seemed alive at all. In the backseat, Meadow slept, the beach towel pulled to her chin. I considered waking her up, just to hear the sound of someone else's voice.

The lights of Plattsburgh relieved me. Plattsburgh is a snarl of a town, surprisingly impoverished, barracks of transient white people hanging about, their children wide-awake all night. The clear lack of a police presence in Plattsburgh suggested it as a good place to stop. I needed a break. And to recover my wits. Meadow slept on. I parked under the spotlights of a heating-oil company parking lot, got out, and walked as far away from the idling car as I responsibly could. The huge drum lights from the port were at my back. My long shadow lay on the scrub grass. And that was when I began to breathe shallowly. My throat tightened. My hand went to my throat. Good God, I thought, not now. This had happened to me before, of course, but not for a long time. It had happened to me a lot when I was little. The cure for this had been— back in the dark days of Soviet-style medicine—long, lonely steam showers, my mother's form a blurry silhouette waiting

for me on the edge of the toilet, periodically asking me if I felt better yet. I do not want to suggest that my life, and the series of mistakes I was making, was fated. And yet, and yet. It had been years since I stood gasping for air like I did standing in the parking lot in Plattsburgh. I felt that I had just woken up in utter darkness only to be blinded by a bright, sourceless light. I was finally awake, but who was that beyond? Who held the spotlight?

So this is what I did: I decided we would go to Canada. Just for a little. I had my passport, and I knew that even if Pop-Pop had alerted the police about Eric Kennedy, no one on God's earth was yet looking for Erik Schroder. And since I lacked Meadow's passport, and since she was asleep, I reasoned I would just scoop her up and lay her in the trunk and drive her across the border. I'd heard you could virtually roll right through the Canadian border. The stop would consist of a friendly chat that would probably go something like this:

Hello there.
Hello, sir.
A German national, are you?
Yes, sir.
(A squint into my face.)
Here for pleasure?
Yes, true. Just wanting much to see this Canada.
(A brief sweep with a flashlight of the empty backseat.)
Well, you go ahead and see it, sir. You have yourself a nice night.

The searchlights at the border were visible down the highway, giving the impression of a distant fire. I pulled over to

the side of the road. I turned around and looked at Meadow asleep in the backseat. I gently shook her leg. No response. I got out of the car, and under no moon I opened the trunk. It was very small. Mini. I made a nest out of what I could—the Lake George towels and some of my friend's forgotten clothes. I moved aside the jumper cables and brushed clean the rough fabric. Then I opened the roadside rear door, crouched in the cab, and lifted my sleeping child into my arms. I carried her out and laid her in the trunk, tucking the towels around each limb. She looked comfortable enough. I patted her shoulder. She would sleep through it, I told myself. The journey over the border would be less than fifteen minutes. And then we would have all the time in the world, how much or how little of it we wanted—no, we'd be *outside* of time; we'd be free of it. I returned to the backseat for Meadow's backpack and tip-toed through the roadside gravel and placed it at her feet, only to find her open eyes staring up at me.

"What are we doing, Daddy?" she whispered. "Why am I in the trunk?"

I stood there looking down at her, one hand on the trunk door. Her eyes were shining and colorless. The taillights of the idling car lit the grass, the road, and my own body, doused with red light.

"Would you mind terribly if—" I cleared my throat. "Would you be uncomfortable if—"

My gut cramped. I took several steps into the grass and vomited. I stayed there bent over in the dark brush for a moment. When I looked back at the car, Meadow was sit-ting upright, her fingers curled over the rubber sealant of the trunk, looking concerned for me.

But tell me, isn't that what childhood *is*? An involuntary adventure? A kidnapping? Before birth, before your specific appearance, what angel asked you, in the astral light of the anteworld, *Excuse me, little presence, would you like to be born now? Would you like to be born into this family or to that one? Into which sort of life? Into which set of circumstances?*

Tell me, when did you consent to your own life?

VIOLATORS

A little German history, if you will. Wars are often about maps—maps and borders—but occasionally they are also about walls. Most Germans cringe at the topic of modern history, and theirs is a villain-shaped shadow few of us have to live with, but let it be said that perhaps the unique result of their defeat at the hands of the Allies after World War II was the consequence of being *divvied up*. For a short time, in fact, before the country split into an East and a West in 1946, it was parceled by four, with a little smackerel of it going even to the French for some reason. And Berlin! Berlin itself was a mirror image of the splintered whole and was also divided fractiously (forgive me if you already know this) into four zones. This incoherence of a city was then marooned inside the erstwhile Soviet zone. Sure, we could consider Germany in terms of "divorce." The "divorce" of Germany led to a kind of "shared custody" in which several monolithic parent powers were meant to maturely resolve disputes that were absurdly at odds with their warring national interests and entrenched ideologies. And so the war grew very cold, and civility impossible, and the mediation process resulted in a kind of bizarre and

hostile parental agreement (see Potsdam) whereby the parents decided to *split up the siblings*, one child going westward and the other shuffling off with some natural reluctance to the east.

So Germany was divided and Berlin was divided and for a while everyone was just trying to move forward and rebuild and forget. (Destroyed buildings, destroyed bodies, a half-destroyed race stacked like planks under the dirt of a black field.) Fairly soon, for reasons I won't go into here mostly because I don't know them, East Germany fell into a state of economic privation, and people were just trying to get their hands on some butter or maybe a banana or something. Of course, after giving this a try, many East Germans became disillusioned with socialism. It was inevitable, West Berlin was just *too close*. In East Berlin, for example, you could smell buttered toast wafting from the apartment buildings along Bernauer Strasse. When, in 1961, it became clear that the East German government was trying to devise a solution for the torrent of jaded East Berliners leaving for West Berlin and democracy every day, rumors of an actual *wall* were born. The GDR head of state and Communist Party boss Walter Ulbricht (1893–1973) answered a reporter's question about rumors that a wall might be built to stop the exodus. Ulbricht's legendary answer, as you may know, was *"Niemand hat die Absicht, eine Mauer zu errichten!"*[6]

And yet a wall was erected. A precast concrete construction with large reinforced concrete and prestressed concrete components. Unlike other great walls (China, Turkey), over the years, this one eventually morphed into something truly

---

6. No one intends to build a *wall* [emphasis mine].

impenetrable, with many innovative add-ons: spotlights, anti-vehicle trenches, wire fencing, protective bunkers, watchtowers, and even a dog run. The Wall was not just a wall but a wide swath of seared and swept land, upon which desperate crossers could be handily sited between crosshairs.

But the East Berliners did not give up the ghost of escape. The impenetrability of the Wall made them want to cross it all the more. Nowhere in the history of oppression do we see as much creativity as we do around crossing the inner German border. Between August of 1961 and November of 1989, thousands of daredevils from all over East Germany tried to make history by flinging themselves over this border in every conceivable manner. Some highlights? 1965: A Leipzig engineer casts a weighted Perlon string from the roof of an East German ministerial building and sends his family one by one down his spontaneous funicular. 1968: Bernd Böttger from Sebnitz attaches an auxiliary engine to a buoy and thereby invents the world's first "aqua-scooter," which pulls Böttger across the Baltic at the lamentable rate of five kilometers per hour. (He lives. I'm only telling you about the ones that lived.) Or how about this one, undertaken in 1975, soon after the East German government signs a pact in Helsinki promising its residents *freedom of movement*: Two brothers in West Germany build a homemade aluminum airplane and cover it with Soviet insignia, then fly the aircraft straight into Treptower Park, where a third long-lost brother and the man's young son clamber aboard. They fly back to West Berlin, the little boy screaming with pleasure and confusion the whole way. That one's famous. And if it's not, it should be.

If there's one thing I'm sure of, it's that making a dusty run for it across the control strip would have been way beneath

my father. My father was a collector, a tinker, a wonk. My father was a squinter, a skeptic, a bender over documents, a taker-apart of small machines. For however long he contemplated our escape—that is to say, mine and his—I imagine that he investigated as much as he could the methods of wall crossings, weighing their relative merits. He would have studied them all: the sprinters, the jumpers, the tunnelers, the train commandeerers, the aviators, the gliders, the swimmers, the divers, the sailors, the bulldozers, the imposters, and the passport falsifiers. An internal GDR memorandum entitled "Overview of Attempted and Successful Border Violations Across the Border Security Installations (December 1974– May 1982)" makes for interesting reading. According to this document, 7,282 "border violators" were arrested during this time. Only 313 violators succeeded in crossing.

It's a slim number, but let's say it's correct.

I'm not telling you all this to brag.

I'm telling you this because I know about borders.

HOWL

So there we were, by the roadside, my daughter and myself. She was sitting obediently in the trunk of a stolen Mini Cooper somewhere just shy of Champlain, New York. And I had my hand on the trunk door and was debating how to explain this. In the end, I was unable to speak a word. An approaching eighteen-wheeler broke the silence between us, grinding up the highway and pouring its headlights across the sad scene. I made no move to hide myself from view. The driver did not stop. A man stuffing a child in the trunk of a car was no business of his!

"Daddy?" Meadow said again, entranced by my scheme even as she detected danger in it. The telltale whistle below her breath betrayed her stress. That teakettle boil, that awful rasp, that constriction.

I reached out my hand. Meadow took it.

"Get out of there," I said, laughing drily. "I don't know *what* I was thinking."

She stepped out of the trunk and balanced on the fender before jumping off. She looked backwards at the road for a

moment, more trucks approaching. Their headlights shone through the gap between her knees.

"Where *are* we?" she said.

"North," I said.

"Oh. Are we going to keep going and going?"

"Not that way," I said, pointing toward the border. "I don't know anymore."

I sat on the fender and cleaned my face with my shirtsleeve. She turned around. "If we kept going, where would we be?"

"Canada," I said.

"And after that?"

"Baffin Bay. I think."

"And after that?"

"Greenland?"

"And after that?"

"Jesus, Meadow, nowhere. The ocean. Come here. You need a puff." I retrieved her backpack from the trunk, took her inhaler from the outside pocket of her knapsack, and shook it. She leaned forward and accepted two spritzes. I tucked the inhaler back where I'd found it, right beside the neatly curled tube of strawberry toothpaste.

"No, *after* the ocean," she said, exhaling medicinally into my face. "On the other side of the North Pole."

"Oh, I see what you mean. Russia."

"And after that?"

"I don't know, Meadow."

"Daddy?"

A line of traffic passed us, coherent, oceanic.

"Daddy?"

"Yes?"

"Your face is wet."

I touched my fingers to my cheeks.

"Oh," I said. "I guess it's because I'm crying. Do you mind?"

"No."

"Good."

We watched the traffic.

"Do you get sad when I'm sad, Meadow?"

"Yes."

"Well, there's really nothing that can be done about that. You just have to stand it."

"OK."

"You just have to stand it. You'll be free of it much later, when your mother and I are gone. It's all right to be relieved when other people die. No one ever tells you that."

She stared back at me.

"Believe me," I said.

"OK."

I wiped my face.

"Look at you—" I plucked at her shirt, sniffling. "Your clothes are still damp. Maybe that's bringing on your asthma. How about you change into your pajamas in the backseat? While I take a look at the map. OK?"

"Don't you know the way back home?"

"I know the way back home. Do as I say. OK?"

Pulling away from the roadside, I made a screeching U-turn. I could feel Meadow watching me. I didn't know what to say about my tears. There is nothing to say about them, even now.

"You know what would cheer me up?" I said.

"What?"

"I'd like to see a very tall mountain. With you."

"All right. Is there one close by?"

"Sure. There are mountains everywhere."

"Good. Because I have school Monday."

"Right, school." Again, in the distance, I could see the orange glow of Plattsburgh. "When are they going to let you out of that place? Don't Catholics believe in summertime? It's hot already, for Pete's sake. The blackberries are out. Outside is life."

"I don't know. June, I think."

"It *is* June, hon. Put on your pajamas, would you?"

In the backseat, Meadow unclasped her belt buckle and placed her glasses to the side. After a series of contortions and arm torques, her head popped out of the head hole and she smoothed down the fabric and replaced her glasses on her face. In the headlights behind us, the crown of her head was a star of static. It's ridiculous, I wanted to say, how many steps there are to everything, how endlessly procedural this life is. I wanted to apologize for it.

"Here's an idea," I said. "Now, you can say yes, or you can say no. Got it?"

"OK."

"Consider this"—I swept my hand toward the windshield— "Mount Washington. Highest peak in the northeastern United States. Home of the highest surface winds ever recorded. And what's great about Mount Washington is you can drive all the way up to the top. Right to the tippy-top, where you can buy fried chicken and a bumper sticker."

Meadow held her position of frozen listening.

"But it might take us a couple days," I said. "If you were willing, we could make a *real* road trip out of it. We could stop here and there. Cause some trouble, you know. It's been a long time since we've—we haven't had much time together. With all the razzle-dazzle between me and your mother."

Meadow was pensive. Her nightgown bore the magnified image of a blond girl singing into a microphone. The girl's pupils were filled in with glitter. Meadow drew her seat belt across her chest and studied me in the rearview mirror.

I smiled gamely. "I am happy to write a note to the nuns."

"I don't get taught by the nuns," she said. "That's just music and religion."

"Then I'll write a note to the Christless laypersons who teach you other subjects."

Meadow gave me a bitter smile. I loved her bitter smiles, signs of a frustrated intelligence. I didn't want her to be frustrated, but if she was intelligent, there wasn't any getting around it. I even had the thought that she was going to refuse me. I suppose, in a way, I trusted her to rescue us.

"All right," she said, shrugging.

"Really? Are you sure? You'd miss a little school."

"It's all right."

"Really? Great. *Great.*"

"Of course," she added, "I'll have to ask Mommy."

My heart sank. She had dutifully found the compromise solution that would keep all of us from getting what we wanted. We were once again prisoners of our own making.

"Absolutely," I said, swallowing bile. "We'll find a pay phone and call Mommy first thing in the morning. See what she says."

"Well, maybe not first thing," she said. "Just sometime along the way."

"OK, sweetheart. It's nice of you to think of Mommy."

"How many days will it take?"

"How many days do you feel like giving it?"

She screwed her eyes. "Six?"

"Six whole days? That's great. That's almost a week."

"It's how old I am."

"Your lucky number. We haven't spent six days together in—in forever."

"And I *don't* learn that much in school. I already know the stuff they're teaching me. Reading and stuff. I already learned when I was a baby."

"I'm sorry, Meadow. That kills me."

"So I *would* like to go to the top of Mount Washington. But I'm hungry. Actually, could I have a donut?"

"Sure. Sure. I'm sure we can find you a donut some-where around here..." We both looked out at the landscape, a thick wall of first-growth forest on either side of the road. "Or maybe in Plattsburgh. I bet there are zillions of donuts in Plattsburgh. You can have them all."

But she was asleep again by the time we reached Platts-burgh. I can only imagine the dreams with which her uncon-scious mind explained the sensations: the thrum of the trucks as they lined up beside the passenger cars, the huge clanging of the ferry's deck as it lowered the ramp, and the way it must have felt to have the car's wheels detach from earth and slide away upon some other substance...

It was 1:05 a.m.

The Plattsburgh–Grand Isle ferry was surprisingly traf-ficked. I pulled onto the deck when I was signaled and shut off the engine and sat with one arm hanging out the open window, the lake breeze sweeping the deck. Meadow slept on in the backseat. Her sleep had already developed a deep, denying quality.

I opened the door and stepped from the car, nodding at the trucker who idled behind us, high in his cab. Then I crossed

the deck and climbed up the metal stairs to the passenger deck. I hid myself in the very corner, from which I could not see the Mini Cooper. I leaned over the railing, looking deep into the lake. It was odd. Suddenly I wanted to get away from her. That is, I wanted to get away from my love for her. I had forgotten about the vortex that gets created when you love a kid. Because I wanted to be with my daughter more than anything, and yet I also wanted to be free of that desire. I wanted to be free of that desire because I knew being with her had an end. You, me, death, her teenage years—what would end it? Whatever it was wouldn't be up to me.

There is no such thing as forgetting.

You just have to stand it.

Lake Champlain was as dark as oil. A necklace of distant lights flickered along its edge. Up on the observation deck, I watched the most curious scarves of spider silk float inches above the black water. There are silent people, and there are also very silent things.[7] The strange silence of this windless lake was broken by the uneven reception of a radio playing pop music somewhere. The music roused me, shook me awake, back from the railing over which I was leaning recklessly. I thought of the truck driver high in his cab and wondered what the hell I was thinking leaving her there even for a second. I ran back down the metal stairs. In the backseat of the Mini Cooper, my daughter was safe and fast asleep. Within sight of the hinterland, the ferry's engine powered down. Now we would simply skid the rest of the way. New York State was behind me. We had entered Vermont.

---

7. Blue herons, grain silos, deserts, angels, monuments, satellites, poems, vigils, statues, moons, poison, burglary, courage, footprints, shipwrecks…

RETICENCE

As I've said elsewhere, my dad was a fairly quiet man. I associate him with silence, since that was the sound-track of our lives together, whenever I wasn't unspooling for him the tales of my schooldays in English he could only half understand. He wore a wool overcoat, and had iron-colored hair on his chest and back, and his beard was the same dark crimson color of the cherry juice he drank each day to ward off gout, and every once in a while, I threw back a glass of the same, wondering if it would thicken my own hair and make me hearty like him, capable of labor. Me, I was always getting sick.[8]

---

8. I never quite got rid of a tendency toward respiratory illness. Part of me thinks that I'd made some kind of connection between being ill and getting attention from women. There was a period of time in West Berlin when I was seven or eight and I got in the habit of going to the school infirmary, which was an alcove with walls painted robin's-egg blue containing two long vinyl daybeds. The nurse was an angel with cold hands who drew her divining rod out of a glass of antiseptic and placed it under my tongue. On my first visit, I was invited to lie down on one of the biers, and there I stayed until my aunt could come and get me. I was an old man, I decided, and the nurse was my wife, and my classmates, my petitioners. Not only did I have the full attention of my nurse, but then I got to go back to the apartment and play whist, no one

Dad was not cruel. He rarely scolded me. He never forced me to do anything, except for once. After that one time, he never directed or guided me at all, and in fact, he seemed to forget the conventions of fatherhood altogether. I missed the pedantic advice he used to give me when I was very little, when we were all together, in East Germany, the cautions, the slaps to the back of the leg, all of it. For all the grimness of our life in Dorchester, his outrage might have reassured me. But the anger in him disappeared as I grew up, and as it did, our history made less and less sense to me. Why had we gone to so much trouble to get here? And so when I say that silence makes me think of my father, maybe I mean silence in the sense of censored speech, censored memory, the static of erased tape.

---

else around, none of my cousins, nor my withholding father, no one but me and my crazy auntie. I must have gotten away with it a half dozen times before the jig was up. *I know what he's suffering from*, my aunt said to the nurse, both of them standing over my prostrate body one afternoon at school, *Wall sickness. Mauerkrankheit*, she said. *No medicine for that.*

ZWEITER TAG OR
DAY TWO

We awoke the next morning in Grand Isle, Vermont, our backs stiff, our car surrounded by chickens. I had parked the car there the previous night in the darkness, and I was glad to see in the daylight that I had hidden us well. The car sat in a patch of sandy ground behind a billboard advertising the Great Vermont Corn Maze. Except for the chickens and the road, there was no sign of civilization.

Now, in any other context, I would have set out trying to secure Meadow a decent breakfast, trying to find a safe and sanitary place for us to wash up and change. But a strange thing happens to people once they start to sleep in a car. A sense of permission seemed to have settled over us both. We had not fled to Canada, but neither had we returned to Albany. We were on a road trip. It suddenly felt as pointless for Meadow to change out of her nightgown and brush her hair as it did for me to start being honest. We set off through the woods behind the billboard. I think we felt—we both felt—excited for the adventure—I think so.

And yes, I planned to call you.

Have you ever seen Vermont hayfields just after they've

been mown, the large sage-colored bales casting their shadows westward at daybreak? Have you seen red barns with their doors open, exhuming a cool, night-fed shade you can feel from far away? We came out of the woods into a sea of tall buttercups, whose sheltered birdsong we could hear over the silence. Lake Champlain glittered through white birch trees at the far edge of the field. Along the puckered furrow of cleared land sat an old white farmhouse in need of fresh paint, and on the slope above this house, a groomed geometry of green and brown farmland gave a shapeliness to the innumerable hillocks. Everything hummed with morning.

"Here," I said to Meadow. "Come up on my shoulders."

I hoisted her skyward. She was heavy, but I found myself glad to labor across the field carrying her like that, because I still could. Everything we did was starting to feel touched with lastness: the last summer I could carry her on my shoulders, the last—or at least finite—days of our togetherness before I would return her to Albany and to our occasional, supervised visitations. Crickets, butterflies, and orange-banded birds burst out of the grasses. Up on my shoulders, my daughter twirled her hair with one hand and surreptitiously sucked her thumb with the other. Her eyes had that loose, satisfied look of her early years, when she gorged on love.

We were halfway across the field when the door to the farmhouse opened and a woman with a low-hanging bosom stood watching us, her face half in shadow. I nodded and pressed on, but two small dogs had been released from the house and were now darting around my ankles amongst the knotted stems.

"Doggies!" cried Meadow. "Daddy! Can I pet them, please can I pet them?"

"No, sweetheart." I glanced over at the woman. "We really should forge ahead."

"Please, Daddy, please! Look how cute and *tiny*."

I stood there while Meadow sank into the grasses petting the dogs, and I tried not to acknowledge their owner watching us. We were trespassers, and I was determined to avoid all imbroglios or anyone who might demand to know who we were and what the hell we were doing. Besides, she looked like the shotgun type. I heard her garbled shouting.

I feigned deafness. "Excuse me?"

"You looking for me?" the woman shouted again.

"No. At least I don't think I am. No."

"Because we got cabins." The woman had stepped off the porch with some effort and down the single stair to the edge of the meadow. "I thought you were looking for our cabins. I rent them. I rent the cabins."

I nodded. I gave Meadow's back a little push.

"Sometimes people just kind of come wandering through. Because they've heard about me in town. That's why I ask." The woman put her hands on the small of her back. She was, I could see now, a rather old woman, her gray hair cut short like a man's. "Because I only want the kind of people who hear about me in town. People who come recommended."

"Sure," I called. "That makes sense."

"All righty, then," she said, and clapped her hands. The dogs ran off, glancing back at us. The woman turned and labored back toward her porch. I once again surveyed the view—the splintery farmhouse, the lake, my daughter, dew netted in her hair.

"Excuse me!" I called, scything my way toward the old woman, until I managed to rip myself free of the field. I swat-

ted the grass from my pant legs. She blinked back at me with opaque blue eyes. "Pardon me for being so slow to respond. My daughter and I—" The field spat forth Meadow, looking impish with thistles in her hair. "My daughter and I are taking a little road trip together and we do, actually *do* need a place to stay. For a day or two before we head on."

The woman's eyes shifted vaguely in Meadow's direction. "How did you hear about me? Someone in town?"

"No," I said. "No, to be honest. I don't even know which town you're talking about. We've been driving all night."

The old woman looked disappointed. "The thing is, I like people to come recommended. You never know. It's just me out here. You never know."

"Oh, I totally understand. But we're just a dad and his little girl, who needs a place to change out of her pj's. She could use a nice little cabin to rest and change."

The woman nodded, but I could tell now she had no idea Meadow was wearing a nightgown. Aha. She was perfect; she couldn't even *see*. I redoubled my efforts.

"This might sound like a whole lot of hooey to you," I said, "but I believe we *were* recommended. By the land. We were drawn to it. Sorry—" I squeezed my eyes with my fingers. "I've been driving all night. I completely understand your policy. Come on, sweetheart."

"Well," the woman said, as if I hadn't spoken at all, "you can come and have a look at Cabin Two. Cabin One is rented, so you don't get a choice. I don't know"—the woman spoke to the ground as she walked—"the other one is rented to someone *else* who wasn't recommended."

"The economy is terrible," I said, taking Meadow's hand. "We've all lost so much."

"I don't offer breakfast or any conveniences," the woman continued. "I don't have innerweb. Hell, I don't even have a phone. But most guests, to tell the truth, seem to get a kick out of that. Where you from?"

I squeezed Meadow's hand, gave her a wink. "Canada," I said.

Meadow's eyes widened, then narrowed with conspiracy.

The old woman led us down a gravel path that ended at the lake in a small horseshoe beach with hard gray sand. On either side of this beach stood what looked like two refurbished tool sheds spruced up with a little latticework. The chocolate brown structures were so small that they appeared as two dollhouses standing in the woods. The old woman grappled for a key ring on her belt and shouldered open the door. Meadow ran inside and bounced upon one of the narrow, iron-framed beds. The room was musty and unswept and smelled of wet wool. An oval rope rug lay on the floor, and a dozen small apothecary bottles lined the sill of the cabin's single window in the dimness.

"Well?" the old woman waited. "What do you say?"

What did I say? What *should* I have said? Should I have said no—no, we'd better turn around and go home? I failed to save my marriage, and I failed to protect my rights as a father, and I failed in my resolve in so many ways, and now my exceptionally intelligent child must return to Our Lady of Chronic Fatigue and her deadening education, and her conventional grandparents, and her merciless mother, and we must never speak of this, and must never wonder what we would have gained if we had just said yes? And I! Should I have said, Actually, I'm needed back at my rental on New Scotland Ave. so that I can spend another evening in the shower stall scrub-

bing the soap scum off the sealant with a toothbrush, a glass of Canadian Club nestled in the soap basket?

I stepped inside the tiny cabin and sneezed from the visible allergens.

"Thank you," I said, pumping the old woman's hand. "We love it."

WHEN IN DOUBT, DON'T

They say the recession made people look inward. Out of work, folks suddenly had time on their hands to contemplate the fabric of their souls. People who had driven themselves into the ground for decades were suddenly baking bread, reading poetry, creating sand mandalas, and asking probing questions of their priests and rabbis. I'm not saying it was good for us. I'm just saying we tried to make the best of it.

As for me, I guess history will count me among the legions of promising young Realtors whose careers were in ascension when the real estate bubble burst. Throughout 2006–2007, I had been selling properties at a steady clip. Just ranches and bungalows in North Albany, condos in refurbished multifamilies in Pine Hills. Small-fry, starter homes, but lots of them. Not bad for someone who was barely trying. At my best, I was representing ten to fifteen properties at a time, all of which vanished from the market before the next insert in the Sunday paper. I was doing so well that I simply stopped taking calls. My success—albeit in a field for which I had little respect—appealed to my latent exceptionalism. And so, although it was the recession that brought me low, I was well into the process

of subverting my career when it struck. In fact, it was probably at the pinnacle of my career (Clebus & Co. Realtor of the Month February 2007) when I lost interest. Having proved myself so handily, it was my nature to grow bored and look for a new challenge.

The moment Meadow was born, I knew she was exceptional. First of all, she didn't cry. Although I understand that a newborn crying is a sign of *life* and of *vigor*, I dreaded the cliché of it. To be honest, I had little interest in her until that moment. I never really wanted children. That is, I never really wanted children, but I wasn't prepared to take a stand about it. I didn't *not* want children. But Meadow didn't cry when she was born, and this piqued my interest. I peered at her in the silver scale as she punched at the emptiness, and I thought, I'll be damned, there's something *in* this.

Then I let two years go by before investing more than a passing interest in her. She was a sweet but somehow not yet relevant presence, not yet *here*. Besides, she was yours, clamped to your breast. A father gets the message.

And so I didn't sweat fatherhood much those early years. I was a provider. It made me proud that I could give you time at home with the baby. I enjoyed my erratic work schedule and used it to further my recreational soccer career. I became friends with my clients and with them took three-hour lunches in the winter, spontaneous trips to Saratoga in the summers. I often came home at the end of the day with cleats over one shoulder, skipping my way up the stairs, and until I heard Meadow's crowing from behind the apartment door, I sometimes forgot that I even had a baby.

You, of course, Laura, had changed. Meadow was your life. After you gave birth to her, you spent a disheveled year

at home. You mashed your own baby food, fretted about environmental poisons, and generally ignored your careerist impulses. Sometimes, when I came home, the kitchen was chaos, as if it had been ransacked, with no sign of either of you. I would climb the stairs, and there at the top, in the steamy bathroom, you and little Meadow would be secreted in the bathtub together, clothes—your big blousy shirts and her little onesies—strewn like lovers' clothes across the threshold.

It doesn't take much effort to go along with someone else's vision of life. For Christ's sakes it doesn't take much effort to go along with anything. But then, one day, a force of reckoning comes to your door demanding a word with you. For me, that day occurred when I came home from soccer and Meadow—eighteen months of age, a whisper of a being—pointed to my sweaty face and said, "Daddy rains." It made me pause, just as I had when she didn't cry. How does a child so young compose such a pretty sentence? She looked up at me. I was thirty-four—not an old man, but old enough to spy the burnt edges on the scroll of my life. This child. Did some clue to my life lie here?

So for *me*, for *us*, the economic slowdown presented an opportunity for spiritual growth in the form of me going bust and you getting a coveted job at the new experimental charter school in North Albany. By springtime of '09, the real estate market was as dry as a desert. It seemed as if its previous health, the happy exchange of sellers and buyers, was a fairy tale. And this is how I came to be Stay-at-Home Dad of the Year. This is how I came to be left on the porch that fall with my three-year-old child, who was really a stranger to me, while her mother drove off in my company car, looking very pretty, actually, in a flounced blouse and touchingly mature pearl earrings.

Do I remember my first days alone with Meadow? I sure do. I remember looking down at her, her thumb snug in her mouth, her Stinky Blanket under the other arm, and me filled with complete terror. The neighborhood was as silent as a tomb. The leaves on the oak trees were still. An acorn pinged off the hood of a car. I could hear my blood in my ears. I waited for someone to approach down the street—anyone. I longed to make the sort of meaningless small talk I was so good at. How would we fill a day, two people with such a different sense of fun? I felt overwhelming pressure to do something outrageous or entertaining. I worried that she would just pick up Stinky Pillow and walk away from me. What I didn't know was that she was helplessly bound to me already. It was *me* who could have wandered away from her. I could have left her outside of the fire station and walked away and— after a year or two of effortful self-justification—would barely have thought of her again.[9] My daughter stood barely looking at me, as if embarrassed by her position, the ligature of her polka-dotted underpants visible above the elastic of her corduroy rompers. My heart flipped. How *abandonable* a child is.

With this vague gleaning of one another's vulnerabilities, we were off. We quickly exhausted the territory of the apartment, whose dolls and crayons had always bored me. To be outside was better. We both could breathe there. We played in the wet sandbox and the wet grass. We discovered that we could stand *inside* the hedge that bordered our property and thereby go unseen by the mail carrier. We discovered that on the *other* side of the hedge, summer's late blackberries still clung to their scary-looking vines. We debated whether or not the

---

9. Maybe I should have done that.

hedge was ours and therefore the blackberries were ours also. (We decided yes.) We found, in the neighbor's yard, an overgrown garden. We discovered that the scent of mint leaves, when crushed between thumb and forefinger, stayed on the skin for hours. We made grass stew. I noticed that my daughter was able to combine her mother's scrupulous attention to detail with her father's relentless sense of wonder. I came to see that her apparent ordinariness (her fondness for glitter and for high-pitched screams of excitement, etc.) was a kind of camouflage for the truer, inner child burdened by extraordinary perception. The child—I quickly came to see—was *gifted*.

O tiny imitator! Compact mirror! Within days Meadow was using words and phrases that I had used casually, almost aloud to myself, thinking she had not understood. A boo-boo was a *laceration*. A burp was an *eructation*. Acorns were *ubiquitous*. I never talked down to her. I had always loved words. My early experiences learning English satisfied me, if nothing else did, by the language's interesting consonance with German. And so, almost casually, I threw in some foreign words, phrases from Spanish, Japanese, and even my buried native tongue. She retained every word. Anything you threw at her stuck. Naturally I wondered what else she might be capable of.

A-B-C-D-E-F-G.

One day, I sat her down with some old Clebus stationery and several sharpened pencils.

"This," I began, "is an *A*. The sound" (I said) "of *A* is *ah* or the sharper *aa*, as in *cat*. If you add a *y*, the sound is the same as how you say the letter—*ay*. Like *day*."

"*Aaay*," she said. "Can I have a graham cracker?"

"Sure you can. Just as soon as we finish what we're doing. *B. B* sounds like *buh. Buh*."

"*Buh.*"

"What other words start with the sound *buh*?"

"Hamburger," she said.

"Good try. Try again."

"Bug."

"Bug! Yes! Bug."

H-I-J-K-LMNO-P.

And by the end of that fall, she could read. She was three years old.

Is it now safe to say that I made my share of mistakes? Sure. Can I now say freely that she took a couple of knocks in my care? That twice I lost her in the Grand Union—I had to do the grocery shopping, too—and she had to be raised on the PA system? That once, at home, we were visited by the fire department for something unwise we did with the smoke detector in the name of science? But the thing I will never apologize for is teaching her to read. I don't care how it makes me look.

Ask her; she'll tell you. We had *fun* together. Our days were full. I was getting the hang of parenting. I was no longer bitter about the busted real estate market or my lack of earning potential. I could accept the unique humiliation of asking my wife for pocket money. I even unearthed my manuscript from beneath its sward of bills and took up—at nap times—my independent research. And all this should have been good but for a single problem.

Q-R-S-T-U-V-W-X-Y, and *Z.*

"Where have you *been*?" you said, your face in a literal sweat, as you stepped out of the apartment and onto the porch. "I've been losing my *mind* here, Eric. Pacing around for two hours. Two hours! It's dark. It's November." You fell to your

knees and began to search your daughter's body with your hands, making her laugh. She was bundled in her parka, hood up and cinched. I was confused. Why wouldn't she be fine?

You looked up at me. "Do you even know what time it is, Eric?"

"I guess we lost track of time, hon. We're sorry."

"*We're* sorry? *She* isn't in charge of getting you guys home on time. Jesus. I was out of my mind with worry. You couldn't have called? You couldn't have left a note? My poor peanut. Are you cold? Where *were* you?"

"The liberary," Meadow said from behind her scarf.

You sighed, routed. As a middle school teacher, you had to support library use.

"Come in, come in," you said, ushering us into the apartment, which glowed with golden light. "You two worry me *sick*."

Throughout the winter, this sort of conversation repeated itself with little variation. I could see your evident exasperation with my time management, lack of schedule, etc., but as far as I was concerned, I was a trustworthy guardian—a man of strong build, multilingual, a good problem solver—so what were you so wound up about? As far as I could tell, a parent got through his or her day via a mix of structure, improvisation, and triage. This took complete concentration. Thinking about *you* or about how *you* would have done it would have been an unhelpful distraction. Did you want us to stay home all day watching the window?

But OK. I really don't mean for this document to devolve into the jeremiad that I was never permitted to deliver in family court. I readily accept the following charges against me, that:

a) I often forgot to leave notes detailing our whereabouts.

b) I sometimes did not remember how much you wanted to see Meadow at the end of the day and therefore our whereabouts should have been at *home*.

c) I occasionally omitted mentioning certain not-so-age-appropriate activities or side trips we took, which you mostly found out anyway from some pal of yours who saw us.

d) I was bad at following instructions, especially as pertained to schedules and quotas (e.g., servings of fresh fruit), and probably, yes, I had a certain passive-aggressive reaction to these rules and hid my resentment of them behind a friendly absentmindedness.

But I *tried*. I took care of her.

One day, while you were correcting me for some oversight after your return home, I watched your pretty face in its shrewish contortions, and your words sort of fell away, and I saw that you were jealous. You were jealous that I got to be with Meadow while you had to content yourself with other people's children. This realization softened me. I felt bad for you, and for what seemed like the Pyrrhic victory of being a working mother. I apologized for teaching Meadow foreign words that we would then use as code in public. I saw, as you did, that this was a wedge. And so I tried to include you more and leave you more notes and account for every hour we spent, and in general, to be smotheringly nice to you. Your happiness was still my central goal. I wanted you to see that you had everything you wanted. A noble job. A gifted

child. A husband who was secure enough to stay at home with his child for a gap year. And a home—we did have a lovely home—a rented duplex on the top two floors of a baby blue tenement on Morning Street.

You cheered up by springtime, but there was still a part of you I couldn't please. There was a part of you I couldn't reach. I began to wonder if what you wanted was another child. Maybe you wanted another chance. Maybe you wanted to make sure one kid belonged to you, only to you. I understood that. I understand possession. After all, I wanted you to belong only to me. I brought up the issue that spring, one night in the kitchenette.

"More children?" you said, turning around, a dish in your hand. "Why do you say 'more'? How many 'more' do you want?"

I took the dish from you to dry it. Again we were cleaning up and trying to talk at the same time, something that probably contributed to our irritability.

"One more, then. One more child. You want to, Laur?"

You looked at me for a long moment. Then you turned back toward the sink, saying, "Oh, Eric." My name, as you turned, was swallowed by the running water. I watched you sort through the dishes caked in spaghetti sauce and waited for you to elaborate.

"You seem discontented," I said.

"Discon*tented*."

"Do you object to that word too?"

"Yes," you said, "I do."

"What's wrong with it?"

"It's so cold is what's wrong with it. Discon*tented*. It's a word someone would use in *Masterpiece Theatre*."

"It's Latinate," I said, shrugging.

"I don't care. I'm your wife, Eric. It's just you and me here. There's no audience. The word you should use with me is *sad*. Or *unhappy*."

"OK." I stacked another dried dish on the countertop. "Are you unhappy?"

You considered it. "No."

"Well, good."

"Lonely sometimes."

"You're lonely? Why are you lonely?"

"I don't know. I feel lonely a lot. When we don't understand each other. I sometimes think we aren't interested in understanding each other, like we used to be. Sometimes I don't understand the things you do. Sometimes you seem like a stranger to me. I can't figure out if I've gotten lazy or if there's a part of you that's hidden from me. Tell me I'm crazy."

You looked over your shoulder at me then. I stared back at you.

"I'm just me," I said. "Eric Kennedy. No big mystery."

You were slow to turn away.

"Maybe I'm just tired," you said, rubbing your temples with wet hands. "I don't know, Eric. I don't know what's wrong. I think about it so much, but I never get *any*where."

I watched your shoulders as you returned to the dishes—scrubbing, rinsing, placing them dripping in the rack. You did, in fact, look lonely. This seemed to me impossible. Impossible in the sense of wondrously bad—*inconceivable*. It seemed inconceivable that two lonely people could *strand* one another in the same kitchen. The naked conversations in which we spent our first year abed were not so long ago. God, Laura, I was interested. I came up behind you and put my arms around

you. I rested my head against yours. We stayed that way for a long time.

"I'm totally devoted to you," I said.

"I know," you said.

"I don't want anything more than this."

"It feels good when you hold me," you said. "It feels good. Don't move."

MERMAN

Meadow and I settled in. We both unpacked our small bags into a shared dresser. Then we got back in the Mini Cooper and I drove an hour south until I found a local credit union. There I took out a cash advance on my credit card, netting two thousand dollars and a roll of quarters. I then drove back north to a Walmart on the outskirts of Swanton. I bought Meadow a proper bathing suit—a two-piece with spangles that you would have hated. I also bought a fresh razor, a flashlight, Tic Tacs, a loaf of Roman Meal, a squirt bottle of mayonnaise, a family-sized package of cheese singles, and a vanilla-flavored Garcia y Vega. We used half the quarters on the plastic horsey ride in the Walmart foyer. Oh, and I let Meadow buy a heavily discounted package of chocolate Easter eggs, which she divested of their pink and blue foil wrappers in silent rapture in the backseat of the Mini Cooper. There. There are your details.

Back at the ranch, I hid half of the cash behind a le Carré novel, and we sat on the ash-colored sand and ate cheese sandwiches and chocolate eggs and I smoked my cigar. Ours was a small, unnavigable cove, and the motorboats we saw in the

lake beyond did not enter. Once, a pair of lady kayakers surprised us through the reeds, but there was something about Meadow standing guard in her spangled bikini, her legs caked with sand, that made them paddle away.

That afternoon, I was every kind of monster. I was a manticore. I was a merman. I was a hippogriff. A leviathan. When we ran out of amphibians, we went on to giants. I was Anteus. Paul Bunyan. Magog. Meadow's job was to slay me. She ran me through with sticks, peppered me with pebbles, she pinecone-bombed me. As a rule, I am very good at dying. I stagger. I fall backwards. I cry chillingly. I float underwater for longer than you thought possible. (You should see me stiffening from tetanus!) Whenever I stayed underwater too long, I could hear Meadow's garbled pleas above me, telling me to cut it out already, and I was strangely satisfied by the limits of the game. I enjoyed playing a game in which my death seemed ludicrous. We dried ourselves off with the scratchy guest towels and watched the stars enter the mind of the sky like a billion epiphanies. And I wondered momentarily if you weren't right, Laura, about a God, because there was someone, someone superhuman, who had kept me from succumbing to the terrible ideations I'd had in the darkest of February.

DRITTER TAG *OR*
DAY THREE

It was late afternoon on our second day in Grand Isle when I became restless. Nothing was wrong; I'd just probably gone too long without adult conversation. I suggested to Meadow we go out for chow. She was game. We clambered into the Mini Cooper and began to make our way down Route 2, snaking back and forth across Lake Champlain, which seemed on the verge of spilling goldenly onto the roads. We drove through first-growth woods whose moss-colored shade itself seemed ancient. It was another glorious day, the third in a row. The light seemed purified. Winter had retreated in a torrent of dirty runoff, leaving the springtime world new and washed, like this.

"For all this country's transgressions," I mused aloud, "for all its abuses, its opportunism, its meanness, it sure is pretty. Don't you think, Butterscotch?"

"It *is* pretty."

"It really is a beautiful country. A lot of people come here, looking for somewhere to be safe and free."

"They come to Ellis Island," Meadow said.

"They used to, sure."

"But if they come from Mexico, guards shoot at them."

I nodded encouragingly. "I don't think they get shot at per se. But yes, it is dangerous to come here sometimes. America can't fit everybody, right?"

"I don't see why not." Meadow gestured out the window. "Plenty of space up here. They could live right there in those woods."

I grinned. We both returned to staring at Vermont.

"You're a sweet kid," I said.

"I know that," she said. "You tell me that all the time."

The countryside receded and exchanged itself for a thicket of small houses, the outskirts of a town we soon discovered was North Hero. The town was, in essence, a barracks-style row of short retail spaces fronted with fluttering awnings. The parochial avenue was the same as in any small American town: a hardware store, a pet-grooming outfit, a coffee shop, an impossibly small public library. Meadow pointed out several eateries, but I kept driving. Just as we were on the verge of reentering endless Vermont countryside, I spied the neon glow I'd been looking for. The wheels whined as I pulled up to the curb.

"Wait here," I said, walking up to the window to give the place a once-over. Through the wrinkled plastic tinting I saw a large man behind the bar pouring a coffee-brown pint of stout.

"Perfect," I said to Meadow, throwing open her door and unsnapping her seat belt. "A cozy little pub. The perfect place for some local color."

Meadow stepped from the car. Her purple velour sweat-pants—the only other change of clothing she had in her over-

night bag—were flecked with sand, and the sides of her unwashed hair had slipped out from her headband. I straightened her glasses and swatted clean her pants.

"There," I said. "You're such a pretty girl. Do you know that?"

"Technically, I'm not so pretty. I'm pretty*ish*. Rapunzel is pretty."

"Rapunzel? Are you serious? What about Maria Callas or Benazir Bhutto or somebody like that?"

"No. Rapunzel is prettiest. I'll show you her in my fairy-tales book when we get back *home* home."

No heads turned when we entered. There was only one grizzled man sitting below the television, staring at the bottles behind the bar, and a booth along the wall in which a single woman applied lipstick from behind a compact mirror. I was overjoyed to see a plastic red basket on the table in front of her. The joint served food.

"Up here, honey." I patted the stool beside mine at the bar.

When the bartender approached, I stuck my hand out. "How's it going?"

"Good." The bartender shook my hand once, hard. "How are you?"

"Very good," I said. "Excellent."

"You'd have to be an asshole to be unhappy on a day like this," said the bartender, flipping a coaster onto the bar. "What can I get you?"

"Canadian Club on the rocks. And my daughter here will have two hot dogs and a Shirley Temple. Isn't that right, sweetheart? Did I get that right?"

The bartender looked at Meadow. "How many cherries

does the little lady want in her Shirley Temple?" he said, pouring me a generous drink. The ice cubes cracked like dry wood in a stove.

Meadow blushed and leaned her face against my arm.

"Come on now," I said, "tell the nice man how many cherries you want. She can be sort of shy at first."

"As many as you want," said the bartender.

Meadow held up six fingers.

"Six!" the bartender bellowed. "That's all?"

Meadow nodded.

"One for every year," I said.

"You're *six*?" The bartender leaned against the bar across from Meadow, his big maw exaggerated in the track lighting. "Well, then you probably already know how the world works, right? You know about gravity? You know about taxes?"

Again Meadow buried her face in my arm. The bartender chuckled and grabbed a pint glass. I gave her shoulder a squeeze, drinking deeply with my free arm. Canadian Club is sweet up front, but somehow I've gotten used to this and can't stand anything drier.

"Isn't this fun?" I said to Meadow. "Isn't this place a riot?"

I turned and surveyed the pub. The lady in the booth had snapped shut her compact mirror and gave me what looked like a wink. I smiled back, but she got up to leave. I tried not to stare at her big blond dandelion hair as it sailed across the mirror behind the bar.

"You count those cherries, sweetheart," the bartender was telling Meadow, sliding her Shirley Temple toward her. "You shouldn't trust anyone over the age of twelve. After twelve, it's lies, lies, lies. You know about Area 51? You know about Roswell?"

The bartender was leaning across the bar again, smiling gamely. He had a wide, ironic face. He looked like he was waiting for something unpredictable to happen.

There are moments—I hate to say it—when a parent's loyalties jump ship, and he just wants to be liked by another grown-up. Even the best parents with excellent parenting styles can't help, on rare occasion, but side with their own kind, those on the downslope of life, and in this process they get the urge to gang up on somebody young, since it's impossible to banish this instinct altogether, this throwing around of one's hard-won experience.

"Well?" the bartender barked at Meadow. "Did I cheat you?"

"Did he give you six cherries?" I prompted her. "Did he steal any?"

"Not that kind of cherry," said the bartender. "You only get one of those."

"Ha." I nudged her with my elbow. "What do you say, Butterscotch?"

Meadow now stared into her drink, stirring it with a straw.

"Cat got your tongue?"

"Thank you," she murmured.

"She speaks!" said the bartender.

"She's shy at first," I said.

"No, she's smart. She knows she shouldn't trust a guy like me. Here. I've got something that'll make her smile." The man reached under the bar and brought out a small windup frog with a silver key in its back. He turned the key and placed the toy on the bar. The frog flipped backwards and landed on its feet. Meadow watched it.

"You like it?"

"Answer the man, sweetheart," I said, taking a draught.

"Do you? Here, it's yours," said the bartender. "My kids are all grown up and refuse to crack a fucking smile. Let me tell you, you've got about six more years and then she'll barely talk to you. So. You folks staying here in North Hero?"

"Sadly, no. We're just passing through. We're on our way to Mount Washington."

"Now, there's a place worth seeing."

"We're making a road trip out of it. Stopping here and there. A father-and-daughter road trip."

"No wife?"

"Sure I've got a wife," I said. "For our last wedding anniversary she gave me a restraining order."

The bartender snorted.

Grinning, I waved my hand. "But I don't like to talk about it in front of the kid."

The bartender shook his head, his laughter dwindling. He was looking ruefully at Meadow, who had finally picked up the frog and was turning its key.

"Kids," the man said. "They ruin your life. Then they're the best thing about what you have left."

"*That*"—I raised my empty glass to him—"is the truth."

We fell into a melancholy silence.

I looked down the bar toward where the old man sat. Hands around a can of Pabst, he studied the muted television. I looked up at the screen. The local news was beginning. I felt a pang of homesickness. For a moment, I missed Albany, its brutal winters, its amateurish politicians. The lead story out of St. Albans appeared to involve a bear attack.

"Funny," I said.

The bartender raised his head. "What is?"

"Pabst beer. 'Pabst' means 'pope' in German. I just thought of it."

"No shit. Pope beer?"

"Pope beer!"

"Maybe the pope blesses it. Holy beer."

"It's like kosher beer, but for Catholics."

"Ha!"

"Ha-ha!"

"Ha! That's the damnedest." Chuckling, the bartender pointed to my glass. "Get you another?"

"You'd better."

"You want a chaser of holy beer with that?"

"Let me think. What would Jesus do?"

The bartender bellowed. I felt a pluck at my arm.

Meadow look up at me. *"Können wir Mommy anrufen?"*

I swallowed. In my stupidity, I thought she had forgotten. No, I hoped she had forgotten.

"Sure. Sure, sweetheart. We can call Mommy."

"I told you she was smart," said the bartender. "What is that, German?"

Just then, someone hollered behind the swinging doors and the bartender went out and then came back with Meadow's hot dogs in a red basket. Meadow perked up at the sight of food. She crawled onto the next stool and got a bottle of ketchup from where it sat with a caddy of miniature jellies between the old man and us. She opened the ketchup bottle and turned it over the basket, thumping the bottom until half the basket was filled with ketchup. I watched her eat. She was completely absorbed. I sipped my fresh drink. The first one had relaxed me, but the second was making me philosophical.

"You're a good daughter," I said. "You know that? You're a good kid, and very responsible."

She looked at me, cramming the end of her hot dog in her mouth.

I lifted my chin toward the bartender. "All right," I said. "I promised the kid I'd call her mother. You've got a phone?"

"Right there next to the lavatory. But maybe you should finish your drink first."

"Ha, right. Hey, throw some water on me if I burst into flames."

I got up and went to the pay phone that hung from the wall. I searched the pocket of my khakis for quarters.

And that's right about when I experienced one of my life's greatest reversals.[10] Because there, in the television over the bar, was my face.

My face. A snapshot taken just before the separation. And because this was an era of significantly better grooming, of my being a hell of a lot more *together*, my hair was cut cleanly, and I looked, to my eye, pretty decent and responsible. I squinted upward at the television. There was my name, my age, race, eye color, etc.

The dial tone roared in my ear.

---

10. I'd like to borrow an example here from poetry. Since poetry is written in lines, sentences spill over from one line to the next, lending a tiny but not insignificant pause right there at the line's precipice. (Stick with me here. I'm just trying to get at how I felt.) Sometimes the subsequent line satisfies the reader's expectation. But sometimes expectation is reversed. I like this example, from Allen Ginsberg:

Here we're overwhelmed

with such unpleasant detail
we dream again of Heaven.
For the world is a mountain

I scanned the bar. The bartender was leaning against the bar with one elbow, staring out the window. Meadow was busy with her hot dogs. But the old barfly in the corner was staring straight at the television, where Meadow's face now appeared, with her trademark red glasses, her hair nicely brushed—her kindergarten portrait, taken the previous fall. The receiver of the telephone slipped from my grip, crashing against the wall's wood paneling.

The bartender turned to look. "She give you a hell of a time?"

"Jesus H.," I said, smiling. "Did she ever. A hell of a time."

I stooped to retrieve the swinging phone, not taking my eyes off the bartender.

"But everything's fine now," I said. "With her, it's all dry lightning."

Walking straight up to the bar, I willed myself not to look up at the television. Meadow watched me closely.

"How does this crazy thing *work*?" I said, picking up the frog.

"You turn the key," Meadow said, tamping her second hot dog in the ketchup.

"Like this?" I placed the wound-up frog on his feet. I

---

of shit: if it's going to
be moved at all, it's got
to be taken by handfuls.

NB the fabulously cruel enjambment of "For the world is a mountain / of shit," in which "of shit" reverses one's own quiet and perhaps more optimistic mental rendering of a mountain made of, you know, boulders and moss and mountain laurel and that kind of thing. When Ginsberg swaps your imagined mountain with shit, you feel...well, I can't say how *you* feel, but I feel disappointed (not with the poem, but with my own tendency to err on the side of the romantic). There are poetic reversals like this in life, is my point. There are pauses between knowing and understanding. Pauses in which we wait for delayed news of ourselves to spark along the sagging wires.

glanced up at the television. Meadow's face and mine were now sharing a split screen, a tip-line telephone number scrolling across us, and I noticed with a flash of remorse that there was no recent photograph of the two of us together, that separate ones had to be used, and that the reason there was no recent photograph of the two of us together was because in the scant time we had together, there was no third person to take such a picture anyway, no picture taker, just our banished lives, cruelly subpar to the life we'd shared before.

Cut to commercial. Laundry detergent. A talking teddy bear.

"Welp," I said, releasing the frog, which immediately malfunctioned, falling to the side and kicking at the air. "Enough shit shooting. We've got to hit the road."

The bartender raised his eyebrows. "So soon?"

"I'm not done with my hot dog," said Meadow.

"No problem. We'll just bring it in the car."

I tossed a pile of money on the bar and grabbed Meadow's arm, firmly. The butt of her hot dog in her hand, she looked up at me with alarm.

"You folks have a good trip," the bartender said. "Come on back."

"We will. We definitely will."

As I backed out of the door, my eyes could not resist being drawn to the profile of the old man at the end of the bar. He stared forward into the glittering liquor bottles before him— a horizon of alcohol—his grizzled neck swallowing the melt from the ice cube he chewed. And with the jangle of the bell tied to the door, the man turned his head with awful slowness, as if just coming awake, and I tried to divine my fate in his buried eyes.

JOHN TORONTO

"Butterscotch?" I said in the darkness. "You still awake?"

Meadow shifted beneath her sheets. "Yep. I'm awake."

I propped myself up on one elbow and looked across at Meadow's bed. "Are you having a nice trip?"

"Oh, yes. I liked playing Merman and I like our new car and I like having so much junk food. And I'm glad Mommy said yes to our vacation. I was worried she'd say no. She must be changing her mind about you. I've *told* her and I've *told* her. I guess it's not hopeless."

I winced in the dark. "No. It's never hopeless."

"But it *is* funny."

"Yes, it is funny," I said. "Life just gets funnier and funnier the longer you live it."

I stared up at the ceiling of our cabin. The night was moonless. As if hearing my guilty misgivings, Meadow clicked on her flashlight. The beam roved across the ceiling, illuminating the cobwebs.

"Hey, Meadow," I said. "How about, if you don't mind, we play pretend while we're on vacation? You can be some other girl you want to be, and I will still be your father but

I'll have a different name, you know, like John. You can pick your own name. Some name you've always liked. And I'll *call* you that and we'll make up stories about our life. Like, you can have the little sister you always wanted—"

"Oh, I don't want one of those anymore."

"All right."

"I would prefer a hermit crab. But I want a real one, not a pretend one."

"Well, what kind of pretend pet would you like to have?"

Meadow thought. "A Portuguese water dog? Like Sasha Obama got?"

"OK, OK. That's great. You'll have a Portuguese water dog back at home. And we'll be from Toronto. And my name will be John, and your name will be—"

"I think you should be mayor."

"Of Toronto?"

"Yes. Mayor John Toronto. And on the Fourth of July, you get to launch the fireworks."

"OK. And your name? What should I call you?"

Meadow considered the ceiling. "Chrissy."

"*Chrissy?* Really?"

Her eyes flashed angrily in the dark.

"OK," I said. "Chrissy is good. In case we need a code name."

"And I have blondish goldenish hair. Like Rapunzel." Meadow sighed. "I'm *wide*-awake, Daddy. I'm absolutely *wired*."

"Me too. Would you like me to read aloud from *Birds Come and Gone*? Maybe that'll put us to sleep."

Wedged next to the le Carré novels of our cabin's small bookshelf, we had discovered an ancient pamphlet of poetry by a dead society lady named Kitty Tinkerton Bridge, who

wrote rhyming poetry about birds. Lacking other appropriate bedtime books, we had read from *Birds Come and Gone* and had both come to appreciate Bridge's amateurish but somewhat musical verse, and it had become a kind of ritual to read from it.

"All right," sighed Meadow. "Read to me."

As I opened the book, I heard the slap of the screen door across the path. Given the otherwise dead silence in our remote cove, I could only assume that the resident of Cabin One was home.

MY FIRST LIE

Technically, fraud is defined not by the act of lying but by *the intent to benefit from lying*. If you lie for fun, or for the various other reasons that we lie (e.g., to avoid physical pain or recrimination, or to perpetuate heartbreaking self-delusion), that is not necessarily *fraud*. I suppose my first *fraudulent* lie was told in a distant wing of the West Berlin Rathaus, in 1975. It also happens to be one of my few clear early memories. My father was speaking with a West German man in civilian clothing. The man had fuzzy hair that he wore in a kind of blond atmosphere around his head, as well as a shirt whose top two or three buttons I assumed had come undone accidentally, because this sort of experimentation with male décolletage had not yet arrived in East Berlin, from whence we had just emigrated hours before. The man and my father had been arguing most of that time. My father's brother-in-law, the man who was to let us live in his garage apartment, had left hours ago, leaving us with his address and assurances that we'd be processed soon. But the blond West German seemed to be losing patience with my father.

"But I need some sort of confirmation, you see."

"You have confirmation," said my father. "You have two exit visas."

"But you are married. There is no certificate of divorce, which you are instructed to produce, not just there, but here. You have nothing—"

"I had one hour to report to Friedrichstrasse. Did you want me to dig up the body?"

My father's voice was rising in pitch, as it did whenever he felt persecuted by other people's stupidity. Finally the sponge-haired man looked at me and called out into the hallway. A pretty brunette came to the door. The blond man whispered something to her, and she smiled at me.

"Well, hello," she said.

She disappeared for a moment, only to return with a small silver canister, which she held out to me. I remember this clearly: The can was aluminum, with a pear-shaped hole for drinking, which was still preserved, until the woman peeled it off, by a tacky silver sticker. The canister was beautiful, a tiny powder keg. I vowed to keep it.

"Thanks!" I exclaimed.

"Drink it. It's juice," said the woman, lingering prettily in the office. "How old are you, sweetie pie?"

I held up one spread hand.

"Five? My, my."

My father glanced down at me in the folding chair beside him, with a look I could only describe as aggrieved, and despite the fact that my cuteness was overshadowing his entreaties, I guzzled my juice with relish.

"What a *Süßer*. What a *strammer kerl*," the woman said to my father, using two phrases that were in German but beyond my ken, because although there was love in East Germany,

sober, private love, for certain, there were—you'll have to believe me—no endearments. I loved the lurid sound of them immediately.

"Look at him," the woman continued. "Sitting so patiently. So poised. His mother would be so proud of him. Don't you think?"

"Yes," said my father, looking pale. "My wife—my late wife—doted upon him."

The man with the blond hair looked down at me in exasperation. "It's true, then, what your father says? Your mommy has died? We need to know that she isn't missing you."

My eyes went wide. I was not surprised by the news that my mother was dead—I knew that was a complete fiction, as I had just seen her that morning—I was only surprised that I was being addressed. After hours of sitting in a windowless room full of folding chairs, my father bargaining with everybody he could find, no one had yet asked a direct question of me.

I clutched my canister. I would keep it forever and I would play with it. We did not have silver juice canisters in East Berlin. I knew that my father and I had an understanding. I would say what he needed me to say and he would protect my right to my juice canister. I could feel his large, fading heat beside me, his hands still smelling—as they would forever after—of the inkpad from the border crossing at Friedrichstrasse.

I looked across the desk at the blond man. He inspired no feeling in me. But when I glanced toward the doorway, I saw the brunette with her soft cheek pressed against the doorjamb. And even though I knew my mother was still *there*—somewhere, on the other side—I slipped into a black-

and-white reality in which I had lost her entirely, which was closer to the truth, anyway.

"Little boy? Can't you speak?"

I burst into tears.

"Oh, leave him alone, Gerhardt," said the woman in the doorway. "For God's sakes. Does it even matter anymore? What are you going to do, send them back?"

VIERTER TAG OR
DAY FOUR

I awoke with a headache, as if I'd been drinking heavily. I sat upright on the edge of my bed for a long time, watching Meadow sleep. Dawn was a reckoning. In the daylight, it was difficult to deny that I had only one clean option. This thing about Meadow being in danger was a misunderstanding. I could clear that up by returning her to Albany as soon as possible. I'd pay fines. Maybe I'd even be arrested. None of that caused the physical aversion I felt just as soon as I pictured myself doing the right thing. Why? Because I wasn't ready to blow up my life. Maybe nobody else cared about it, but it was my life. My lovingly constructed American life. I wanted to keep being who I was. I wanted to keep being Eric Kennedy. If I went back now, they'd make me be Schroder. And claiming that name would be part of my punishment, a ceremonial rite. And no one would listen to me when I would tell them, But I am not Schroder, no one would understand what I meant by that. It's your legal name, they'd say. I understand that it's my legal name, I'd say. And they'd say, Are you really in any position to object?

In the warped glass of the window over Meadow's bed, I

spied my face, gazing back at me plaintively. I ran my hand around my jaw. I gave that sad sack face a couple fit slaps that brought water to my eyes. Harder, I thought. You're not even capable of hitting hard enough. I stopped to catch my breath.

"John fucking Toronto," I muttered, getting up to shave.

Meadow and I headed out into a hazy morning. I couldn't muster the same enthusiasm as I had the day before. I kept staring with preoccupation out at the lake, wondering which way they'd come from. Maybe this was just the imprinting of my childhood's apparat, but it seemed to me that if you scratched anybody deep enough, you'd reveal some criminality, a questionable exchange or evasion, a moment where he or she bent the law at its most flexible joint. And so I had believed—right up to the moment when I saw myself on TV—that I had not "kidnapped" Meadow but that I was merely very, very late to return her from an agreed-upon visit.

"Daddy," Meadow said, shaking me by the wrist. "Aren't we going to Mount Washington yet?"

"Not today," I said. "I just feel like kicking around here."

"But how many days do we have left?"

"Plenty."

"How many is plenty?"

"We've got plenty of time, OK? Why don't you go play?"

"I want to play with *you*."

"I've got a headache."

"Why does your head ache, Daddy?"

"I don't know, Meadow. Maybe because you keep asking me questions. Now, please. Leave me alone. I need some time to think. Don't you ever just want to be alone?"

Her face clouded. Fine, I thought, I hurt her feelings. Fine. She had, to my mind, another long, blessed day, an entire

beach all to herself. She had her whole life. She walked down the beach, moping, kicking sand, digging up rocks, not going very far.

That's when a tall woman in a sheer nightgown emerged from Cabin One, her arms stretched expressively over her head.

"Well, *hi*," she said when she saw me. "I've got neighbors."

Meadow and I both jumped. I stuffed my hands in my pockets, and Meadow, who'd been squatting in the water smiting two rocks together, drew to standing.

"Hi," I said.

The woman walked in a lazy path toward the beach, which was not ten steps from her door, and stood there on the grassy rise between Meadow and me, her hands on her hips. I could see the outline of darker panties beneath her nightgown. The woman seemed unconcerned by this.

"*Hey*," she said, shaking a finger at us. "Isn't that funny? I saw you guys yesterday. At that bar in town. I remember you because I thought, how funny to bring a little kid into a bar. How old-school. Like we're back in County Cork or something." The woman looked down now at Meadow, who stood in her spangled bikini, rubbing one bare leg cricket-style against the other. "But I bet you had fun, didn't you, hon? You didn't want to be left out, did you? No. I'll tell you what. You can learn a lot in a bar."

Meadow's eyes grew large behind her glasses. Our statuesque neighbor looked even more impressive from her knoll, staring back at us with the smile from her previous question still on her lips. Was she pretty? Not technically. She was too formidable to be pretty. I ran over the scene from the bar in my mind. I remembered a blond woman in the booth, yes.

Hadn't she left before the news story about us aired? I walked toward her, my hand extended.

"Hi," I said. "My name's John." I gave an inner wince. "John Toronto."

She took my hand firmly. "Hi. I'm April. April Los Angeles."

"OK," I said, taking my hand back quickly. I waved it toward Meadow. "And that's my daughter, Chrissy."

"Hey, Chrissy!" the woman shouted.

Meadow shifted her weight from one leg to the other. Then she came closer, if only to get a better look.

"So what do you want to be famous for, Chrissy?"

Meadow squinted. "Excuse me?"

"When you grow up. What do you want to be famous for? Everybody wants to be famous for something."

"I want to be a lepidopterist." Not unkindly, Meadow added, "Lepidopterists study butterflies."

"You're not going to be famous for *that*." The woman laughed huskily in Meadow's direction. "Forgive me for not raising the pitch of my voice when I talk to you, sweetheart. I don't do baby talk. Then again, you don't seem the type of child who likes to be bullshat. Are you? Look how erect you're standing. Puts me to shame." She then turned to me and said, "Why do all young girls want to work with animals?"

I grinned. "Maybe because they're beautiful and gentle and the world is harsh and cruel?"

April touched me on the arm. Now that we were standing side by side, she seemed less Amazonian. I glanced again at the nightgown, which while not entirely sheer was definitely not outdoor wear.

"Well, it's true, isn't it?" she agreed. "I myself once ran

a very successful pet hotel. I'll tell you about it when I get back."

The woman stood unmoving.

"Oh," I said. "Where are you going?"

"To get some groceries in Swanton. I'm out. Do you guys have a piece of bread or something? I'll pay you back. You need anything? I'll get it for you. I'm *starved*."

It was Meadow who went into our cabin and got our neighbor two pieces of Roman Meal. She placed them on the plastic card table beside the Weber grill and spread them with mayonnaise, then topped each with a slice of cheese, then stood watching while April devoured her sandwich.

"I'm going to get us some meat to grill," April said, kicking the Weber. "I'll make you two a feast, you'll see."

Meadow stood observing the woman in her quiet, anthropological way. For a six-year-old, she was a pretty good judge of character. If she had said to me, *This woman is bad news*, I would have taken her word for it. But a lonely man is not a skeptical one. Sitting beside her in a matching plastic lawn chair, I inhaled deeply, disguising as a sigh my desire to take this woman in, even just the smell of her, to say *Let's!* to somebody, to say *Let's!* to the giving and the getting. My brain seemed to flicker and go out. So what, it had done little for me so far.

When Meadow was small, she'd gone through a phase of being fascinated with the human body, especially the innards. She wanted to know where pee and poop came from, and how the heart worked, and all that. We went to the library to browse the collection of anatomical drawings, murmuring over the bladders and bones and organs and meat-red muscle. When we got to a drawing of the brain, she became solemn.

"That's the brain," I said.

"I already know about the brain," she said.

"Oh yeah? Tell me about the brain. Tell me what the brain does."

She was three and already slightly myopic. The following year, she'd be prescribed eyeglasses, but before that, she would crawl up really close to other people's faces when she spoke to them, I guess so she could see them better, but we didn't know that. We thought it was sweet. I remember her best like this, close-up and breathing in my face, her brown eyes wide set and serious.

"The brain," she told me, "is the thing that makes ice."

LOVE SONGS

Requested items April brought back for us from Swanton, with receipt and exact change: carrot sticks, seedless green grapes, a stack of bologna, Progresso low-sodium Italian wedding soup, cheddar-flavored popcorn, a twelve-pack of Diet Pepsi, a sweatshirt, and a sand pail. My plan was to regroup. I would figure out an exit strategy. We would get out of this cleanly. We would have fun in the meantime. We would figure it out.

"So, *John*." April poked the coals in the grill with a stick. "What brings you and Chrissy this way?"

I shrugged. "Just a trip. A field trip. A trip through fields. Collect some butterflies. Befriend some tall women."

She snorted. "Tell some tall tales."

I sighed, held it, and breathed out. "You? What are you doing out this way?"

"Passing through, just like you."

She smiled at me through the smoke. I felt my face get hot. She talked like someone who knew me a lot better than she did. She made me jumpy, and at the same time, I was not in a position to refuse a friend. I glanced over at Meadow,

who was wearing her new sweatshirt with the tags still on and filling up her new sand pail. The spoils from Swanton had won Meadow over. She'd also been allowed into April's cabin, where she'd been spritzed with some heavy fragrance that I could still smell over the creosote. I hate to say it; it felt nice—seductively nice—to be three again. To have a female influence around.

"You're lucky to me meet me, you know," April said. "I'm actually pretty famous."

I grinned and took a pull from my Diet Pepsi. "Bullshit."

"Am too. You don't recognize my name?"

"I don't know your name."

"April Almond."

"Doesn't ring a bell."

She placed the top back on the grill. "April A.?"

"Stumped," I said.

She leaned in. "Don't you know the song, by the Minor Miracles? 'Oh yeah / Spring again, cares are gone away-hay. Hey now / Like a flower / Here comes April A.'" She stepped back, gesturing at her chest with a spatula. "That's me."

"No shit." The rest of the song came to me unbidden, a B-side hit I had memorized in my impressionable first years as an English speaker. "'Ayyyy-pril Ayyyy,'" I sang. "'Whose-a gonna be your lover *next* time...' Wow. When was that? Nineteen eighty-three? Eighty-four?"

"American Top Forty for three weeks in 1981."

She turned and settled into one of the plastic chairs we'd pulled up to the grill.

"So tell me the story," I said. "How you got a song written about you."

"I was nineteen," she said. "It's a long story."

A quick calculation put her deep in her forties. In truth, she looked older. Her hair drizzled down her back in gelled curls. The hair color itself was blond in the majority, but was also shot through with streaks of red and brown, giving it a kind of camo effect. Her face was diamond shaped, two generous cheeks tapering down to an expressive chin, and a brow that lacked worry. She did indeed seem like a person who'd had a lot of fun over the years. A person who might have possibly inspired a rock song. Even the way she sat invited you to look at her, one slightly sunburned thigh thrown across the other, her foot twisting in its gladiator-style sandal. She had changed into denim shorts so brief that the white squares of the inner pockets hung below the ragged hem. Her short, busty torso was covered in a blousy tunic. She had good, youthful legs. It was her legs, I decided, that must have inspired the Minor Miracles. My eyes reluctantly wandered away from them. But she had already caught me watching.

"Let's make us a drink," she said, smiling.

She came back with two old jelly jars full of a glowing greenish yellowish liquid.

"Mountain Dew and vodka," she said.

The way she said *vokka* was familiar to me. "You're not really from Los Angeles, are you?"

"I didn't say I was. I was born and raised in Plattsburgh."

"No kidding. We just came through there. What's the story in Plattsburgh? Why's everybody living in barracks?"

"Those," she said, raising her bright green drink, "are the remains of the Plattsburgh military base. The base got closed in the eighties and I guess they decided to keep the barracks. Just move right on in. Instant ghetto. How's your drink?"

"It's very— I'm very grateful for it."

"Huh? Do you like it or not?"

"Yes." I took an acid sip. "Do you have some extra, for my daughter? I mean, without the vodka. She loves Mountain Dew, for some reason. Her mother would die. She's a health nut, her mother."

"Sure." April went into the hut and came back with another glass. She walked a couple of yards down the gravel path and gave a husky shout: "Hey, *Chrissy*!"

Naturally, Meadow did not respond. She was crouched over her bucket, her back to us. From where we sat, she looked like two knees and a spine.

"Sweetheart," I called. "Want some Mountain Dew with your dinner?"

"Sure!" Meadow did not turn around. "I found a frog!"

"Great," I said. "What kind?"

"Well, it's *huge*. Huge and warty."

"Is it a toad?" April asked.

Meadow looked sadly over her shoulder at April. "There is no scientific difference between a frog and a toad."

"Well, good, because I always get them confused."

"Come on and show him to us!"

"He's kind of brown on the back but has a green mouth."

"Sounds like a bullfrog."

"I'm going to keep him," Meadow shouted. "Just like I kept the mouse."

Then the image blazed in the evening: the mouse that I'd caught beneath the kitchen sink in Pine Hills and none of us had the heart to kill. We'd bought it a plastic box and a wheel and a whole world of wood chips. And where I saw the mouse in the box I also saw you, Laura, reaching in, your sleeve rolled up, cupping the thing in one hand, speaking to it in tender tones.

Silence.

"Why so quiet, John? You seem lost in thought."

I looked over at my companion. "I was thinking about your legs."

"Ha! Sure you were."

"You have very nice legs, April A."

"Go on."

"You know, I always wondered where you girls went."

"What girls?"

"The subjects of love songs."

"You're joking, but actually, I tried getting a group of us together about ten years ago. Lola. Sharona. Roxanne. Roseanna. Don't forget *Layla.*"

"Peggy Sue!"

"Peggy Sue's probably dead, for Christ's sakes. They wrote her song in the fifties, John. Where've you been?"

"Were those women real? I thought they were just made-up songs."

"Some of them are real. I'm real, aren't I? I thought it would make a good reality TV show, you know, to trace the girls through their lives and see what happened to them. And how the song shaped their lives."

"And? What happened to your idea?"

"Well, let's say there was a certain amount of skepticism. Subterfuge. Jealousy. Agents intervened. The girls themselves, they took it took too personally. I don't think they ever understood what they were."

I looked at her with amusement.

"They were *muses.* There was a *cause.*"

"A cause?"

"Rock and fucking roll was the cause. You, John. At six-

teen, in your underpants, playing air guitar in your bedroom. *You* were the cause. It's not *funny*." April took a sip of her vokka. "Of course, you don't earn a living as a muse. Nobody writes you a check for it. Do you think the Minor Miracles were going to send me royalties? No. And so. I found jobs like everyone else."

"Were you at Woodstock?" I grinned.

"How old do you think I am, you piece of shit? No. But I did Burning Man once or twice. All I got out of that was a snakebite and a yeast infection."

I laughed and finished my drink, cracking the last ice cube with my back molar.

When I looked over at her, she was staring at me, stirring her drink with her finger.

"So," she said. "Later, after milk and cookies, I hope you come back and see me, John." She smiled at me over the rim of the glass. "I hope you knock on the door. And say my name. I'll wait up for you. I'll wait up for you, and I'll think about you. And then you'll knock on the door and say my name. And we'll see what happens. Maybe something nice."

"Sounds good," I said.

She laughed ruefully. "Oh, John Toronto, you are one strange man."

It was late before we had finished our steaks and cleaned up as best we could with only the use of bathroom sinks and bug lights. Meadow was delaying bedtime with some questionable frog care. I watched her in the iodine yellow light, squatting over the bucket, talking to it. Finally I wrangled her into her nightgown and tucked her into her bed.

"April's going to teach me how to change my hair," she said.

"What's wrong with your hair?" I said, smoothing it down at the top of her head.

"I want it to look like hers. Yellow."

"Oh. Really?"

"She gave me the bottle for it. The yellow comes in a bottle."

"No, I like yours how it is," I said. But I wasn't really listening. I was starting to experience a certain notorious foregleam, whetted by the short distance between my and April's cabins. I slid off the creaky bedsprings and gave Meadow a peck. "Good night, then, sweets."

She clicked on her flashlight. "Where are you going, Daddy?"

"Right over there. To talk to April. Could you not shine that in my face, please? I don't like lights in my face."

"Can you read me one more poem from *Birds Come and Gone*?"

"No. It's late. The birds came and went. Close your eyes, and before you know it, it will be morning."

"Can I come with you?"

"Not on your life."

"When will you be back?"

"Soon. Or, as you would say, soon*ish*."

"I'm afraid to sleep alone."

"You won't sleep alone. Like I said, I'll be back really soon."

"Just one more poem?"

"Meadow—"

"Can you at least stand outside the door until I fall asleep?"

"OK. OK. I'll be right outside. Now, go to sleep."

Except for the light in April's cabin, the night was completely dark. The lamplight spilled across the short distance and exposed me to the night. One movement and April would be able to see me from under the hem of her lacy window treatment. I cleared my throat. The lake lapped against the little beach, unseen, darker than the sky. I leaned against a tree with large, bald roots, kicking the dirt that formed a little collar around the barbecue. I could hear Meadow talking to herself, the beam of her flashlight roving the ceiling of the cabin. After a couple of extremely long minutes, the beam settled and I could hear only the lake. Three, four, five paces later, I'd crossed a realm.

April opened the door and stood behind the screen, a drink in one hand and a rolled-up celebrity magazine in the other. She pushed the screen door open with it.

"You're supposed to wait for me to knock," I said.

"I couldn't stand the suspense."

"I was hoping to get your autograph."

April beamed. "I'll do you one better."

The headboard was cheap and loud and her legs were very long and she was strong and tawdry and enthusiastic and neither of us was very clean or polite and it occurred to me it had been a long, long, long time since I'd made love like that, I mean without apprehension, without bracing myself for some kind of fallout. It had been a long time since I'd visited that vast, unregulated sexual territory between two willing people—no hazards, no rattlesnakes, no treachery. But I remembered it. There is even a photograph of it. A Delaware Bay motel en route to Albany from Virginia Beach. We didn't have a camera, so we bought a disposable one in the motel lobby, along with a package of pistachios and a liter of root

beer. In the shower, we stood cleaning the highway off one another. I found black grit in the corners of your eyes, and inside the carpet of your hair. I shampooed you brutishly, a real amateur; you just laughed. The sun gives us a day, but who fashioned the hour? What is supposed to be accomplished within its parameters? How long is an hour supposed to *feel*? That hour—the one in which we lay on the bed afterward, staring at each other in the underwater light particular to roadside motel rooms—that hour seems to still be taking place endlessly, and it is a kind of invigorating torture to me, and I can't get rid of it.

How did you get rid of it?

"Why are you crying, hon?" April was saying now. "Don't cry. Come on, John. That makes me feel like shit."

"I'm sorry," I said, wiping my face. "I'm sorry. You're gorgeous. You're good. I like you. It's just— It's been a long time since I felt so"—I searched for the word—"acceptable."

"All right. Sure. That's all right."

"You make me feel acceptable. Do you know what I mean?"

"Not really. I just make love because I like to do it."

"Well, that's good. Good for you. I'm just a lot sadder than I appear. Ergo the random outbursts—" Here I leaned over her naked body for a deep drink of vodka from the bedside table.

"Come here," April said, pulling me to her by the neck, and I lay across her like that, crying and apologizing, and topping off our drink and listening to her talk until everything smoothed out and made a sort of sense, and that was me falling asleep. My dreams were only mildly disturbed as the body beside me stirred and resettled and the night labored on and I

pretty much forgot I had a daughter and more importantly I believed she had forgotten about me.

I didn't wake up until the morning, when dim light fell across my face.

Disoriented, I looked up. There was my daughter in the doorway, staring at me, her hair scorched white.

SILENCE THEORY

It occurs to me that I haven't really mentioned my research here in the body of my text. I don't want to burden the prospective listener with subjects too esoteric, but on the other hand, it seems that my not mentioning my research belies some form of embarrassment? And given that I woke up today regretting yesterday's confessions (see pages 147–8, re: Delaware Bay) and am now practically impaired with bitterness that a) I felt such tender things about you, Laura, in the first place and b) I then immortalized them by writing them down, I think now would be a good time to change the subject. Let's not forget that my audience here is diverse. I've got a legal obligation to humanize myself. For my own defense. Other people might want to know, how did I contribute to society? What did I care about?

I care about pauses. Actually, I collect pauses. Back in the year 1990, fresh out of Mune, after studying many of the most significant moments in human history, I thought it might be cool to collect all those moments—literary, cultural, political—when something was *not* said or *not* done. Hesitations, standstills, lulls, ellipses. All kinds of inactivity. I called it "Pausology:

An Experimental Encyclopedia." The work stemmed from my longtime interest in the concept of "eventlessness" (which I would define as moments in history when nothing was happening, producing a significant insignificance).

At first I thought I was doing something groundbreaking. I was writing antihistory. History's negative. Then I realized the obvious, that the material I was trying to collect was totally undocumented. One summer I hired a research assistant through my old prof at Mune, and we spent most of the summer just trying to figure out how to begin. After Meadow was born, I had to adjust my ambitions and reckon with the fact that there was no way that my encyclopedia would ever be "complete." And after a while, looking over the bits and pieces of promising chapterlets and indexes, I thought, well it could make for an interesting coffee table book. I don't know. People kept asking me, "How's the book? Making progress on that book?" The truth is, I had told too many people about it to stop.[11]

For all of his brilliant writing, playwright and unofficial pausologist Harold Pinter loved moments in which the characters did not speak, leaving us now with plays chock-full of excruciating or "pregnant" pauses. Although Pinter later came to repudiate his famous pauses, he happily wrote 140 of them into *Betrayal* and 224 into *The Homecoming*, which, if faithfully

---

11. In source material as ancient as Pseudo-Dionysius, the researcher can find evidence of an ongoing debate that is probably at the heart of my personal interest in silence studies. We've heard that talk is silver, but silence is golden. As someone who is widely considered talkative—*too* talkative—the suggestion is provocative to me: Do I say *less* than a silent person? Is silence truth, *in itself*? That is, is silence the sole expression of the incommensurability of the truth with our rudimentary powers to speak it? Do I have a mouth that can talk like that? Do you have ears that can listen like that?

acted, led to some satirically long, theater-clearing perfor-
mances that will fuel bad undergraduate repertoires for gen-
erations to come. I'd like to draw a connection here between
dramatic pauses and marital pauses. Both dramatic and marital
pauses vary in duration; the shortest, or most minor, are easily ignorable ("...") but do signal some form of inner struggle;
other beats are longer and more loaded with effortful suppres-
sion or confusion (*pause*), but the longest pauses (*silence*) are
the ones no one should have to bear, and speaking personally
I would have rather been flayed alive than to stand there with
my wife having *nothing to say*, as in nothing *left* to say.

Therefore, anyone interested in Pinterian pauses could save
the cost of the ticket and spend an evening witnessing someone's disintegrating marriage. Here's an excerpt from mine:

Ham Sandwich: A Marriage
for Laura

WOMAN
Looking up from her schoolwork
Oh. I didn't know you were here.

MAN
Yes. I'm...here.

WOMAN
Well...you might as well sit.

MAN
Where?

WOMAN
Anywhere.

MAN
Next to you?
Silence

WOMAN
Is she asleep?
MAN
Who?
WOMAN
Our little girl.
MAN
Oh, yes. She was very tired. But happy.
WOMAN
Happy... Happy...
Silence
MAN
And you?
WOMAN
Startled
Me?
MAN
Are you...?
WOMAN
I don't know.
Pause
I don't know.
MAN
Might we...
WOMAN
Oh. I don't know anymore.
MAN
Do you...
WOMAN
No.
Pause

Not anymore. I . . .

Silence

Pause

MAN

Well. Would you like a ham sandwich? I'm going into the kitchen. I could . . .

WOMAN

Yes. All right. Thank you. A ham sandwich would be nice.

MAN

All right.

He stands

WOMAN

Wait.

MAN

What is it?

WOMAN

I don't really want a ham sandwich. I'm not hungry.

MAN

Well. Would you like another kind of sandwich? Egg salad? Roast beef? What about an ice cream sandwich?

WOMAN

Like I said. I'm not hungry.

MAN

What about a pretzel? A fruitcake? Lamb with mint jelly? WHY IS EVERYTHING I OFFER YOU INSUFFICIENT?

Silence

END OF PLAY

★   ★   ★

But that's not very funny.[12]

Well, Harold Pinter wasn't a very funny playwright either.

I've always been fascinated by—and uncomfortable with—pauses. My research forced me to see that short pockets of silence were everywhere and that even sound needs silence *in order to be sound*. There are tiny silences all over this page. Between paragraphs. Between these very words. Still, they can be lonesome. So for all my project's shortcomings, I'd say the worst is that I haven't shaken the lonesome feeling that pauses give me. Sometimes I still wish there weren't any silences at all. And so it is with some reluctance that I give you this one.

---

12. Maybe you've heard this one:

An elderly man was feeling ill and had his wife drive him to the doctor. After the exam, the doctor sent the man to a waiting area without saying much and asked to see his wife.

"What is it?" she asked when they were alone. "Is it serious?"

"It's very serious," said the doctor. "He has a very rare condition that will kill him within three months. Only one thing can save him—you must have intimate marital relations with him twice a day, every day. That and only that will keep him alive."

She nodded, left the room, and went back out to see her husband in the waiting area.

"What did the doctor say?" the man asked anxiously.

She looked at him sadly.

(Pause.)

"He said you're going to die."

MEN AND WOMEN

When dressing in your underclothes, you used to loop both straps of your bra over your shoulders and then bend over, catching your breasts, as it were. Then you would reach around and hook the clasp, adjust the fit of the cups, and then you would stand, perfected. I often watched this ritual from the bed. I would wait for it. I liked the way it evoked a bow, the way that when you stood, you seemed to invite applause. I appreciate the tease of undressing, but there is nothing so transfixing as a woman dressing, article by article, fitting her toe through the ruffled hole of the panty, or drawing closed a zipper, pinky erect, saying, with her whole form, *Maybe later*. Of course I never really felt worthy of all that. It always seemed to me that as a man I was so much uglier in comparison. Take my male *toilet*. I would stand there in the bathroom with white bits of deodorant caught in my underarm hair, penetrating my own nostril with the whirring pole of an electric nose-hair trimmer. You left a scent of camellia in your wake. I left tiny whiskers in mine. My footfalls were heavy. Yours were soundless. You could handle glass. I looked like an idiot holding a champagne flute, a real gorilla. I'm grateful, really, and also sad, that you were so beautiful.

FÜNFTER TAG *OR*
DAY FIVE

The beautiful weather could not last forever. While April and I slept, clouds slid into the sky above Lake Champlain, and with them, the mood had darkened. Back in Cabin Two, Meadow rattled the bottles in the half fridge, looking for something not there. She was tired of cheese sandwiches. Why hadn't I bought any cereal? she wanted to know. Normal people eat cereal for breakfast. And fruit. Fresh fruit. Three to five servings a day. Everybody knows that. I watched her move about the cabin, still trying to get used to the color of her hair. Unfortunately, it wasn't goldenish like Rapunzel's. It was a parched color, like dried corn stalks. She must have done it wrong. I followed her around, holding the dry rope of it in my hands. Glancing in the bathroom, the smeared towels and sink basin made me feel sick.

After she'd walked in on me and April, I'd dressed quickly, and run after her. And now she would barely look at me, and I could understand why. I was in need of a shower. And a Laundromat. No. I was in need of a bonfire. I needed to burn my clothes and start over. I smelled of cigars and April and rain and vokka and my face was bloated as it is sometimes in

the mornings after drinking. Meadow sat at the tiny cocktail table that functioned as the cabin's dining area, resting her big white head against the heel of her palm as she bit off the corner of the last piece of Roman Meal, staring down at the plastic tablecloth. Jesus, I thought, what would her mother think? I was almost more afraid of that than of legal ramifications.

And our getaway car! I looked out the window to where the thing sat in the mist. What sort of rube steals a car with a white racing stripe? The car was useless. We had driven it all over North Hero, and earlier, to Swanton. It was a moving trap, a fucking advertisement. The only place in which I knew we were invisible was right where we were, but we couldn't stay here. I could see that Meadow had lost the fragile enthusiasm she'd first had for our trip. Hell, she'd been doing me a favor the whole time. I could see that.

But what did *I* want? Just a little more time. But for what? What spectacular thing was I going to do with it? I didn't want to be exposed—how much I was about to lose—but I knew I was going to lose it, now or later. I grabbed a nearby chair back, squeezing until it hurt. There was something more to do. I wasn't *done*.

"Meadow," I said. "Look at me, please."

Not changing her position, she looked at me.

"Why are you sad? Don't you like your hair?"

Her hand flew to her head and brought a swath of it to her face. "Actually. I like it lots."

"Well, maybe we should change it back. I hate to say it, but I kind of miss your real hair—"

"No. No, thank you." She shook her head firmly. Her eyes moistened, but she refused tears. She seemed shy of me, as if

she'd realized that her association with me was far less beneficial to her than she'd previously thought.

"So. What is it? What's wrong?"

She shrugged. "I just don't understand why we have to be friends with April."

"Oh," I said, relieved. "Well, we *don't* have to be friends with April. April and I are ships in the night. April and I are— two articles of clothing that got accidentally tangled up in the dryer. April and I just had some comfort to give each other. I had some comfort to give her, and she had some comfort to give me. Do you know what I mean?"

"No. Why go to all the trouble? Why not just keep it and comfort yourself?"

"I *do* comfort myself," I said, my voice thick with my own double meaning. "I comfort myself all too often. It's not the same. Everyone wants to be comforted by someone else."

"Why?"

"Why?" Frustrated, I grabbed the air with both hands. "Why? What's *wrong* with you? Don't you like to be held and kissed? Don't you like to be babied sometimes by me or your mom, or by Mom-Mom or Pop-Pop or Stinky Blanket?"

I saw her memory snag on the words, and her eyes filled up instantaneously with tears.

"Oh, no," I said, grabbing her hands. "Oh boy. I didn't mean to—"

"I miss my mommy," she said, tears falling onto the tabletop. "I miss Mom-Mom and Pop-Pop. I don't like this vacation anymore. I don't *care* about Mount Washington. I don't want to go there anymore. I don't want to go there with you. You're not good." She looked at me with an expression of

disapproval I'd never seen on her face before. "You're not good! You told me you were going to be right back! That I wouldn't be alone!"

"Oh, Meadow. Please—"

"And you were nowhere! You were *away*."

She snapped her hands back from mine and swiped at her eyes. She stood up and walked out. The slam of the cabin door resounded through the cove.

I grabbed my wallet and keys and followed. She was already indistinct in the morning haze, marching toward the road. She was carrying, with some difficulty, the bucket with the frog in it.

"Hey," I said, catching up to her. "Let me help you. Tell me the plan. Talk to me. What are we doing?"

She kept walking, her eyes red but dry. I peered into the bucket. The frog was floating spread-eagled in two inches of water. Meadow had covered the top of the pail with salvaged chicken wire to prevent his escape, but it looked to me like he was pretty much dead. I took hold of the handle, careful not to touch her hand. We entered the field we'd crossed with her on my shoulders days before. This time, we skirted the edge, passing the frugally darkened windows of our hostess's farmhouse. We were soon on the main dirt road, walking uphill. Cows observed us from behind electrified wire. I was surprised at how fast Meadow could walk without stopping, and how far. After some outbuildings on the crest of the hill, the road began to dip again, and we could see, in a field below us, a small pond.

"Good," said Meadow, as if she'd known it would be there. "That's where we'll put him. Then he can have the place to himself and he can start his own family."

"Or maybe he'll become a poet and write a book called *Frogs Come and Gone*."

"No," she said, eyes narrowing. "He hates poetry. All frogs do. Amphibians are allergic to poetry." She took a couple of steps forward and then looked up at me, hard. "You can come. But only if you don't touch him with dry hands. That'll kill him."

I fell to one knee. "Sweetheart," I said. "If you want, when we get back to the cabin, we can pack up, and I'll take you straight home. I'll take you straight home to Mommy. I want you to be happy. I don't want you to be angry at me. Say the word."

She said nothing, but the expression in her eyes softened, and she finally wiped her brow with the arm of her oversized sweatshirt. She gave the bucket a yank.

"Come on," she said, and we continued to the pond, over which the sun was now wearing through cloud cover.

THE TANGERINE AND
THE FOX

Listen. I don't see myself as some kind of Socrates, but from my point of view, it doesn't seem fair to hold a child back from her natural curiosities. Some kids—kids like Meadow—like to ask the hard questions whether or not you've brushed up for them. Take the example of the tangerine. She saw a forgotten tangerine that had pruned and hardened in the fruit bowl back in Pine Hills, and she wanted to know what would happen to it next. Would the tangerine keep shrinking and finally disappear? We observed it. We noticed that approximately seven days after we first observed the process of hardening, a process of softening began.

"Decomposition," I said. "The reverse of growing. But first the dead thing has to dry out. Like with rigor mortis."

"Rigamordis?"

"Yeah. When a body dies, the body first becomes stiff, like"—and here I did a vampy imitation of a dead body, which made her laugh—"and eventually the same thing happens to the body that happened to the tangerine."

"It gets stiff; then it gets mushy."

"Yes," I said. "Everything that dies eventually gets mushy."

Her eyes grew wide. "Even we will?"

"Yes," I said. "Even we will get mushy someday. Every-thing dies that is alive. It's important to accept that up front. You do less running."

Soon after, when we found the dead fox in the backyard, I tried to use the fox as an advanced example of the tangerine. We put it in an old milk crate and put it respectfully behind the lawn-mower shed. And we watched it, day to day, as the sun burned away its flesh and flies took it away in infinitesimal pieces and the wind blew away its form, until it was almost a carpet of copper fur, sinking back toward the earth. We spent hours watching the fox decompose. I know it sounds weird, but it didn't feel weird at the time. In fact, I thought of the fox as something of a pedagogical success. Which is ironic, as vis-à-vis you, her mother, made tense by advanced stages of marital conflict, the fox was The Final Straw.

"I need to talk to you," you said one morning, your eyes hard.

We were at the breakfast table. It was a Saturday, early summer. You were almost done with your first year of teach-ing, and while we should have been looking forward to the summertime together, the time seemed, to me, touched with a danger I couldn't fully admit. Weekends had become a strain. You'd let me sleep in. Then when I awoke, you'd suit up for a run. This morning that I remember, Meadow must have filled you in on some of our recent experiments while I was still in bed. You gave me a significant stare across the table.

"Meadow," you said, tapping her leg. "It's almost time for *Dora*. You can go and watch *Dora* while me and Daddy have some sharing time."

I smirked. *Sharing time* had such a punitive ring to it, I could hardly hear it without laughing. Your speech had become rife with institutionalisms. I watched Meadow wipe her mouth and push off from the table, her cane-juice-sweetened Os distended in their inch of milk. After she was gone, you leaned in.

"What are you doing?"

"Eating breakfast."

"What are you doing collecting dead animals? What the hell makes you think that's a good idea? Who are you trying to turn her into, Wednesday Addams?"

"That's funny, Laura."

"This is *not* funny. I have *had* it."

"Had it with what? It's nature. Death is natural. She's not scared of it. She's wiser for it."

"She's not supposed to be wise. She's supposed to be three and silly and to laugh a lot and not worry."

"Well, she asked."

"I don't believe you," you said. "That's the problem. *I don't believe you anymore.*" You pressed both hands to your brow. "I don't believe you. I don't trust you. *Help me*, Eric."

I sat there wishing for something to do, a satisfying punishment of the sort we used to get in grade school in Dorchester when we were bad or rude, and we were instructed to endlessly rewrite our error until we had filled pages and pages with the chant

> I pushed in line
> I pushed in line
> I pushed in line

I pushed in line
I pushed in line
I pushed in line

We'd write until our hands ached, and we were totally purged, ready to begin again, ready to be better.

I looked up to see tears dripping from your jaw, untouched. You toyed with the handle of your coffee mug.

"Please don't cry, Laura. It was just a dead animal."

"No," you said. "No, it was not."

"I'm not sure what you want," I said. "Something that I can actually give you."

"I want to know how this happened. How we became so different. So opposite. How this huge space grew between us." You looked at me pleadingly. "Were we always like this? I don't think so. I miss who I thought you were."

And then you just let go, you just let yourself sob.

It's not totally relevant for me to sit here and describe what it feels like to watch your wife cry in despair about something you did—no—some way that you *are* that doesn't even seem strange or remarkable to you. Despite the fact that I have clearly lost the PR battle here—I mean, I *broke the law*, in countless ways—I'm still curious to know whether or not I did the wrong thing with the fox. Because in the end I really don't know what I should have said, and I spend a fair amount of time sitting here wondering how I could have been more like who you thought I was, which sometimes feels productive, and sometimes feels like a rare form of self-battery. And so I have devised a multiple-choice questionnaire, for the reader of this document, whomever she may be if she is not

you, Laura, in an effort to conduct, as it were, a sort of study. Here it is:

Is it appropriate to tell a three-year-old child that everything that is alive will die and decompose, including the human body?

Yes or no?

If no, why?

a) Because that is a lie. A dead body does not decompose, but rather is borne off completely intact on the shoulders of a bevy of celestial heartthrobs.

b) Because the question is irrelevant. The teacher has been discredited, for reasons that have multiplied exponentially since then, and therefore whatever he said, whatever factoids he once offered his exceptionally intelligent child, were spurious.

c) Because a guy in his position really should have deferred to his wife, and if he had a brain in his head, he would have known that his wife wasn't going to like it, and the fact that he went ahead and desecrated a dead fox is proof that he probably didn't love *her* anymore anyway, or had given up on *her*, or had given up on her ability to accept him for who he was, and the fact that they were fighting so viciously over a science experiment was probably a red herring, and underneath it they were probably asking each other the standard late-stage question: Why don't you love me? / Why don't *you* love *me*?

Circle your answer and return to:

Erik Schroder RN # 331890
CCI ALBANY
COUNTY CORRECTIONAL INSTITUTION
P.O. BOX 3404
ALBANY, NY 12227

ANOTHER SURPRISE

The frog was still alive. When Meadow settled the bucket into the pond water and removed the chicken wire, he startled to life and began to rapidly stroke away from us, deep into the murk. We turned around and traced our steps toward the dirt road.

Just as we reached the road, we heard a car approaching. The car came rapidly over the rise and sped past us, only to come to a dusty halt farther on. Taillights flicked on; the driver turned around and backed up, rolling down the passenger-side window. It was April.

"Well, hello again," she said.

I couldn't help but smile. I leaned over and put my hand on the roof of her car. Her arm was hooked over the seat back. Since I'd last seen her, she'd changed into a long, angel-sleeved sheath of yellow, green, and red. In the backseat, I saw her belongings: several crates, a sleeping mat, a duffel bag, a bunch of celebrity magazines.

"I was trying to get used to the idea that I'd never see you again," I said.

"Not necessary," she said. "Get on in. I can move all that junk."

I shook my head. "Thanks. But we were just about to head back and clear out ourselves. You know, head home. Time's up."

April leaned forward and gave Meadow a warm smile. "Hey, Chrissy."

"Hi," said Meadow, hanging back but smiling a little.

April waved me around the car. "Com'ere," she said. "I should tell you something."

I walked to the driver's side, and leaned forward.

She spoke into my ear. "So. If you head back now, you will be greeted by three Vermont State troopers. Three squad cars. The one came first, and the others came with their sirens off. They've already been inside your cabin. I'd say whatever you had in there is now property of the state. Cheese singles and all. There will be more coming soon, is my guess. That poor lady is in a state. She kept saying she had a bad feeling about you."

I raised my head. The top of the dirt road ended in sky. Everything was quiet.

April leaned forward to peer at Meadow, who was toying with her bucket. "Find any butterflies, baby?"

"No." Meadow inched closer to the car. "But we freed the frog."

"Good. That's good. That's *right*." She looked up at me. "So, Sir John. What will you do? You've got about sixty seconds before I take off. I can't believe I'm even talking to you."

I opened my mouth, but I could not speak. My mind jammed. All I could think of was—the old lady had a bad

feeling about me? April sighed and got out of the car. She moved the duffel into the trunk. Then she gestured to the open door.

"You should see your face," she said to me.

"I have some things—," I said. "Some things in the cabin—"

"So what?" April said. "They're gone. They're not yours anymore."

Meadow was staring at me. Her face must have mirrored mine, if only because mine frightened her so much. That's when I thought of it, of what I had left to do.

"Get in, sweetheart," I said.

"And don't slam the door," added April.

"Be quiet."

"Why, Daddy? What's wrong?"

"Get *in*."

And there they were—male voices, down by the water, amplified by the lake, sounding closer than they were. They sounded as if they were right beside us on the road, invisible men. The dogs were barking out of their minds.

I couldn't buckle my seat belt. I couldn't feel my fingers. I tried and tried. We were already moving very fast by then.

FALLING ROCK

"The road for all seasons and reasons," Route 2 sweeps you through Vermont's niche industries, a series of diverse, minor attractions like the winery at Calais or the "cornfusing" corn maze at Danville. And if the traveler doesn't have time to stop, if he is, in fact, desperately trying to cross state lines, he may just gaze out the car window at the legendary Vermont woodland, through which, if he lives that long, the traveler may return on a charter bus from his retirement home in some distant leaf-peeping season. And if he closes his eyes, he can see it already, although it is only June: autumn's mosaic of yellow and copper and red, the sad magic of it.

Meadow had not spoken a word to me since the outskirts of Burlington. She sat steely eyed in the backseat, her hands clutched in her lap, looking small and unfamiliar without the added height of her booster seat. I had tried to speak to her several times, but at the sound of my voice she snapped her head to the side. She'd been upset to abandon her backpack ("and my *tooth*brush and my new bi*k*ini"). All she now possessed, in fact, was an empty bucket. As for me, I carried only my wallet and keys and the clothes I'd been wearing for four

days—a pair of flat-fronted khakis, still rolled to the knee and wet with pond water, and a blue-checkered collared shirt with a wilted buttercup in the breast pocket. Everything else in our cabin was currently being turned inside out by some square-jawed woodhick with a CB radio. (*Found something, Dawson.*) Of course, at the core of this, there was an image that made my stomach tighten. (*What is it, Peterson? Looks like a passport.*) I saw him coming toward me—not the cop, the boy—in his knee-high athletic socks, his knockoff Bruins jersey, circling me like some hungry fish.

Erik Schroder, it says. Who the hell is Erik Schroder?

"What's that sign mean?" Meadow said suddenly, pointing out the window.

We were driving through a mountain pass of blasted granite.

I cleared my throat, trying to summon a steady voice. "Falling rock."

"Oh great," Meadow said. "Now rocks are going to fall on us, too?"

The wind was high, swabbing the clouds back and forth across the sun. Whenever we plunged into shadow, Meadow's eyeglasses became reflective, giving her face a cold, mechanical look.

"April's driving too fast," she muttered. "She's driving too fast to miss the falling rocks."

"Hey," April said into the rearview mirror. "As my mother used to say, don't should on me, and I won't should on you."

Meadow crossed her arms and snapped her head to the side again. "I don't care what your mother used to say."

We plunged back into silence. Probably none of us, in our whole lives, had ever gone so long without talking. I glanced

over at April, who was holding on to the steering wheel with a high two-handed grip like an old lady. Was I *that* bad, was I *that* desperate, to become the goodwill case of a woman like her?

"Hey, April," Meadow said darkly.

"Yeah, hon?"

"Chrissy's not my real name."

April laughed. "I didn't think it was, honey."

I didn't turn around.

"My name is Meadow. Meadow Kennedy."

"Well," said April, "my name *really is* April Almond. Even though it sounds made up." She laughed again, this time a little uncomfortably. "Funny how people are always trying to tell me the truth, even when they shouldn't."

"My daddy doesn't always tell the truth. He tried to shut me in the trunk of a car once."

I swung around. "What?"

"You *did*."

"But I *didn't*. I mean, I didn't shut you in it. And besides, I've apologized for that several times." I looked at April. "I apologized for that."

"Don't tell *me* about it," said April.

"And Mommy said you lied sometimes."

"When?"

"When I was little. And you took me all sorts of places."

"Like the *library*? When I was taking *care* of you? And she was at *work*?"

"No. Like the church where everybody was crying? Mommy said that was *not* for kids."

Again I turned to April. "An AA meeting. I went to support a friend."

"You took her to an AA meeting?"

"A mistake."

"Well, I told Mommy *all* about it," Meadow declared.

"You can't tell Mommy things like that, Meadow. She doesn't understand them out of context."

"Still!" Meadow shrieked. "You're not supposed to lie. If it was good you would have told!"

"All right, all right," April said. "You know what? I really don't want to know any more about all this. I'm sure you are both very important people. You deserve a ticker-tape parade for living, OK? Anyway, cheer up. We're heading to New Hampshire, a great state. We'll drive over the Kancamagus. Gorgeous. You won't believe it. Much better than this. The White Mountains blow the Green Mountains out of the water. Who wants to listen to the radio?"

She screwed irritably at the dials. In the distance, mountains tumbled into mountains. The nearest ranges were dark and green, the farther ranges fainter and higher, echoed by fainter mountains farther still, the jagged horizon a series of studies for a mountain.

"I want to thank you," I said to April, my voice thick and wounded. "You've been—you've been—"

"No problem. You're welcome."

"I'm not a bad person."

April sighed. "You may or may not be a bad person. You're just a lot less bad than the other people I know."

"Well, thanks."

"Like I said."

"I mean, thanks for taking us to your place. I just need a quiet place to stay. To collect my thoughts."

"You won't be staying anywhere, John." April turned and

looked at me hard. Then she glanced backwards at Meadow, who was scrutinizing us from behind. Finally, Meadow rolled her head away and pretended to stare at the landscape. April turned up the volume on the radio. "And I didn't say the place was mine. The place is my cousin's. A camp near Ragged Mountain."

"No, listen. I don't want to involve anyone else."

"My cousin's not there. It's a long story, but let's just say he's in Georgia. I check in on his place now and again."

"Better to stay at a motel. You can drop us off at any motel."

"Slow down. At my cousin's place, you'll have privacy. You can give her a home-cooked meal, and you can think about where to go next. But you won't be able to *stay* anywhere, is all I'm saying. I mean, if your idea is that you're going to keep running. With or without her. There are lots of people out there living like that." She dropped her voice to a whisper. "Jesus. I'm not going to force your hand. But *she* will. Look at her."

I looked. My daughter's arms were wrapped around her orange bucket. Her mouth was set in a wry smile, and I could almost hear her making wild promises to herself. Her white hair was being sucked in ribbons out the window, giving her a bizarre, mythical look. This, I thought, *this* is what I wanted? This rumpled, sandy child with an abnormally high tolerance for upsetting turns of fate? With a sick twisting in my conscience I saw that I had been waiting to see if she could do it, if she had the capacity to tolerate the world as it was according to me—a mess, a random and catastrophic mess—and if she could stand it. And there she was in the backseat, standing it, the third in a trio of missing persons, and there she would be, in some ways, forever, wouldn't she? Because when she was

older, might her familiarity with people like me or April con-
sign her to their company, so that she would be drawn to them
and would travel with them in their VW vans or the sidecars
of their motorcycles, forever along the edges of things, until
she would be, in the end, more comfortable with freaks and
eccentrics than with the main army? I shuddered inwardly,
experiencing the first cold pall of regret, a sense that this victory was the wrong victory, a sense that *you had been right*.

We arrived in St. Johnsbury in the late afternoon. April pulled
up to a coffee shop across from a white New England public academy and took Meadow inside to use the bathroom.
School was letting out for the day, buses lined up along the
street, parents gathering slowly.

I sat and watched the parents gather. Several of them wore
muddy work clothes and trucker hats. Some of the women
were visibly pregnant. They stood together, murmuring. I
rolled down the window and tried not to stare.

A flash of blond hair behind the café window. Meadow
had turned around and was talking to someone I could not
see in the interior of the coffee shop. A waitress? She was nodding. What was she being asked? She reached out her hands,
accepting something.

Say it, I thought. Go ahead and say whatever they teach
you to say to save yourself.

Then there was April behind the glass, smiling through
fresh lipstick, joking, explaining, scooting Meadow along.
Cowbells jangled. A man on the street tipped back his hat,
and out came my daughter, holding a donut.

RAGGED MOUNTAIN

We arrived at the camp in darkness. In the headlights, the place looked as if someone had extracted an apartment from the worst Dorchester housing project and rebuilt it cinder block by cinder block in the middle of a field in New Hampshire, and then covered it up with dirt, like a cairn. The car ground to a halt and our tense silence acquired another layer. April shoved the gearshift into park, took a tube of lipstick out of her purse, and ran it back and forth across her lower lip.

"Well," she said, "if you think it looks bad now, you should see it in the light of day."

"Somebody lives here?" Meadow wanted to know.

"Sure. My cousin raised both his kids here. The setting is really pretty. Over that way"—she gestured into the darkness—"there's a little brook with real fish. And that way, a hill they liked to sled on. They had everything. A vegetable garden. Tomatoes. Carrots. Dill. Bird feeders. A smokehouse. It was real country living." She turned to me. "You ever heard of the back-to-the-earth movement? Those couples who sold

everything and made their houses out of fieldstones and all their kids ran around naked and they just lived off the land?"

I nodded, still unable to speak.

"Well, I think my cousin was going for something like that. It all went to hell, of course, but you can't blame him for trying. There were good times. I used to come out here with my boyfriends. I even brought J.J. Torraine from the Minor Miracles, back in the day. All *right*." She clapped her hands. "Let's go in. Leave those headlights on, would you, so we can see. You can carry my duffel, John. And you—little Miss Butterfly—well, you bring your bucket."

In this way, April motivated us out of our paralysis, and we walked toward the structure in a single line, illuminated in the headlights. In front of me, Meadow's skinny legs marched below the sagging hem of her oversized sweatshirt. The tag on the back of the neckline was sticking out. Suddenly there was the snap of a sizeable branch as something large moved in the woods. We froze.

"What the hell was that?" I whispered.

I saw Meadow's expression in the lights—frightened, but also defiant, almost satisfied. Like she was thinking, just you go ahead and try me.

"A moose, probably," April said, working on the padlock that hung from the front door. From what I could see, the camp's door was some piece of leather-covered salvage, orna- mented with brass bolts, as if it had been pillaged from a church.

When April turned on the lights, we found ourselves in the midst of a strange room. Strewn with small domestic arti- facts, left in a hurry, it seemed like some Pompeiian scene, something almost curated—there was a book opened on a table, a worn dog bed still holding its rump-sized impres-

sion, and a number of coats hanging from hooks along the wall. Other than these objects, the room was not pretty. The carpeting was of a dark, indoor/outdoor variety, the cinder blocks were unpainted even in the interior, and the drop ceiling was missing one or two panels, revealing strips of pink insulation and wiring. The room seemed to function as an all-purpose family room, with cabinets, a countertop, a propane tank, and what looked like an icebox lined up on the far wall, serving as the kitchen. It was clear that the place had been built and maintained by someone who did not know what he was doing. As confirmation of this fact, a large aluminum canoe, pushed up against the far wall and filled with cushions, seemed the only discretionary piece of furniture in the room.

"Your bed," April said, gesturing to the canoe.

"A canoe? I'm sleeping in that canoe?"

"What? He took the bars out of it."

Here I laughed, a little aggressively. "And what does Meadow get to sleep in? A kayak?"

"No, she gets a couple bales of hay out back." April rolled her eyes. "Kidding. She gets a nice little bed, right there through that door. My cousin saved the best for his kids. But he liked to sleep in a canoe. I never asked why."

"Sure. Ha. Why pry?"

"You've got a problem with this place, John Toronto?"

"No," I said, rubbing my head. "No."

April turned to Meadow. "Hon, go ahead, through that door. Go see your room."

Meadow stepped forward. I could see that her reaction to the strange home was the same as mine: What had *happened* to these people? Where had they gone so quickly? It made you

think they had been endangered, but not for anything they did. Just because they were a family, and the chances were somehow cosmically against their togetherness. She pushed back the accordion door toward which she'd been directed and turned on the light with her shirtsleeve. That room glowed in a warmer, less fluorescent light, revealing a bunk bed and a red beanbag chair. April and I came to the door.

"Like it, hon?"

Meadow nodded.

"I know there's some toys around here. Good ones. Do you like Lincoln Logs? Look." April pulled a sagging box from a shelf and dropped it on the floor. "I always liked to build when I was your age. Do you like to build shit?"

Meadow nodded. She reached into the box and began to remove the notched plastic logs. When she seemed absorbed, April stood up and wiped her hands.

"All righty," she said, and walked out.

I followed her into the kitchen area. She opened some cabinets.

"Yum," she said, "baked beans."

"This is kind of you," I said. "Very, very kind."

She shrugged. She pulled a can opener from the coffee can in which it stood, and ground away at the tin top. The can opened. She sniffed inside.

"If you don't mind, I'd love it if you watched your language around the girl."

"You watch your language," said April. "*You're* the fucking outlaw."

"You have a right to be mad at me," I said.

"I'm not mad, OK? Just hungry and tired."

"She *is* my daughter, you know. I didn't steal her. And I'd never hurt her."

"I don't want to hear about it."

"The problem is between me and my ex. She tried to keep me from seeing her. And now, if I go back, I bet I'll never see her again."

Sighing, April plugged in the hot plate and sloshed two cans of beans into a frying pan. I reached into the coffee can and gave her a spoon.

"Thanks," she said.

"I'll tell you what I'm guilty of. I am guilty of— I am guilty of exceeding my legally allotted visitation period. That's it. And stealing a car. And falsifying my entire identity." Here, I laughed. A long, wrung-out laugh, a laugh long delayed. I laughed so long and with such rue that April passed me a dish-rag to wipe my eyes. I had to lean with both hands against the countertop until I could pull myself together.

"Thanks," I said, slowing to a chuckle. "Thanks. Thank you."

"Here," she said, getting another spoon from the coffee can and dipping it into the beans. "Take. Eat. This is my body."

She put the spoon in my mouth. The beans were sweet and warm.

"Thank you," I said, leaning against her. "Thank you so much."

The spoon and the pot in her hands, she couldn't hug me back. I stood there against her anyway, my nose in her hair.

"Hi," I said.

"Focus, John. Set the table."

She handed me another spoon. I went to the table and took

another look around the room. In a flash, I thought, it's not so bad. We could stay here for a little if we had to. It wouldn't take much to make it nicer. A couple of gallons of paint, a sheepskin rug, lamplight maybe.

"So are you sure your cousin won't be back tonight?"

"Yes, I'm sure."

"When will he be back?"

"Unless he gets parole, not for four more years."

I turned and stared at her. "He's in jail?"

"Oh, John. Don't look so shocked. Look, you're breaking my heart."

April turned off the hot plate, walked over to me, and took my face in her hands.

"Poor John," she said, kissing me on both cheeks. "You are the worst criminal I've ever known."

I fell against her. We leaned on each other, equal weights. I felt my throat tighten. I covered my eyes with my hands.

"I'm a mess," I said, into her hair. "A disaster. Everything I touch turns to shit."

"No. I'm sure that's not true."

"I just wanted some time with my daughter. I just wanted to have a vacation with my daughter. *I* wanted to decide that. I'm her *father*. I taught her to *read*. I stayed up with her when she was sick. There's been a mistake here, you know—a very grave mistake—a miscarriage—"

"You should have gone to court or something. You should have gotten a better lawyer or something. You shouldn't have nabbed your own daughter."

"Please." I pushed her away gently. "Please don't take the other side. The whole world is going to take the other side."

"Don't flatter yourself. The whole world won't be paying attention. Miss Butterfly?"

Meadow's voice sounded small from the farther room. "Yes?"

"Would you like some dinner?"

"No, thank you."

"You should eat."

"I'm not hungry, thank you."

April rolled her eyes. "I'm not even going to say anything. All she eats is donuts. When is the last time she had a vegetable?"

Grinning, I took up my spoon. "You know what? My wife would like you, if she knew you. Even though you're pretty much polar opposites. I think she would like you. At least, she'd be grateful to you for looking after Meadow."

April lifted a heap of baked beans on her spoon and blew on it. "Quit looking so grateful. It's not like I'm in love with you."

I grinned. "I should have married you. I should have married someone like you. I should have married a woman with a sense of humor."

"I don't need to get married. I've already got a rock song named after me."

I watched her across the table, one hand pinning back her hair, her lips blowing little rapid puffs toward her spoon.

"Hey. Do you want to—" I gestured toward the canoe. "After—"

Now April laughed. "Ho-di-ho-*ho*. I'm not having any more sex with you, Toronto. Especially not in a canoe. The only thing I'm going to do with my ass tonight is save it."

"Oh. OK. That's too bad."

"It *is* too bad, you know."

"I like you very much."

This seemed to make April a little sad. "Hey. How about you go put your kid to bed? We'll catch up after that. Here. Bring her these." She pushed a bowl of beans across the table. "She's probably starving, but too mad to say so. If I were you, I might try to make things right, while I had a chance. Say what you need to. After a lot of trial and error I found the 'truth will out,' as they say."

I sat there for a moment.

"Sorry," she said. "Did I overstep?"

"No. No, you didn't. In fact, I was—I was thinking the same thing."

I stood up. I walked to the door of Meadow's room. Then I stopped and came back and put my hand on the back of April's neck. I looked down at her big face, and I smiled. There was a pause—and I mention it here because, well, it was distinctly un-Pinteresque—light, merciful, safe.

"Everything about you is big," I told her.

"Thanks, I guess."

"Yes, it's a compliment. You're just a little bit *more* than most people."

And that was the last time I ever saw April A.

Who's gonna wanna be your lover next time?

April had been right about the White Mountains. There was something about them, something mysterious, legend mak-

ing. We had driven through their southern boundary all that afternoon into the evening, along the Kancamagus. To our left rose the promontories of the Franconia Range. The wind was high, and you could feel it hit the car. The silence was broken only when April would say, gesturing with her chin, "There's Moosilauke. And that one's Osceola." *Moosilauke. Osceola.* Words Meadow and I would have laughed about, had we been on speaking terms. I knew that Mount Washington towered to the north of us. But we couldn't go there, not anymore. Not in the spirit we had intended.

Now I came to the door of Meadow's erstwhile bedroom. She had abandoned an impressive metropolis of Lincoln Logs on the floor and was lying on the bottom bunk of the bed, one arm thrown over her face.

"You awake?" I whispered.

A lamp sat on a bureau in the corner of the room. I stepped forward and pulled the chain. She drew her arm from her face.

"You want some dinner?" I said, raising the bowl.

She glanced at me but said nothing.

"You're still not speaking to me?"

She shrugged and rolled to her side, poking the pillow on which her head rested.

At sunset, nearly out of the mountains, April had announced that she needed to pee and without further comment turned off the highway onto a gravel road bordered by wild rhododendron. We drove into a parking area and got out. April ran into the woods in her fluttering kaftan. Meadow and I walked uphill in silence. When we crested the hill, we were looking at the surface of a crater lake, which sat as smooth as glass inside the mountaintop, as if just the tip of the mountain had been sliced off and filled with rainwater.

Large clouds raced overhead in galvanic wind, sweeping purple shadows across the lake. The lake closed and opened with
the moving clouds; it almost felt like we were racing through
years. Meadow reached out for my hand. This surprised me—
that's why I remember it—that she still had some need for me,
however inscrutable, however ambivalent. And I remember
her reaching out for me as the reason that I did everything
thereafter, which led me to the place in which I now find
myself, writing this document. Because I see that moment as
the beginning of my disappearance. I mean the disappearance
of who I'd been. Of course, I'm still *here*—everyone knows
perfectly well where I am—but when she touched my hand, I
felt a falling away of my exterior, of my deception.

In the darkness outside of the camp, I heard a door slam.
I squinted through the plastic sheeting to try and see if it was
true, if April was leaving us. She started the engine and idled
only for a moment before she left us there, just the two of us
again, in the shadow of Ragged Mountain. And in this way,
my last escape route was cut off. I stared at my dim reflection
in the plastic.

"Meadow," I said. "There are some things I should probably tell you."

SECHSTER TAG *OR*
DAY SIX

I don't want to be singled out. I mean, I'm afraid that I've made myself too exceptional and that you won't see me for what I am. Other than my famous last name, there is almost nothing that distinguishes me from all the other sad men and women who have languished in the American family court system. The irremediable decisions, the obedience required by law, in matters of greatest urgency. The issue here is deeper, don't you think? It is beyond me.

The average American marriage has a life span of seven years. Seven is, of course, an inherently symbolic number. There were Seven Wonders of the Ancient World. Seven hills of Rome. The number seven is all over religion (seven days of Creation, seven skies in Islam, seven chakras, and of course, seven sins that are deadly). Let's take our marriage as a beau ideal of divorce, ending promptly in its seventh year. Its conclusion had a slow, balletic quality. As I've said elsewhere, I hardly felt like I was a player in it. And yet, in the year of our parting, Meadow's fifth year on earth, we joined one million other couples in legal separation or divorce, thereby conscripting our daughter into the ranks of the ten million

children living with separated or divorced parents, undoubt-
edly the largest subset she'll ever belong to. They say that one
out of every seven of those divorces involves a custody battle.
This means that in the same year, about two hundred thousand disgruntled parents took their petitions through courts of
family law, paying tens of thousands of dollars to end up more
frustrated than they were when they began. They became
damaged people, really. Deranged people. Because, of course,
there is one thing that really deranges us, and that is the disappearance of love.

Even in the year we separated, the year in which you
unstuck yourself of me, I never imagined my relationship
with Meadow would be jeopardized. She and I were close. Of
course we were; we'd just spent an entire year together. Even
when that was over, and I'd gone back to work as planned,
and she was enrolled over my objections in the Catholic pre-
school, I believed that our bond was strong. Hers and mine,
that is. Our bond—mine and yours, Laura—was tenuous at
best. While I worked, back on the real estate hustle with a
couple other survivors from Clebus, you spent quality time
with Meadow after school. When I returned, you gathered
up your grading and retreated to the bedroom. So? So what?
Love ebbs and flows, right? Alienation from others kicks in a
sporting self-reliance. I started playing soccer again. I flirted
heavily with the girlfriends who came to watch. The boys
seemed much younger to me than they had two years before.
I kept wallet-sized photos of Meadow for anyone who'd look.
I told myself that the frost that had fallen upon my marriage
was natural. A natural evolutionary phase.

From my current position, I see things more clearly now.
I think of you. I think of me. I think of Mama. I think of

Daddy. I think of Mama, and Daddy, and how the brain makes ice. I think of *Vogelgesang*. *Ich denke an die Vögel wie sie in Treptower Park gesungen haben*. And I think of childhood's density.

If my parents had loved one another once, that truth was quickly buried under too many other things to be of use to me. I remember sitting with my chin on my knees, gazing at the two of them engrossed in separate tasks, Daddy staring into a broken Swiss watch with a headlamp, Mama reading a black market fashion magazine, marveling at their silence. How could two beings be so quiet? How could they concentrate for so long without stirring? It never occurred to me that I was also concentrating. I was concentrating on them. I would lose myself in watching them, wondering what fascinated them so much, and when they might utter a word to one another. I could feel my eyelids swipe the surface of my retinas. I could hear houseflies searing themselves inside the lozenge-shaped sconce overhead. I could hear the banging of pots in apartments on either side of ours. Finally, my mother would look up and give me a kick with her shoe. *Snap out of it*, she'd say.

Did I love her? Oh, very much. Of this no one ever tried to dissuade me. I loved her and I loved my father and I loved my *Opa* and I loved the teacher of my nursery school and I loved the sheepdog she relied upon to watch us when she went to do something else. I loved sitting at my mother's feet, pulling along a series of wooden blocks sewn together with a string, a kind of Cubist caterpillar, while her foot bounced idly in its fashionable boot, a pat of grass stuck to the bottom of the high, stacked heel. Who *she* was, however, remains hotly disputed. A tart. A fanatic. A collaborator. A communist. It's

very hard to reconcile all this with the mother who walked me around Treptower Park, the material of her synthetic bell-bottoms sounding a reassuring washboard rhythm beside me. This was the woman who taught me how to ask, before falling upon some pup on the street, "Is your dog friendly?," the same woman who—I can only assume—taught me to hold a pen, to read, to write, to waltz, to tie a shoelace, to look both ways before crossing a street. A woman who does that—who teaches you to tie your laces—has a soul. She has a soul even if, as my father once told me in a rage, she did fall in love with some high-ranking party functionary who seduced her with packages of white chocolate.

But what about this affair with the communist? Was he the villain? How could he be if, in the end, with his intervention, we did not have to hijack a bus or a train or dig a tunnel or swim across the Spree in wet suits in order to get to West Berlin, which was my father's enduring dream? Instead, we were granted two exit visas and exactly one hour to get to Friedrichstrasse station. My father had been trying to get visas for us for years. Our suitcases—three of them—had long gathered dust in the pantry. Finally, after years of being rejected, his application dragged out, his career stagnant, our family ostracized by neighbors, here was a bureaucratic change of heart. A miracle. And a mystery.[13]

Whatever the case, it was a nagging thought of mine that I didn't have the whole story on my mother. Seeing as I was five the last time I saw her, too young for explanations even if she had wanted to offer them, I had never heard her speak of

---

13. The son in me likes to think: *a sacrifice*. She did what she had to. She played a role. She was a decoy. A mother would do that. Wouldn't a mother do that, in extraordinary circumstances?

my going away. But she knew about it. I mean, she was *there*.
She walked me to the nursery school, at the door of which we
were intercepted by my father, who traded me for an envelope. I do not know what was in that envelope. Money for
the bribe? Her own exit visa, to use when it was safe? For as
long as we were in West Berlin, I kept expecting her to follow, but she never did. I think Dad expected her too. We
were granted residency in West Berlin but did not qualify for
financial benefits, and so we lived in a state of disorientation
and near poverty above the garage of my father's wonderfully
unstable sister.

West Berlin was crowded, full of artists, gays, old people,
and anyone trying to escape the draft. My father, essentially a
conservative man, was shocked. How irritating it must have
been to recall the propaganda from the other side, warnings
that the Wall existed to keep out saboteurs, enemies of the
people. But I remember life in West Berlin at that time as intimate, surreal, and a little dangerous. Dad was either working
or scouring for work, a hard thing to find in such a place and
time, while my aunt was at home burnishing her idiosyncra-
sies.[14] My aunt had three sons. I played with these baby saboteurs day and night. I recall a vacuum of supervision. Jumping

---

14. My aunt was funny. She was nothing like her fastidious brother. She
disliked cooking and cleaning. The only things she enjoyed were smoking,
talking, and games of chance. When it was discovered that it was my eighth
birthday, my aunt rose from her card table and declared she was going to bake
me a cake. I followed her into the kitchen in a state of hope and disbelief. She
pushed a tower of dirty dishes into the concrete sink basin and rubbed her
hands together. *An egg?* I suggested, trying to jog her memory. *An egg*, she said,
bending toward the icebox. *Flour?* I climbed the cupboards to look for flour. She
had no butter, but she did possess a bottle of vegetable oil, as well as a packet
of colored sugar that we planned to sprinkle on top. There was the matter of
the cake tin. Clattering aluminum followed. She stood, beaming. Here was

out of the window onto a pile of mattresses. The sight of an old wooden cask rolling toward me in a game with rotating victims. By then, the Wall, which stood there in silence at the dead end of certain streets, had become the largest public art surface in the world.[15]

---

something that would work. *Eureka,* she said. *First we've just got to clean the mouse shit out of it.*

Sometimes, she and I would go to Kreuzberg to walk among the Turks. It was said that if West Berlin was the insane asylum of the Federal Republic, then Kreuzberg was the lockdown room. Where had all these people come from, in their headscarves and wide-legged pants, and why were they grazing their goats in Viktoriapark? On weekends, the Turks turned stretches of the Landwehr Canal into a giant souk. My aunt and I loved it there, and we spent afternoons rubbing the fabrics and wooden carvings and murmuring to one another. I did whatever she did, which meant that we both looked crazy, or at least starved for sense impression, which was true, since when you went into Kreuzberg you realized how strange the rest of West Berlin was, not just leached of color and scent, but wrongheaded, mishmoshed, half-resurrected by attempts to switch out the old, bombed-out cathedrals with modern boxes of concrete and metal, a project that would never succeed, because there was too much dust and history in that island of a city, too much backward-leaning ballast. It took a particular kind of mind-set to appreciate the architectural disharmony of West Berlin. My aunt possessed that mind-set. She shared it with the punks and skinheads and radicals that populated Kreuzberg along with the Turks. She'd take me down to the abandoned U-Bahn station at Bülowstrasse, where we'd buy kebabs and stare at the inert turnstiles, strains of the Clash reverberating through the corridors. This was my life. My island life.

15. Even the wind couldn't pass through the Wall, but instead blew back at us in a tunnel, picking up bits of dirt and paper, contributing to the eerie impression that the graffiti-filled structure resembled a very long subway. Kids bounced balls against it. People grew shade plants beside it. But whatever the Wall was or wasn't, whatever it resembled, however impassable or foreboding it was, it was also, for me, an outrageously small margin that separated me from my mother, a margin that probably drove me a little bit crazy, which is an admission I do not intend to seem exculpatory, i.e., a burgeoning insanity defense. After all, it's easy to avoid going crazy. All you have to do is pretend that whatever is making you crazy is impotent. After a year or two, I played there near the Wall paying it no attention, as I would have ignored a disapprov-

We waited four years.

By the end of that time, I guess he couldn't stand it. He'd begun to send off sheets of correspondence to prospective sponsors in the U.S. and Australia. It was 1979, and if you had said to any German on the street, *Just you wait, that Wall will come down in ten years*, he would have laughed in your face. The occasional scientist or prima ballerina on tour would defect, bringing the world news of the deprivations of material and human rights that existed behind the Iron Curtain. Plus, they needed electricians in Boston. So we left. I pulled on my wind-breaker and the stiff imitation jeans we called "Texas pants," stacked up my comics, and said good-bye to my cousins.

Among all the surprises that were in store for me—because I was living in the sort of childhood where nobody explained things to children—was the mind-blowing sensation of lift-off, leaving Tegel Airport with Dad via airplane, 1979. Until the plane tilted back, as if in prostration to the sun, I did not with my whole mind understand that we were going to actually *ascend*. As the forward thrust pressed me back against my seat, I nearly passed out from confusion and a sudden sense of betrayal. The yolk of my heart came loose. I could feel this yolk at my center become unmoored in my chest, too slippery to catch, too delicate to clutch. I said nothing to my father, who was staring out the portal window in silence. The plane seared the sky. We went up. "Lift," said my father, for

---

ing grown-up who stood there blocking the sun with his shoulders, until day by day I literally forgot that it was a Wall in the sense of a thing that separates; that is to say, I forgot there was anything on the other side. I forgot that I had ever been on the other side. Being there would have been impossible; there was nothing there. There was a wall, and beyond the wall was the end of reality, as in the dream wherein the door of your sweet house opens onto a desert.

some reason. I said nothing, hoping he would not turn his head from the portal window and see my stricken face. Lift. And as he said this, one wing of the plane tilted precipitously earthward, causing my father and me to hang there over the suddenly exposed realm of a disappearing Germany. Below us, a civilization of cities, timberland, and autobahns, clearly of a piece, indiscriminate, utterly undivided. Then the vision was gone, hidden by clouds. My father did not speak. I could feel the ascending plane penetrating the clouds with minimal resistance, like the ripping free of webbing or a weak embrace. Up, up, up we went, until the plane seemed to relax and take a seat in the air, coasting within some great corridor of migratory birds across the North Sea, and I knew we would never, ever return.

For the first year or two of our new lives in Boston, I developed a renewed interest in my mother. Maybe the plan was that she'd meet us *here*. I used to study every woman her age on the streets of Savin Hill. I studied mothers with young children. I watched the mothers and I watched the children. I waited for understanding. I tried to jog my own fading memory. But study of these people yielded nothing. The women seemed busy and irritable. They rarely laughed or talked to anybody. They dragged their children so fast they looked like tippling monkeys. I watched them all, and I loved them all, and I wanted them all, until finally I hated them all and was relieved to side with my father. And I held my breath, and I hid deep down inside myself, and soon enough, I got out of Dorchester. I moved to Albany and returned to Boston exactly twice—once, soon after graduating from Mune to pack away my things so Dad could inhabit the bedroom, and again when I was twenty-six and my father needed cataract surgery. I

still called him. I touched base. But Dad rarely called me and never demanded more from me. Namely, he never demanded an explanation about why I'd fled. It was almost as if he knew I was hiding something, and he sympathized.

And then I met a beautiful girl in Washington Park and a complete break was necessary. There was no other choice. Because there was no way I was going to jeopardize the thing I had going—a serious relationship with a serious American girl, one so smart she required graduate school to tame her mind, one who liked to bake her bare feet on the dashboard when we drove, one who gave me, several years later, a beautiful child with a perfect, four-chambered heart. And although I often thought of getting back in touch with my father, there was no clear way to do it. Even if I could sit with him in the old way, at the card table overlooking Savin Hill Road, then what? There would be an expectation that we see one another again, and another conspiracy would be conceived and aborted, followed by another long silence.

All this was very much on my mind when Meadow and I boarded the bus at Conway. The night before, I had promised her that we had one final stop to make before returning home. We were Boston bound. There, I told her, she would at long last meet someone very special to me. Someone I loved and, because of my own bad choices, had kept her from knowing. And if there was one last thing I wanted to do, it was to correct this error, if she would just bear with me a little longer. I wanted her to meet my father.

Maybe she believed me and saw herself back in the arms of her mother within a day or two. Or maybe she did not believe me at all, and it was merely that her patience had been stretched to the point of breaking, and she had simply snapped

free of all survivalist anxieties. I don't know, but *we held hands*. We *held hands* when we were picked up on the road near Mount Ragged by a handyman on his way to Conway. We *held hands* when we stood at the ticket window in an overcast New England town. And when the southbound bus pulled up that afternoon, we *held hands* as we climbed the rubber-coated steps into the cool tunnel of the bus. We carried nothing. We moved instinctively to the back, Meadow stroking the black velvet of the seatbacks as she walked. We settled in with a half dozen other wayfarers heading south, and soon the bus started forward. I think she sensed the difficulty ahead for me, personally. The difficulty of the things I had to say to her.

Before we'd even left Conway, I felt her eyes trained on me.

Ha, I thought, the kid's got the mind of a trap.

"*Tell* me," she said. "You said you'd tell me things."

"Did I?"

"You did. You did. Don't tease, Daddy."

"OK," I said. "My Life Story. You ready?"

She nodded and did not look away.

"So I've been thinking of how to begin this story, and because it's such a *long* story, I think it needs an invocation." I raised my hands. "Tell me, O Muse, of that ingenious hero who traveled far and wide after he had sacked the famous town of Troy, New York!"

Meadow did not smile.

"Ha," I said. "I'll be here all night."

"*Tell me.*"

"All right. Listen. Jesus, Meadow. I've never been more nervous in my life."

"Don't be nervous, Daddy." She took my hand. "You're my dad."

Tears bit my eyes. I can't explain how it felt to prepare myself to utter words that I had never really spoken—not in English—names, places, truths that I had really never forced into sound. Would they even come out as words? If I spoke certain truths, wouldn't time freeze, and nightmare soldiers board the bus and drag me away, back to the past for some ritual in which I would die, die or be sacrificed? I knew I was no match for my own lies. Why in the world, then, would I take my chances against them?

Because of a little girl.

I looked at my daughter.

"Go on," she said.

"I have not, as you once noted, always told the truth."

Meadow waited.

"I have told stories, in fact, that were elaborate—you could say—fictions, and although these fictions were not meant to defraud or to injure, I always knew—I knew in fact—that they would. Which is an admission that I—even now—can't put straight to you, because I think it might be possible—it's possible that if I made it explicit, if I took the blame, I would be singled out, struck down, and die."

Her eyes widened. "Don't do that."

"No, it's fear. It's my *fear*. I don't think saying certain things out loud will really kill me. Maybe I'm worried that you will reject me, and that would feel like a death. You're sort of all I've got." My eyes slid subtly in her direction. Look at you, I thought, trying to secure amnesty from a child.

But she—gifted she—only shrugged. "I guess you just have to try your best."

I smiled. "Right you are. OK," I said. "Let me put it to you this way. Do you remember how for a while you wanted

a baby sister? You wanted one so badly, and you thought about it so much, that sometimes it felt to you like you really *did* have a baby sister? And how sometimes you would even talk about your baby sister to other people, perfect strangers, and you would kind of forget to tell them that you were pretending? And they would believe that you really did have a baby sister and would ask you questions about her, like how old she was or what her name was? And you realized that you knew the answers? Because when other people believed you, even though you knew she was make-believe, she seemed realer—that is, realer to *you*. Do you know what I mean?"

She nodded.

"Great," I said, wiping my brow. "Great. You comfy? Nice bus."

"Uh-huh."

"So, a couple things. Firstly. I used to tell you about Twelve Hills, where I grew up. I didn't exactly grow up *in* Twelve Hills. I *wished* I had grown up in a place like Twelve Hills. But instead, I grew up not too far away, in a place called Dorchester, which you will see soon. And before that, long before that"—I cleared my throat—"I was born, in Germany."

"Oh." She looked confused. "So you never lived on Cape Cod?"

"No. But hell, I visited it once or twice. I loved the names out there. Cotuit. Barnstable. Wellfleet. Do you know much about the Kennedy family, your sort-of namesake? They had a compound in Hyannis Port. A very important family. John F. Kennedy was the thirty-fifth president of the United States. Germans love Kennedy. When there were bad men ruling Germany, he went to Germany's great city, and he said, I am

from here! Everyone is from here! We are all slaves until we are all free! President Kennedy was a real German hero."

"So President Kennedy was German too?"

"No." I looked at my hands. "Uh, yes and no. You know what? That's a great theoretical question. Listen. I don't want to confuse you with geopolitics. The person I want to tell you about is your grandfather. Not Pop-Pop, and not the gentleman from Twelve Hills. Your *other* grandfather. *He's* the German. His name—his name—is Otto Schroder. That's who I'd like you to meet."

"Otto Schroder," she said, screwing up her eyes. "He's my grandfather?"

"Yes," I said.

"Then how many grandfathers do I have?"

"Well, two. Or three. It depends on how important Grandpa Kennedy is to you. The point is—the problem is—you've never met either of them but Pop-Pop. And I owe you—I owe you an apology."

I stopped to compose myself, staring over her shoulder at the receding foothills of the White Mountains.

"I owe you an apology because I kept you from information that's your birthright. I kept you from information that helps you know who you are. For you not to have this—for me to take this from you—well, I hope someday you'll forgive me. You're only six. Hopefully you'll forget some of the stuff I said and did?"

Her eyes narrowed. "What about Grandma?"

"Grandma?" I winced. "You mean Mom-Mom?"

"No."

"You mean Grandma Kennedy? Buried in Twelve Hills?"

"No."

"Ah. You mean Otto's wife."

And while I had thought that the worst part of this conversation would be beginning it, I realized suddenly that hers was the name I could not say. I shut my eyes. In the darkness of my mind, I heard the sound of her company, that rhythmic sound of her walking beside me amidst the cheerful, unoppressed birdsong in Treptower Park, and I knew that the most excruciating pain of my life was the fact that I did not even know if this woman was alive or dead. I didn't know if I wanted her to be alive or dead. All I knew was that for as long as I was Eric Kennedy, she was neither living nor dead. When I was Eric Kennedy, she did not exist at all.

Meadow touched my arm. "Daddy?"

My eyes opened. "I'm sorry," I said.

"It's all right."

"I can't tell that part yet. I have to begin—elsewhere."

Silence.

Meadow turned to me with a smile. "So, did you have any pets in Germany?"

"Pets!" I laughed. "I did. When I lived with cousins in West Berlin, they had a little rat terrier named Brutus."

"Brutus!"

"Brutus could walk across the room on his hind legs."

"That's *crazy.*"

"And when I was a boy in Dorchester, my father let me keep a snake. Ha! Haven't thought of him in years. He ate crickets. But I loved him. Snakes are very good pets, actually."

"So are mice and frogs."

"I'll bet."

"And what about your school? Your *real* school, Daddy, not your pretend one."

"I wasn't very happy at school. I wasn't happy in Dorchester."

"Why not?"

"I don't know. Nobody liked me. I was a stranger."

"Were you sad all the time?"

"I—I—" A shrieking laugh came out of me. "Sorry. This is even harder than I thought."

I remember how the shades were drawn on the Works Progress–era school building on the corner of Tuttle and Savin Hill Road at the end of each day, as if signaling the end of that day's guardianship, and how the pretty teachers would all leave the building afterward, while I would remain standing there, awaiting something, some hugely unmet need. After a long time, I would cross the pedestrian bridge over the oceanic traffic of the expressway, winding my way down to the waterfront of Dorchester Bay. Funny to call it a bay. It was more like a tidal pool ringed by the expressway and a beach of hard-packed sand. When I was a teenager, they cleaned up the area, adding a long white stretch of pavement intended for strolling and decorated with benches and heavy, maritime chains strung through small concrete abutments. Even though I was often alone, well into my adolescence, being alone didn't matter at the waterfront. You could walk around anonymously and root for whatever team you wanted at McConnell Park. Maybe you'd see someone you knew.

I opened my eyes and smiled at my daughter. "No. I wasn't sad all the time."

"Oh, that's good."

"When it snowed, you couldn't even tell whose house was whose. We all lived really close together. Snowball fights were epic. Whole armies of kids. Catapults. Forts. There was always something going on."

"I like school," Meadow said, pulling a swath of scorched blond hair over her shoulder.

"You do?"

"I do. I *do* like school. But I don't always tell the truth either."

I let my head fall back against the seat, grateful to let her talk, grateful that she was speaking to me at all. "What do you mean?"

"I pretend I don't know things, like how to read. If I read things out loud, they say I'm a know-it-all."

I said nothing.

"I don't want them to say mean things about me. So I pretend I don't read the words or know what the big words mean. I pretend I can't see. Then they call me Four Eyes."

"Oh, Meadow. That kills me. We should find you a school that can handle a child like you. A gifted child. You're *gifted.*"

Her face clouded. "I don't want a new school. I like my school."

"Why do you like your school if you can't be yourself there?"

"My friends are there."

"Then you should skip a grade. *Something.*"

"I don't want to skip a grade. Then I wouldn't be in class with my friends."

"Why are you punishing yourself for being smart?"

"You *always* say that. You always *say* that. You always say the same things! I listen to you, but you don't listen to me!"

She crossed her arms and snapped her head toward the window. Just like that, I had lost hold of her.

"I'm sorry," I said.

Beneath us, the bus engine labored in a lower gear. We

passed a sign for Albany, New Hampshire, but neither of us made a joke about it.

"You deserve a better father. But instead you got me."

She looked down at her lap, her eyes glassy. Then she tilted her head just a touch to the side, as if accepting a counter-argument from her more dutiful self, giving me—because she couldn't help it—yet one more benefit of the doubt.

"Listen," I said. "It would take too long for me to apologize for everything. It would take my whole life. And we've only got"—I checked my watch—"two hours and fifteen minutes until we get to Boston. Which parts do you want to hear about?"

She looked up, out the window. "I want to hear about the times you were happy."

I nodded. The bus turned toward someplace called Tamworth.

"I'll tell you about happiness," I said. "The time I was most happy in my life was when I met your mother."

She smiled but did not turn her head.

"Now, every little thing about your mom and me is true. No take-backs."

She turned now, her gums showing. "Tell me."

"We met because a boy fell out of a tree."

"You're teasing."

"Am not. A boy plopped out of a tree and broke his wrist, and your mother was helping him. Everybody—everybody was watching—and I saw her and I fell in love with her on the spot..."

All the way to Nashua, I told her about it. The gifts of tea and apricots, the honeymoon in Virginia Beach, the tidal pools, your pregnant cravings, your enormous belly, her birth,

how she didn't cry when she was born, the pretty music of her favorite mobile, the birth of Stinky Blanket, the smell of calendula oil, winters, branches, and good silences.

A middle-aged woman got on in Nashua. She wore a white cardigan and store-fresh jeans and carried her purse clamped between breast and elbow. From the looks of her, I hoped she'd content herself with a seat farther up the bus. But after rejecting the other seats for some reason or another, she settled down diagonally from us.

After a while, I noticed this woman staring at us. I looked at her, and she smiled tightly and returned to her magazine. My blood went cold. Here was exactly the sort of zealot who would watch television shows in which regular people are encouraged to help apprehend fugitives.

"Heading to Boston?" she asked finally, creasing her magazine against her leg.

I tried to ignore her.

"Are you heading to Boston?" she asked, louder.

"Excuse me?"

"I said are you going to Boston."

"Yes, we are."

"You don't have any games or anything for the little girl? You don't have any pencils or paper for her to draw on?"

"No. Games? I—no, I don't."

The woman cocked her head backwards in chagrin. "Such a long trip. A long time for a little girl to sit with nothing to do." She began to dig in her purse. "Let me see if I have something for her to draw with. Would you like a colored pencil, sweetheart? Ugh. All I've got is a pen, and nothing to draw on."

"We'll be all right," I said, relieved.

The woman shrugged. "Still."

"Thanks for your concern."

"Still. It's a long trip without anything to do."

I turned and looked at Meadow, who was grinning. I winked at her.

"Hey, Daddy," she whispered.

"What?"

She waved me closer. "You know what that lady doesn't know about us?"

"What?"

Then she brought her face very close to mine, just like she used to do before she got her glasses, and put one hand on my shoulder. "She doesn't know how big our imaginations are."

RAPUNZEL

We stood outside of South Station, wearing matching green shamrock baseball caps that I'd bought at a kiosk. I grabbed Meadow's hand.

"By God, Boston has a *smell*," I said. "Do you smell that? It's kind of boggy or peaty. Not gassy, like New York."

It was a windy, late afternoon, but the sun still shone on Boston. I'd planned to go straight to Dad, but once I stepped out into Boston, I thought of everything that my real past now offered up in a fascinating if slightly down-market passel of attractions. Hell, this was way better than an aristocratic country-club childhood on the Cape—this was *Boston*, seat of Colonial America, home of the Red Sox. We wandered into the city's small but festive Chinatown and walked with throngs of tourists along Essex until I caught the splinter of someone's gaze, someone looking at us wrong. I turned down toward Harrison Ave. toward Kneeland, which felt safer. I was not safer in Boston than I was in the wilds of the Northeast Kingdom, but I felt safer, because Boston was the city of my youth, and when I was still quite young, over no objections from my father, I often took the T all the way to town from Savin Hill, not far, not far at all.

We went out of our way to stop in front of the John Hancock building and let its mirrors make us dizzy. We walked all the way to Copley Square and stared at the library, whose facade glowed as bone white as any Coliseum with the last afternoon light. There we bought roasted cashews from a cart and sat eating them amongst the drunks and the pigeons. We walked into the Copley Plaza Hotel and pretended we were guests. We tried to count the crystals on the chandelier. I inquired about the cost of staying overnight and, flipping through my billfold, thought better of it. The paucity of my funds turned a screw of anxiety. I'd lost a thousand bucks behind a le Carré novel on a shelf in Vermont. I knew time was running out. I knew this was our grand finale. I wanted her to have anything she wanted.

After a scoop of ice cream for her and some Canadian Club for me in the Ivy Room, we set off again. Trekking down Boylston Street, Meadow began to lag behind.

"Daddy. I'm tired."

"Tired? What do you need? You need to do the Dew?"

"We've been walking a long time."

"Come on," I said. "You're fine. You're on fire. We're almost to the Common. Don't you want to ride the swan boats? You haven't visited Boston until you've done that." I squinted at the sky. The boats had probably stopped running for the day.

"And *then* can we go to Grandpa Otto's house?"

"Don't worry," I said. "We'll get there soon."

"All right. Can I ride your shoulders, Daddy?"

"Sure, Butterscotch. Up we go."

And I was her camel, and we were crossing the Sahara, and she laughed when I ran beneath the willows, galloping

through the swarms of strolling people across the stone bridge of the lagoon in the Public Gardens, saying, "Pardon me, excuse me, pardon me, camel behind you." We slipped into line just as the attendant drew the cordon closed behind us, and we rode on the last swan boat of the day, sliding across the lagoon trailed by a line of sooty-looking goslings.

It was dark by the time we reached Beacon Street. We walked along the northern border of the Common while I tried to orient myself. A man stood under the streetlight dressed as a turn-of-the-twentieth-century valet. Two pale gray horses waited behind him, wearing red paper cones on the crests of their heads.

"Excuse me. Are we near the T stop?" I asked the man.

"Not too far. You can cut across right there to Park Street Station."

"Is that the Red Line? Green?"

"Both."

"Does the Red Line still go out to Savin Hill Road?"

"Sounds right, bud. Is that in Dorchester?"

"Yeah. I haven't been home in a long time."

I watched Meadow edge up to the horses. They swung their blinkered faces toward her. The nearer horse's hindquarter shuddered as she touched it.

"Hey, what about you?"

"Me?" the man asked.

"Can you take us to Dorchester?"

"Are you kidding? You don't know much about horses, do you?"

I smiled. "No, I don't. How much would it cost me?"

"It would cost you the price of a new horse." The man laughed. "That's a new one, though."

"Just wanted to make a big entrance, I guess."

The man was still laughing good-naturedly. "That's a new one, bud. Thanks."

Now Meadow leaned her head against my side. "Are we going to see Grandpa Otto now?"

I put my hand on the top of her head. I'd let it get too late, far later than Dad would possibly be up. I could say now that I'd had a presentiment, that I wasn't ready to face what awaited. But the truth is, I was just happy to be back—to be back *home*—and even the memory of myself as an outcast and a monster seemed exaggerated, merely the same way everybody feels, on some level, at that age. I looked down at my daughter, who stood belly out, rubbing her paunch. It was her—it was returning with her—that made me feel I'd outstripped all that.

"Unfortunately," I said, "Daddy lost track of time. I know Grandpa Otto and I know he goes to bed early. Tomorrow we'll go. Bright and early. Besides, we're not ready. Your clothes are looking a little pooped out. We've got to buy you a new dress."

A faint smile. "A new dress?"

"A fancy new dress, don't you think? With hoops and bows. And a muff. So you can meet your grandfather in style. I'll take you to Filene's. It was—or it used to be—right off the Common. Excuse me." I pointed, asking the driver, "Is Filene's still this way?"

"You mean Macy's? On Winter Street? It's a Macy's now."

Satin dresses with multiple petticoats. Velvet cloaks with silver toggles. Dresses with hoops. Dresses with matching gloves

or coin purses. Meadow ran around the racks before she was calm enough to touch anything. At that hour, the children's department was empty, with one or two weary saleswomen neatening the inventory. I nodded and tried to look unassuming, but when I saw Meadow pressing one of the dresses against herself and smiling, I couldn't keep myself from bellowing, "Try it on!"

I was studying a brochure of Boston hotels when she emerged.

"Will you look at that," I said, trying not to tear up.

The dress was turquoise and hung just below her knees. The top of it was satin, but there was a shimmery netting over the skirt, the faux crystals of which glinted beneath the department store track lighting. The apron of the dress was as flat and smooth as her chest, cinched at the waist by a silver buckle. Over this, she wore a short matching turquoise jacket. The effect of the dress was somehow made sweeter by the dingy ankle socks she had not thought to remove in the dressing room.

"Your grandfather is going to love you," I murmured. "He's going to think you're the bee's knees."

She was turning back and forth before the three-way mirror, not listening, her shoulders pinched forward, chin tucked under. Three Meadows, three turquoise dresses. Three fathers, looking on. Three red eyeglasses and six dirty socks, three manes of peroxided hair. I'm not sure if I've ever loved her more.

"I look like Rapunzel. Don't I? Don't I look like Rapunzel finally, Daddy?"

EMERGENCY

I'd gotten used to the silence between us, Laura. I knew it was cruel not to call you, to tell you that Meadow was all right, that it wasn't as bad as you were thinking. But I was used to your absence, and we were both used to cruelty by then, I mean the casual cruelty of people dismantling their life together. Odd, how there's so much deliberating before a divorce. Such a lot of shilly-shallying, nobody wanting to be the bad guy. But then once the declarations are made, the lines are drawn, a desperate power grab commences, and there's no more chivalry, no more nuance, no more delicacy. Only winning or losing.

I sat in that hotel room staring at the telephone. I wanted to call you. Not because I was scared and knew I was in deep, and not even because I knew it was the right thing, but because I wanted to talk about Meadow with you. I wanted to talk to the only other person who had the same investment in Meadow as I did. I wanted to talk about small things, about how she swam in her clothes, or about her habit of starting sentences with adverbs like *actually* or *technically*. I wanted to tell someone stories about what she did or said and have that person respond with the same rush of tenderness that I felt

when these things were happening in front of me. I wanted to tell someone about the turquoise dress. She was wearing it now, complete with dirty bobby socks, as she ate a package of Fritos in front of the television, straddled on the floor. I wanted to tell someone how glamorous and incongruous she'd looked wearing her gown in the lobby of the Best Western.

Instead, I put the telephone back in its cradle. I lay down on the bed and crossed my hands over my chest and got very quiet. It was over, our marriage. I could not be married to Meadow's mother anymore. I could not be married to that notion. I couldn't call you anymore to talk about the small things.

I rolled over and faced the wall. Cartoon voices quarreled from the TV, and Meadow guffawed. I could hear luggage wheels squeaking down the hallway. I tried to focus on what I had committed to doing by coming to Boston.

Dad, I thought. My father. *Vater*. How to prepare for you? I wondered if he would look the same. I wondered if his English had improved. I wondered if he'd remarried, if maybe he had finally reciprocated the attentions of the Caribbean woman who lived in the apartment below ours and who adored my father despite his comical stiffness in her presence. I did not wonder if my father would be angry with me for my long silence. I did not want to flatter myself with the thought that he would be angry about it. In fact, the more I thought about him, the more certain I became that he would not be changed at all, and the happier I grew about that, whereas when I was a boy, I wanted him so badly to be different.

I was disoriented when I awoke, fully dressed atop the made bed. It was late, but the television was still playing, volume

off. Jets of damp air came through the vents below the window. Meadow was sitting upright across from me in her bed, still in her dress, looking stricken.

"What is it?" I said.

She looked at me hazily but did not answer.

"What *is* it?"

I stood and leaned in to her face and took her by the shoulders. After a long pause, she drew a shallow breath.

"I'm fine," she wheezed. Her breath sounded broken.

I stood up.

"What?" I said. "OK."

I turned in a circle, trying to remember where we were.

"We're in Boston," I said.

"I'm fine I'm fine I'm fine."

This time, the words left her spent, hanging slightly forward.

"You *are* fine," I said. "Of *course* you're fine."

I turned on the lamp by her bedside.

"No." She squinted. "Turn it off, Daddy. Too bright."

"You're right," I said, obeying, leaving us again in the flickering darkness. "I bet you, if we sit here, and I tell you a long, interesting story, you'll be able to breathe normally and fall right back to sleep. All right? Scoot over. And sit up straight. That always helps you breathe, doesn't it? To sit up?"

She mustered a smile, and I fluffed the pillows all around her.

Dear God, I thought. Not this.

"My story," I said, "is called 'The Camel of Boston Common.'"

I waited. I could hear her rasp in the darkness. Stay calm, I told myself. Staying calm would be my only important

function. Her affliction—can I call it that?—was something that had manifested itself when she was about four, somewhere during the final act of her parents' marriage, and perhaps for this reason, I never thought of her asthma as entirely physical. I mean, I related to it metaphorically, the threat of spiritual suffocation. Which is not to say I ignored medical solutions. I'd been there when the treatments were prescribed—a small albuterol inhaler to which she immediately affixed glittery stickers. Not a serious case, the pediatrician had said. Could be a lot worse. But she should keep this with her *at all times*.

"Once upon a time, there was a camel who got lost in Boston. He—uh—he had never been to Boston before, so he did not know that the people of Boston are prejudiced against camels. In fact, there was a shoot-to-kill order on camels—an obscure law that camel activists had tried to repeal but kept falling short of the votes they needed given the cronyism and general anti-camel sentiment in Faneuil Hall. How are you doing?"

With a wheezy inhalation, she nodded.

"OK? Great. OK. So this camel—his name was Alal—had gotten bizarrely, totally lost in Boston, separated from his, what, his *herd*. But everywhere he went, people were so rude to him, calling him Humpback and Goat-Hoof, and nobody would tell him which way to the Sahara. Somewhere around the corner of Boylston and Arlington he spied a nice little patch of grass. This was, as everybody knows, Boston Common."

"Daddy?"

"Yes, Butterscotch."

"Can I have my inhaler?"

I swallowed the stone in my throat. "As you may remem-

ber," I said, "your inhaler is in your backpack. Which is in Vermont."

She turned her head toward me, her cheek pressed against her hand, and sighed like a very old soul.

"We can get you a new inhaler, of course. But we can't get a new one right now. I mean, it's three o'clock in the morning. We'll find a pharmacy first thing in the morning."

She stared at me in the flickering light. Her gaze, somewhat vacant and dry, gave me pause.

"Don't be scared," I said.

She nodded.

"Don't be scared. That makes it worse."

"It feels like—someone is—tying—"

"Tying—"

"—tyingmythroatupwithstring."

"Oh, Meadow, I wouldn't let anyone do that. OK? Don't let yourself imagine that." I sat upright. "I know just what'll help."

I went into the bathroom and turned on the shower spigots, calling out toward the bedroom, "I used to have trouble breathing when I was a boy, too. Did I ever tell you that? This was back in East Germany. We didn't have very advanced medicine back then. We didn't have inhalers. Things got bad enough, they'd take you to the hospital and intubate you." I came out of the bathroom, peeled back the bedspread, and gently scooped her up. "So of course, my mother tried to find home remedies. Eucalyptus. Prayers to the Moon God, what have you. But the only thing that seemed to help"—I placed Meadow on the cold tiles of the bathroom—"was a nice hot steam shower."

She was an absurdly colored bird in the steam. I helped her

off with her little jacket, and then she stepped out of the collapsed dress. She stood trembling in her underpants, not even bothering to cover her chest. I could see the strain of her ribs under her skin.

"If this doesn't help, I'll take you straight to the hospital."

She inhaled. "Idon'twanttogotothehospital."

"Boy oh boy. Let me tell you, neither do I. So let's stay positive. Upsie-daisy."

I lifted her into the bathtub and she stood in the basin with her hands drawn up under her chin. Her eyeglasses instantly fogged. I reached in to remove them from her face, and as I did so, I grew slightly dizzy myself, remembering those distant treatments.

"You inhale the steam," I said, "and I'll just sit right here on the toilet. Very dignified."

She said nothing. I closed the plastic curtain and sat beside the bathtub on the cold toilet lid. The shower curtain billowed out of the basin. From its tattered hem water was pouring brokenly. A dirty tributary pushed across the tiles toward the door. I could hear the sound of water upon my daughter's skull.

We'd done everything the doctor said. She had a couple minor attacks, so we bought a HEPA filter and gave away the mouse and didn't feed her gluten, and then we got divorced. I could still remember those and other emergencies as clearly as if they had just occurred: a bad burn once when she tried to fry some Play-Doh, the time she ingested a Christmas rose at her grandmother's and we wept all the way to the hospital, several horrible fevers, in which we experienced ghoulish waking visions throughout the night vigil as if we had, according to our prayers, changed places with her. In a bygone era, we

would have lost her ten times over. And yet we never did. We never did. Whatever force took her to that edge always brought her back to us.

"Butterscotch?"

"Yes?"

"Does the steam seem to be helping?"

"Yeah."

"Good."

"But—"

"But what."

"I feel spinnish."

"You want a chair in there? Something to sit on?"

"Yeah."

Spinnish, I thought, stepping out into the room. This cannot be good. I had come to rely—I see this now—on that bracing shot of the inhaler, and had forgotten—had I ever truly learned it—the true nature of her illness, what was physically happening to her, what should be done about it. I believed—I remembered—that steam showers had helped *me* when I was sick as a child, but sick with what? Pertussis? I had grown out of my case. Dorchester had cured me of it, whatever it was. I had grown out of it, or it had been bullied out of me, and so I kept expecting her to grow out of it, but look, she hadn't, and the truth is I really didn't know what the hell to do.

That's when I heard the thud in the bathroom.

The rings screamed against the rod as I pushed the curtain aside. She was on her belly in the basin, under the deluge of water, her hair slicked down over her back and face and darkened by water. She turned her head to me slowly, dawningly, her under-eyes bruised.

"All righty," I said. "Off we go."

"Where?"

"For help."

"No," she rasped.

"We're going," I said, taking hold of her slippery arm.

"No!"

"We are going! We are going! Stand *up*."

"No!" She yanked her arm back.

"Stand up, God *damn you*!"

I turned off the spigot, wrapped her in a towel to get a grip on her, and took her back into the bedroom. She struggled meekly, nakedly, her underwear soaked through.

"Stop it!" I cried. "Stop kicking me!"

I tugged on her purple pants and the sweatshirt from the Swanton Walmart. Her sodden underwear soaked through immediately. I attempted to towel-dry her hair, but she covered her head with her hands, as if she was being gratuitously attacked. We were enemies now. And there, cold and wet on the bed she wanted to cling to, the grave injustice of her position became evident to her, which was that not only could she not have her bed, but neither could she have the comfort she wanted most in the world. Raising her chin to the ceiling, bringing her knees to her chest, she gave a long, chilling cry for it.

"*MOMMY!*"

"Shhh, Meadow. Shhhhhh."

"*MOMMY!*" she hollered again. "*MOMMY! MOMMY!*"

She kicked her legs out straight, her nostrils as wide as marbles. She stayed stiff like that, back arched in apoplexy, her eyes open and staring. I heard the literal rattle of her spent breath. She fell silent.

Out the door, the dead thud of the bolt behind me, down

the stairs, two flights only, where the drowsy concierge turned his face from the television, a solicitous smile lingering upon it even after he saw my daughter limp in my arms, uncomprehending. Meadow's wet head staining my shirtfront. Her eyes were open but vacant. "Talk to me!" I said. She wouldn't talk to me.

"Where's the nearest hospital?"

The man stood, a sandwich falling from his lap.

"Close," he said. "Mass General. You need a taxi?"

"Please. Please. Help me."

No taxis waited outside. The Best Western fronted the wharf between the expressway and the Charlestown Bridge. A million cars passing above us on concrete stanchions on either side, but not a single one on our deserted street right below.

"Call an ambulance," I said. "Call a taxi. Anything."

"Right away. But—"

"But what?"

"You could run. Might be faster. Look."

I looked toward the illuminated tip of the building toward which he pointed. The building seemed very close, but even as I began to run, I understood that it looked far closer than it really was.

I ran out of the isolated underpass and onto another street with little traffic, all of it slick with midnight moisture, upon which the traffic lights slid and blurred my depth perception. I stumbled. A horn blared. Meadow was passive in my arms. Her weight felt neutral, inanimate. It was as if she did not care if we fell, or if we were hit, and she did not care if we made it to the hospital or not. It was as if she did not really believe in the hospital anyway. And I wondered—in that split frame with which a man lucidly witnesses his own downfall—if it was

possible that she did not believe in me anymore either. She suspected but could not yet confirm some future in which I was gone, banished. Discredited. Locked away. And she—adult Meadow—living in a garden apartment, years hence, unmarried perhaps, childless, would say to herself, and I gave years of my life over to *him*? To reckoning with *him*? Or, aging herself, she might even laugh with the sudden realization that a certain amount of time had indeed been shaved off the back end of her life—a year or two, maybe more—years she had donated to her father when she was a child, by dint of her love for him and her inexhaustible mercy, in order to sustain him, before she fully understood the terms of the transfer. This form of self-cannibalizing that children do, well, it's one reason I ran. I mean, ran from Dorchester.

The headlights were blinding. The squad car had already passed us and made a U-turn and was driving back toward us so damningly I could barely walk forward anymore. With Meadow in my arms I could not shield my eyes. Meadow pressed her face against my chest. A door opened and a figure was coming toward us brandishing a smaller light.

"You two all right?" the policeman asked, sweeping my face.

"We'll be fine. Please. I can't see."

"You don't look fine."

"We need to get to the hospital."

He peered into Meadow's face with his flashlight. "Is she conscious?"

"Yes. We're just—" I tried to step past him, toward the glowing building, which seemed to flare, to signal to us. "Please! Let us go."

The man looked surprised. Why wouldn't he let us go?

Didn't I understand he was here to help? The clean-shaven skin over his ears jumped with his pulse.

"I'll do you one better," he said. "Get on in. I'll drive you."

"No, thank you."

"Come on now. You'd better, sir. She doesn't look good."

"It's her asthma. It's just asthma. But it won't stop."

We sat in the backseat. Meadow seemed momentarily revived by the police car, curling her fingers around the black grate.

"Heading southbound on Staniford," the cop intoned to his CB radio. "Heading to Mass General with a female minor, seven or eight years of age—"

"We don't have her inhaler with us," I said. "She can't breathe."

"Subject might need oxygenation."

Abruptly, Meadow lay down in my lap. The action terrified me, it was so final. She murmured something.

I bent down to hear. "What'd you say, baby? What'd you say?"

"You're my home," she said, distinctly.

"Oh. Oh my sweetheart. What do you mean?"

"You're where I live, you and Mommy."

"Oh. All right. Don't try to talk."

She started to cry. A high, weak scratch of a cry, no air in it.

"Am I going to die?"

"Please, Meadow. I'm sorry!"

"Am I going to, Daddy?"

"Don't *say* that."

Her eyes closed.

"Her eyes closed," I said to the policeman.

"Almost there," he said.

"She's going to die! Drive faster!"

"We're almost there, sir." He swiped his CB radio off the dash. "Twenty-two to dispatch. Arriving to Blossom Street entrance of Mass General. That's Blossom Street..."

They had to pry my hands from her shoulders. I was shaking her too hard. She was moving along very quickly now in the hallway on her back. They tried to lose me. I wouldn't let them, though. They didn't understand. There was no way I was going to let her die. I had ahold of the corner of the gurney. I was trying to help them push but I was also falling down, falling into nothingness. The policeman was jogging along beside me. Everybody was running.

"No way am I going to let her out of my sight," I said to the policeman, who now seemed, since he'd signed on for the next chapter, like someone I could talk to.

"Nobody's going to take her from you, sir," he said.

"They'll have to kill me first."

"Nobody's going to do anything but help her. Relax."

"Come this way," one of the nurses said, the one holding the mask over Meadow's face, as she tacked sharply into a bright room, and my child was rolled into the astonishing light.

PEDIATRICS

A hospital never grows dark. Never completely. The clock hands move; night settles in. Trays are brought and cleared through the not-dark, and the not-silence prevails—the blips, the squeaks, the billows of assisted breathing. In pediatrics, the rituals of bedtime follow snack time. A child pauses outside the door in footed pajamas, thoughtfully brushing his teeth and staring…Shuddering, I lowered my head into my hands. If I stayed quiet, if I stayed very still…We were sharing a room with a boy whom no one had yet visited. He slept under his tucked sheet, his dark, perfected face framed by the pillow as if by frilled wax paper. He seemed so totally alone. But *I* couldn't watch over him. If some sylph were to come floating to the door, I would have said, Take *him*. Take *him*!

Other times we'd sat like this, by the bed all night, gagged with worry, measuring that inconceivable interval between the call to the pediatrician and the waiting. Those infant fevers. How *hot* she used to get. We were sure she'd be a pile of ashes by morning. I remember the drowsy doctor, himself due to the breakfast table within an hour or two, telling us over the telephone to be ready to take her to the hospital if

her condition worsened. Throughout the stubborn night we would wait for things to worsen, a night-light for our vigil. And stalking the corners of our quiet sickbed conversations were all the little children who'd tiptoed past their parents on nights like these, centuries ago, all the little invisible souls, running away, laughing. And yet we never lost her.

There was a knock on the door.

"Hey, Dad."

I looked up to see a petite, Slavic-looking woman. We shook hands. Her bones seemed as hollow as a bird's.

"Doctor," I said, standing woozily, upsetting the empty coffee cup I'd left on Meadow's swivel tray. "Come in, come in. I'm so glad to see you. Thank you so much. Thank God for you and your hospital."

The doctor's face assumed a troubled look. "I'm really glad you made it to us. But we're not in the clear."

The doctor frowned at her chart, and then we sat, the doctor on one side of sleeping Meadow and myself on the other. For a moment we both examined her placid face, my eyes flickering between her face and the doctor's.

"We had to give your daughter some heavy stuff to get her breathing again," the doctor said. "Not just the intravenous drug—the magnesium sulfate—also, we gave her ketamine, a dissociative anesthetic. We couldn't hesitate. These drugs prevent respiratory arrest, but they are brutal drugs. Hard on a two-hundred-pound adult. As in everything, Dad, there's a corollary. In pediatrics, you can't push too hard. But you have to push hard enough."

"I understand," I said. "God, you look so young for a doctor."

The doctor smiled, again with the woeful look. "OK," she said. "I need to know why you didn't come in earlier."

I paused. "Earlier?"

"You said—you told us when you first came in—that she has suffered previous asthmatic attacks. You know—I'm sure you know—how serious her illness is? That thousands of children die every year from asthmatic suffocation?"

"You won't believe this," I said. "But we lost her inhaler in the Common. In the *lagoon*. Today."

"You mean yesterday."

"Yesterday. Slipped out of her backpack. Into the lagoon."

"Goodness."

"To be honest, she hasn't had an attack that severe since— since never. At least, I've never seen it like that."

"Well, that's because of her inhaler. Because it saves her life when you use it. And sure, it's no crime to lose it. But you cannot wait to get her help. You have to get help immediately."

"I hear you." I nodded. "I failed her."

"I'm not saying that."

"But I did fail her. *I'm* saying that."

"Listen. I have kids, too. I've made mistakes. I hold no one to an impossible standard. But you and me are lucky because we get another chance. Some kids don't get better. Intervention can fail."

My eyes drifted toward the sleeping boy who shared our room.

"So. She'll be all right?"

"Yes, she will. But she needs to stabilize."

Just then, Meadow yawned.

"Look." I laughed. "We're boring her."

"Ha," the doctor said. "That's a great sign. She's still sleeping, but more lightly."

"So we'll be able to leave soon? I personally get really

antsy in hospitals. And her mother would really love to have her back home as soon as possible."

"We'll see. Get some sleep, Dad. This place really hops in the morning."

As I watched Meadow stir and her sleep get lighter and I saw what I thought was the end in sight, I said to myself, *I will never sleep I will never fall asleep again*, and yet somehow I fell asleep. I dreamed explicitly. I was walking away. Right up Storrow Drive and into the woods. I gave up on all this. I slipped my shape. I was made new. No one ever saw me again.

The squeegee of officious shoes awakened me. Someone had entered the room while I was dozing. I lifted the tonnage of my skull and prepared a smile. Who was it but my friend the policeman. I could see him better now, in the light of day, his close-shaven face shining. I saw that he was about my age. As he offered a few unpoetic comments, I heard in his voice that familiar Dorchester twang, which I'd pinpoint at somewhere around, say, the corner of Dorchester and Victoria, and I wondered if we knew each other when we were kids. I wondered if he was someone with whom I sat beside some Madonna statuette eating salted pips. Someone who shared his freestanding basketball hoop with me when no one else was around. Someone with whom I traded racial insults (Mick! Nazi!). Now he was saying how he was glad everything came out OK. And I was thanking him for saving my daughter's life. And meaning it. Because I was thinking, yes, I *do* get another chance, it is *not* too late, and today—today—I will visit that old house on Savin Hill Road and I will climb those well-worn stairs, and see my father, and show him his granddaughter, and something will be put right, something will be finished...

"Can we step out into the hall?" the cop asked.

"Sure," I said, not moving. "Everything all right?"

"I just need to write up a report. I've got to account for my time."

"Sure." I smiled at him, trying to read his expression. Both sincere and opaque.

"I don't think there's any trouble here," he clarified. "I don't think you've done anything wrong. This is protocol."

"Well, sure." Now I stood. "I completely understand."

A nurse in pastel pink came to the door with a tray of apple juice and soda crackers and peered at Meadow. "Anybody awake yet?"

"Not yet," I said. "Is that normal?"

We traded places at the bedside.

"She's gonna be fine," said the nurse. She flipped through the clipboard at the foot of the bed. "She'll rouse soon. It's just time to check her vitals."

I left the room with a foreboding that surprised me.

The cop and I stepped into the hall. I explained it to him like this: My daughter and I had taken the bus down from Conway the previous morning, just a father-and-daughter Saturday trip into Boston for the sights (swan boats, roasted cashews, the chandelier at the Copley, etc., etc.), and had lost her inhaler in the lagoon, and maybe it was petting the horses that kicked up her asthma. But I noticed that after several minutes of him writing up his report with an awkward leftie scrawl, he had stopped writing and was listening to me with a kind of strained interest. He asked where was the girl's mother and I said she was back in Conway with our other little one, waiting for the two of us to be discharged. We were both shaken up over what happened, I told him, but we knew

that Mass General was one of the best hospitals in the world and besides we were never going to go anywhere without her inhaler again. And then he finally asked for my name and I put out my hand and said, "John Torraine." We shook hands. "And your daughter is?" "Jessie. Jessie. Short for Jessica. But she hates being called Jessica," I added. Then the cop told me he was all set but that I was eventually going to have to fill out some paperwork for the hospital. I didn't have insurance, I said, but you could bet I was good for it. He said I could work that end out with the hospital.

Finally, he let me go.

I walked back into the room shaken. Then I stopped short. Meadow was awake. The nurse in pink was leaning over her, having just placed her glasses back on her nose. Meadow, now tilted upright on the mechanical bed, beamed with restored sight.

"Daddy!" she whispered.

I went over to the bed and clasped her skinny arm, which looked brown against the white linen. I wanted to cry. I wanted to cry for years.

"Jesus Christ, it's good to see you," I said.

"Good to see you too, Daddy."

I fluffed the pillow below her head, uselessly. I brought my forehead to hers.

"OK," I said. "It's OK."

"OK," she said, hoarsely.

"OK." Finally, I laughed. "This is wonderful."

The nurse laughed too. "It is wonderful," she said. "Just wonderful." She gathered her instruments. "Meadow was just asking me where her daddy was."

I drew back, looking now at the nurse, my smile still arrayed.

"Well, here I am," I said, after a long moment.

"Just like I said," said the nurse.

"Just like you said," murmured Meadow, nuzzling the pillows with both cheeks.

Then I said, half-choked, "I'd never leave you."

"I know *that*," Meadow said. She lifted her arm. "Look, I got a bracelet."

As the nurse was passing me I reached out and grasped her shoulder more firmly than I'd meant to. She raised her eyes with a glimmer of alarm.

"Sorry," I said, pulling back. "God, sorry to, like, *grab* you." I brushed my damp forehead with my wrist. "I was just wondering if we might be able to go now."

The woman smiled. "You want to leave right now?"

"Is that possible?"

"Let me get someone. OK?"

"OK, sure. Who?"

"Well, I've got to talk to the doc. Let's see if the doc can come take a peek at her. OK?"

"OK, great. Great. You're going to go ask the doctor now?"

The woman looked over her shoulder, striding out. "Absolutely."

I turned back to my daughter, who was walking her fingers through the air, her cheeks in high color, like a girl in a fairy tale. I went to the door and looked both ways down the hall. No rushing, no alarms, only an intake nurse sitting nearby in a cone of light, shuffling papers. Dawn was breaking in the eastern windows. A discreet light. Go in there and pick her up, I thought, and run. Or run yourself. Now. There are the stairs. There is the elevator. She said her name. Meadow had. *She said her real name.* I stepped back into the room. Meadow

was sucking apple juice through a curly straw, tethered by the wrist to an IV. Dear God, I thought. OK, ten minutes. Ten more minutes, then we're gone. I found her clothes in a white plastic bag hanging inside a child-sized wardrobe. "Scootch down," I said, and yanked up the sheets from the foot of the bed. She was incurious as I slid her purple sweatpants up underneath her floral johnny. And then I stopped. The vents by the window came on, blowing gusts of dry, hot air into the room. I did not pick her up and I did not run. I did not run away alone, one selfish survivor, one perfected criminal. Instead, I sat. My aging knees creaked. The boy on the other side of the curtain sighed in his sleep.

"Meadow," I said. "Give me your hand."

She did. It was small and dark and coldish.

I pressed it against my cheek. She fell in and out of sleep.

I don't recall how much time passed. Fifteen minutes. Fifteen years.

Someone cleared his throat in the doorway. Without turning around, I knew exactly who it was. The guy just couldn't stay away. I tried to clear my expression of open dislike, and looked over my shoulder.

"I was hoping you were the doctor," I said.

The cop returned my expression with nothing, absolutely zero.

He stood awkwardly for a moment in the doorway, and then told me that there was some hospital paperwork to complete and he was just there to show me where it was. Couldn't I fill out the paperwork here in the pediatric ward? I asked. My daughter was wakeful now and I didn't want to leave her alone.

He said, "It'll only take a minute." He said, "Come this way."

I stood and leaned down close to Meadow.

"Sweetheart," I whispered.

Her eyes fluttered open.

"I've got to go somewhere for one minute. OK?"

She nodded. "OK."

"I'll be right back," I said.

"You'll be right back?"

"Yes," I said.

She covered my hand with her own. "You promise?"

"I promise."

That's what I said.

The intake nurse looked up at me when I emerged from the room and then hastily looked away. There was no other soul in sight.

The hallway was endless. As we walked, the subtext between us seemed to deepen prismatically. My escort walked very close to me but with a casual roll. I felt his canvas jacket brush my bare arm and heard the jangle of all of his violent instruments. We turned a corner. Another hall. The tension made my bowels cramp. I almost stopped. I almost stopped and grabbed his arm and cried, *What the hell do you want from me?* But suddenly, he halted. He pointed me toward a set of swinging doors at the end of the hallway. He told me to walk right through and I'd see the registration desk. I tried to hide my surprise. He was letting me go? Had I passed a test by walking down that gauntlet? I nodded to him. I walked the twenty or so paces without glancing back. As I pushed through the doors and stepped into the glass-ceilinged solarium, I was thinking, maybe sometimes you just have to believe everything is going to be OK.

I guess I startled the officers that were waiting for me.

They didn't seem quite prepared as I strode into the solarium. There were two of them, a large black man and a broad-backed white woman, talking quietly in relaxed poses, and they had to leap over the chairs when I saw them and turned and ran. Then all was clear. The animosity was clear, the struggle. I was already back through the swinging doors and running toward the pediatric unit with a good lead when they pursued with their whole lot of noise. People stared and froze. They neither moved to stop me nor got out of my way. A doctor leaning over a gurney in the hallway held a bladder of fluid over his head to avoid dropping it. Onlookers seemed paralyzed, not knowing which of us was the aggressor. Look. Look at me. Imagine me. A man of forty, in beach-crusted khakis and a checkered shirt. I skidded into Meadow's hallway, and there, in a brilliant end around, my familiar opponent approached me with both hands out.

"Let me talk to my daughter," I said.

"Back it up," he shouted, one hand open. "Back it *way* up. How the hell did you get back here?"

The other two officers arrived and yanked my shoulders backwards. At their touch, I felt my gut soften and the hope run out of me. My knees relaxed, forcing the officers to bear me up, holding me around the waist. *At last*, observed my inner tormenter, *the embrace that ends every love story.*

"Hold on," said the cop in charge. "Hold on. Not here, guys. Settle down."

"*Please*," I begged him. "Give me one minute to say good-bye."

"Not on your life. You get back. *Back up.* We're not going to do this here, guys."

Now I pressed forward against the commanding officer,

in some sort of abject supplication, my chin on his shoulder. Leaning against him intimately like that, I could see past him down the hallway. In the distance, a security guard stood outside Meadow's room, watching me. The doctor in the white coat closed Meadow's door and slipped away. A nurse came out of the nearest room with a tray of Dixie cups. Seeing me, she hurried back into the room, shutting the door behind her. Doors shut all along the corridor.

"She'll think I've left her," I wept into my captor's ear. "She'll think I abandoned her. I told her I'd be right back! I promised!"

"You are in big fucking trouble, buddy. You've got other things to worry about."

"You don't understand," I said. "I don't care about other things. There are *no other things*."

"Calm down. If you stay calm, we can walk out of here. We removed you from the room to avoid upsetting the little girl."

"But she'll be upset when she finds out her father is gone!"

"You are *not* calling the shots."

"*Please.*"

"Pipe down."

"Then call her mother," I say.

"She's on her way. She's been located. She's been waiting by the phone for a week."

"Let me stay until she gets here. I want to explain this all myself."

"Are you *kidding* me? Don't you know you're all over the news?"

"Call my father. He lives here, in Boston. He's family."

"Not on your life."

I nodded, staring at the hands that covered me.

Then I screamed, "MEADOW KENNEDY! I'M RIGHT HERE! YOUR FATHER IS RIGHT HERE!"

Immediately I was thrown against the wall.

I was pinned. I was crying. I found myself trying to reason with the police officers, but nothing came out except whispers. Amazing how they moved me, dragging me like a child by the underarms. My feet slipped on the linoleum. I tried to keep up, but my emotions—sudden, explosive—scrambled physical sensation. The officers opened the swinging doors with my head, and we were back in the bright solarium, and it was daybreak.

"OK, OK," I said. "Look. I'm calm now. I'm *very* calm. Let me walk."

They paused to look at me, adjusting their grips. We were standing together in front of a semicircle of chairs, a dozen innocent bystanders reading their morning papers, looking on, dumbfounded.

"I'm very calm," I said. "And I see the police car waiting for me. I will calmly walk right out of here if you could just tell my daughter something for me. I would appreciate it if you would at least give her a message. All right?"

The policeman shrugged.

"Do any of you speak German?"

A look of antipathy from all three of them.

"Good. Then tell her this, please: *Ich liebe Dich und werde Dich immer lieben.* And tell her, also: *Danke. Danke. Es war meine schönste Zeit.*[16] OK? Please. Please tell her that."

---

16. I love you and I will always love you. Thank you. Thank you. This was the best part of my life.

Again, I'm crying.

"What the fuck."

"You are a nutcase, buddy. You are in for a world of shit."

"Tell *her*. It's for *her*."

"Jesus Christ."

"Let me write it down," I cried. "You can give it to her. She'll understand."

"Hey," one of the younger cops said, pushing me through the revolving doors and into the cold air. "How about you do yourself a favor and shut the hell up?"

REASONS TO BE SILENT

U nfortunately, there comes a point in every research project where one's own personal interests are a liability. One loses the scent of the original project, sometimes never to return. For a year or so, I thought I might expand my "Experimental Encyclopedia" to include not just famous silent moments but also famous silent persons or groups of silent persons.[17] But I got hung up on one thing or another, for example some fascinating and finally fruitless investigations about Abbas Diadochus, fifth-century bishop of Photiki. As I had throughout my project, I found myself less interested in the breadth or completeness of my research and more interested in the curlicues of interesting shit I learned paging through moldering books and obsolete science.

At the same time, the researcher is a *searcher*. He never quite knows what he's looking for, or why. After I accepted

---

17. Monks, Quakers, Buddhists, Apaches, George Harrison, aboriginal widows, my dad, Abbot Rancé of La Trappe, Isaac Luria, Abraham Lincoln, Capricorns, the late Platonists, to name a few. You could count yourself as silent, Reader, but according to Milroy-Dudek (1993), *listenership* is not a form of silence, sorry.

the essential dilettantism of my project, I still mulled over its subject with genuine wonder. In the beginning, I thought silence was generic. But soon I saw the inverse. *Sound* was generic. Sound was *obvious*. But silence. There were so many forms of it. Principled silence. Practical silence. Necessary silence. Ritual silence. Religious silence. The silence of incalculable grief.

Let me expand:

PRINCIPLED SILENCE

Pythagoras himself was not a silent man, but back in ancient Greece, he taught legions of young men about the rigors of silence. He called his students "listeners." For five years at a time, Pythagoras's students observed complete silence. Their teachers would ask them questions they were prohibited from answering, and these questions banged around in their heads for five years, so that by the time their silence was over, you can bet they had some hefty answers. Of course, once the students graduated, they found themselves at a stark conversational loss with everyone they had known before. People wanted the listeners to explain what they'd learned by being silent for five years. But you just really couldn't explain pure silence. It was like trying to send a parcel of light through the mail. And anyway, why should there be a shortcut? If you want to understand, why don't *you* stop talking for half a decade? It was soon decreed among Pythagoreans that it was *not lawful to extend to the casual person things which were obtained with such great labors and such diligent assiduity.*

Tell me about it.

THE SILENCE OF FEAR

In the Gulag, a brilliant middle-aged woman who had once been a music teacher in a noted Baltic conservatory was

serving a decade of hard labor for some transgression against the Communist Party for which she was never formally charged but was sure she was guilty of anyway. Some sort of thought crime, some manifestation of her rage. After long days of crushing big rocks into smaller rocks with a medium-sized rock, the woman would spend her free time in the barracks working on her pet project—a silent piano. She made the body of the piano out of a previous prisoner's wooden crate. The keys she labored on for months apiece, filing down thin planks and tongue depressors. The box was solid, as were the keys—white and black—as responsive as real piano keys. It's just that the instrument didn't produce sound. Well, at first it didn't. And then one day she was able to play the entirety of the Handel Variations. She realized that she had developed an ability to create silent music. And thereafter, long after she returned to her life of privation, she always referred to herself, much to the surprise of others, as "lucky."

THE SILENCE OF SOLITUDE

Hermits and recluses fall into this category, though you could also call their silence principled, practical, or ritual. On a personal note, years ago, after a long depression, my friend—the buddy from Loudonville, whose Mini Cooper I stole—decided to go live in the desert for a while, to see if it would help him. He'd recently lost his parents, his girlfriend had left him, and it was just a bad time. That, plus he was born sad. So he went to the desert. He brought a tent, many books, sufficient water and food. During the day, he sat and listened to the silence. Now, he had expected it to be silent in the desert. But he was surprised at how quickly the silence began to gnaw at him. He felt that he was being confronted by the essential indifference of the cosmos. And so, to his chagrin, he started

making up little songs, things like "You Don't Love My Big Toe" or "Someone's Abusing My Appliances." These songs embarrassed him not because they were polluting the silence he had come to study, but because they were so childish. After a while, my friend packed up his things and headed home. He had learned something. He didn't know what he had learned, but he felt better.

I think what he learned was that he would always be sad.

A man steps into the room in which I'm sitting and says, "Your father is dead."

"The hell he is," I say.

"He died three years ago. Here is the death certificate. Otto Schroder. Isn't that your father?"

The room I'm sitting in is dim, with no natural light. I bend toward the paper he slides toward me without touching it, despite the fact that my handcuffs were removed hours ago.

"No," I say.

"No? That's not your father?"

I stare at the paper.

"No," I say again.

The man sits across from me. "Do you know there's a warrant for your arrest in three states? New York. Vermont. New Hampshire. Depending on the statutes, you could get charged with kidnapping in the second degree. The maximum for that is twenty-five years."

I say nothing. My head begins to spin.

I have been sitting relatively motionless in a holding room somewhere in the basement of the Nashua Street Jail, with no water, no food, and no human contact. When they first

brought me into this building, I was ushered into the room with a virtual cortege, a crowd of people. This graying man was not among them.

"Who are you anyway?" I say.

"Lieutenant Stavros. Who are *you*?"

"What sort of name is Stavros?"

"Greek. What sort of name is Schroder?"

"German," I say. "I'm German. A resident alien. Isn't my confession sort of just a formality at this point? I mean, you have my passport, don't you?"

"Tell me about Erik Schroder. Tell me why you're running from him."

"Sure." I shrug. "I'll tell you everything."

"What?" The man seems caught off guard.

"I'll tell you whatever you want to know."

"OK. But could you wait a minute? I need to go get a couple people."

"Sure. Go ahead."

The man stands. "I'm sorry about your father," he says. "Would you like me to get the chaplain for you? We've got a good one."

"Why would I? I'm totally fine. I don't believe your document is authentic."

The man looks baffled. "You don't?"

"No. It's some kind of ploy. Psychological torture. I want its authenticity confirmed by an independent party. And," I say, raising a finger, "I want to speak to my daughter."

The man hesitates for a moment.

"Are you serious?" he asks.

"Yes, I'm serious."

He's looking at me closely. "I've got to be honest with you.

It's going to be a hell of a long time before that happens. Your daughter was the victim of a crime *you* committed."

"That's not how I see it."

"It doesn't matter how you see it."

"I'm her *father.*"

"You're in jail. You have the rights of a person in jail. Those rights aren't the same as the ones you had yesterday."

I pull myself up as straight as possible.

"Then I would like to speak to a lawyer," I say. "A good one. Your best."

The man sighs and reaches for the door.

He leaves.

He does not come back for a long, long time.

THE SILENCE OF MOURNING

Have you ever heard of Bob Kaufman? He was a poet no one's ever heard of. He once took a legendary vow of silence that lasted ten years.

Born to a Catholic African-American mother and a German Orthodox Jewish dad, Bob Kaufman lived a revolutionary and drug-addled life as a beatnik in San Francisco in the 1950s and '60s. Although his biography is full of disappearances and lacunae, some of us know him as the author of *Solitudes Crowded with Loneliness* or maybe the *Abomunist Manifesto*? He was always writing and reciting poetry in unlikely places. Rooftops. Street corners. The day President Kennedy was shot, Bob Kaufman took a vow of silence. For ten years, he spoke to no one. He recited no poems. Nobody even knows where the hell he went.

The day the Vietnam War ended, Bob Kaufman walked

into a coffee shop and recited a poem, gifting his most glorious moment to a bunch of tired strangers. After that, his life cycled through periods of methadone addiction, poverty, and creative inspiration. It was as if he was trying to erase his life as he lived. He wrote his poems on napkins and newspapers, things that blow away. "I want to be anonymous," he once declared. "My ambition is to be completely forgotten."

DEEP-DOWN THINGS

"OK," my court-appointed lawyer says. "It's true, about your father. He passed away three years ago. I suppose with no forwarding address for you—with no other living relatives— Look, it's no one's fault. It's just something that happened. He died of natural causes. The medical report says complications from pneumonia. He was seventy-two."

I say nothing. My lawyer adjusts his seat. He's an absurdly young guy. Slim, olive skinned. Pakistani, I decide. A public defender, fresh out of law school. They've called him in to get my extradition going, to get me moving along. After that, I'll need to find a new lawyer—not Thron, but somebody more qualified to deal with somebody like me. Somebody with lots of layers. I look at my lawyer's fingernails (immaculate), his tie (silk), and finally his face, which stares back at me in abject receptivity. But I'm looking at him from the bottom of a well. There is nothing in the world somebody so young and pleasant can do for me.

"I'm sorry," he says, finally. "My office is trying to track down your father's effects. Whatever is left belongs to you. Maybe seeing these things will give you some resolution?"

I say nothing. My lawyer looks uncomfortable. I feel bad for him. His youthful looks must piss him off sometimes.

"As for your estranged wife," he continues, "she's, well, distraught. She wants to cooperate fully with the prosecuting authority, which is Albany County, where you'll be heading, just as soon"—he looks over his shoulder, as if my custodian, the stork of the criminal justice system, has missed his cue to enter—"just as soon as someone is available to drive you. There will be a preliminary hearing. And your wife will have to testify at that hearing. But you could always hope"—my lawyer pauses, groping for the bright side—"that when she calms down—when she becomes less angry—she might not want you put away forever. I mean"—my lawyer laughs self-consciously—"you *can't* be put away forever. Twenty-five years is the maximum for a class-E felony. Of course, that sounds like forever. A charge of custodial interference— instead of kidnapping—has a maximum sentence of four years. Much better, right?"

I stare back at him.

"There are potential fraud charges. You are living under a false name. That puts you under immediate suspicion. Truth be told, you might have to defend yourself twice. Both as Eric Kennedy, and as—as"—he checks his notes—"Schroder."

I clear my throat but do not reply.

"Your participation is going to be important. So your lawyers can do everything for your defense. You need to paint the whole picture here. Of your marriage and your family life and most especially your past—" He pauses, looking at me closely, waiting. "You could get as little as a year if your story holds water. You told investigators yesterday that you were

willing to give your statement. Then it appears you changed your mind."

I say nothing. I consider explaining: *Listen, it's not personal. I have simply taken a vow of silence. I will not utter a word until I hear from my daughter or my wife. Someone I can trust. Someone I know.*

"Consider you wife's current position," he continues. "She's just discovered that you are not who you said you were. Your entire identity—your past, everything—is not what you said it was. Even her own last name, her married name, is an invention."

Nothing I haven't already thought of myself, I want to tell him.

(Mountebank! Huckster! Swindler! Cheat!)

"But also—and I don't yet have kids myself, Mr. Kennedy, so I can't really get an angle on this—she *could* claim that you put your daughter in grave danger, which would up your sentence significantly. You ended up in the ER. Your daughter's life was in danger. This could be seen many different ways, in a trial. They could use medical experts—"

A flash of anger enters the young man's eyes.

"Maybe you could nod or something, Mr. Schroder, if you follow me?"

I say nothing. I don't nod.

"You don't feel like talking," he says. "Fine."

He takes out a yellow legal pad and a pen. He slides them toward me across the table.

"Then write it down," he says. "Write it. The whole thing."

I stare at him.

"You know," he continues, "I was thinking about this case last night and—to be honest, it's one of my first, and I'm just here to advise you on your extradition, really—but it's a compelling story. I kept thinking about it. I was thinking, if *I* were this guy's wife, and I loved him once, and actually, I never suspected that he was anyone other than the person he said he was, what would I want him to say to me now?" My lawyer leans back against his chair and crosses his legs, relaxed now that he's lost a clear victory, and opens his hands in a disarming gesture of wonder. Perhaps because I've been so silent, he imagines he is talking to himself, in my presence. "Would I want him to beg for forgiveness? Yes. Would I want him to tell me who he really is and why he lied to me? Yes. But most of all, I would want to know *everything* about the days in which I was apart from my daughter. Everything. I would want to know what routes she traveled, what the weather was like, what she ate, who she talked to, whether or not she had fun. Whether or not she brushed her teeth. If she was *hurt*. If she cried." Lacking a window, he stares toward the ceiling vent. "Because it's the not knowing that's the worst part, isn't it? The not knowing eats at us."

For a moment, neither of us speaks. My lawyer seems to have forgotten about me and tilts his chair onto its back legs with his toes, like a boy.

"After that," he says, "after I knew everything, I might be able to think of *you* again. As a person I knew once. I might be able to spare you a little sympathy. To accept your apology, assuming—"

The young man stops midsentence. Finally, he smiles. I have scooted the pad of paper toward me and have taken up the pen.

I begin to write.

What follows is a record of where Meadow and I have been since our disappearance.

As it turns out, it's a long story.

I don't know how it ends yet. But it begins with love.

YOU AND I AND WINTER MORNINGS

In the first trimester of your pregnancy, all you wanted was nectarines, nectarines, nectarines. In your third, you developed a taste for lousy movies from the 1980s starring B-list actors like Kurt Russell. As soon as you became pregnant, your entire personality changed. Your eyes lost their defiance, your voice its snip. I loved Pregnant You. Pregnant You was, despite her poor taste, a slower, more loveable creature. Your fatigue made you cuddly. Your bulk made you quick to accept help. Out from under the glare of your own cerebral self-scrutiny, you became downright friendly, and for once, it was *I* who had to wait for *you*, as you lingered in conversation with clerks and gas station attendants, as the blue rope of frozen Slurpee spiraled into your twenty-two-ounce cup. And so it was early on in your pregnancy that I understood the neutralizing effect this change was to have on you. You had been zapped by that great normalizer: parenthood.

We are all, all of us, bodies. None of us gets to not have one. We all enter life in the same way, and we all leave by dying. Maybe your pregnant body forced you to see that you were just like everybody else, when it came down to it. You

had always wanted to belong. Maybe this wanting to belong was one reason we spent most of your final trimester watching the local AAA baseball team from the bleachers of their tidy stadium. My Realtor's hours made such afternoons possible for us. For a while, I enjoyed my own role as your elbow holder, teller of jokes, fetcher of French fries. But as the summer wore on and you did not stop attending the games, I have to admit I became confused. I don't like baseball, and you knew that. (The sport makes me antsy, with its suspicious lack of action surrounded by tense silence, the occasional foul ball concussing someone in the bleachers.) But you. Was that really you beside me, cheering for the players by name?

But when I tried to get out of it, you insisted I come. You got nervous without me, you said. You felt vulnerable by yourself and pregnant. Besides, you loved my company. My tall tales, my jokes, my store of factoids, my talent for funny accents. And so I kept going with you, but suspiciously. Had you detected something in me, some foreign strain? I was so careful about my accent, careful about my Germanness; for thirty years I'd practiced, but maybe I'd missed something obvious. Something hiding in plain sight. I used to look around the hot aluminum bleachers at the bristle-headed American men and wonder apprehensively if I was supposed to be more like them, if that was really what you wanted, and if I could do it.

What was so unacceptable about the way I was? I thought I was doing pretty well. I was doing well at work. Granted, it was a bull market, but I was selling houses as fast as I represented them. Just little ranches and bungalows, but it was adding up. People seemed to like me. Long before energy conservation was a trendy cause célèbre, I had a wonky, teacherly way of

getting clients to think about the potential hidden efficiencies (e.g., untapped groundwater for the garden). Simultaneously, I stirred within them the collector's sense of priority. *Look at that leaded window*, I would say. *Look at that forgotten hayloft. Come see this yellowed lithograph of a beautiful dead woman I found in an attic.* Plus, I was young and handsomeish. Conventional, clean of shirt. My hair had darkened with age but was still a dark blond, almost iron blond at the roots. In my sky blue chamois shirts and my Wellingtons, my name stenciled on the side of a clean Saturn, above the reputable name of Clebus & Co., I was a member of the community.

But sometimes, in the middle of a baseball game, sitting there with my paper cone of French fries, smiling at all the potential clients, I felt dread. What had we *done*? Why not just go on, you and I? You and I and winter mornings, and the newspaper, and talking, and not talking, and poetry, and the absentminded overwatering of flowers? Why didn't we have the guts to grow old that way? Why have a *child*? Why try to take that summit?

But we were already too far along. That is, you were too far along. Eight months pregnant, you were a beautiful bell jar, shielding your sweet. You were a snake that had fallen in love with what it had swallowed. Leaning back on the bleachers, elbows squared, you looked out over your own horizon, your T-shirt barely up to the task at hand, one strip of skin visible above the hem of your elastic shorts. At various points in the game, you'd scream—*go go go go go!* And your enthusiasm almost made me feel better. You, this graceful vision of life, screaming at people who couldn't even hear you. I tried to relax and enjoy the conclusion of your pregnancy. But in the end, my fear of fatherhood was only a heightened version

of any other man's. The presentiments, in general, are true: You will fall in love with the thing that is out to get you.

Go go go go go!

You. You know who you are. That youngish man thrown into the unknown when suddenly, one innocent night, it comes. The visitor comes.

To the hospital! Gather your things! Your overnight bag! Turn off the lights. Don't dally! You dash to the door only to realize you've forgotten your wife, that mystic bent over and moaning in the kitchen. She refuses to move, but she must move! Give her a second! She is shaking; is this normal? No! No, it is not normal at all! But somehow the telephone has been covered with butter and cannot be gripped and therefore the hospital cannot be consulted and the ambulance cannot be summoned. Far better to unbend the woman and force her into the car! Far faster than waiting for an ambulance! But is she, like the potential paralytic, not to be moved? Might her standing *break* the baby? Several awkward moments pass as your wife gazes at the linoleum. Her expression is that of a toreador who has just been gored. Can she speak? No! Is this normal? Information sighs out of your head like air from a tire. All you can think of to say is *I loved you*, and by this you mean, I tried as best as I could, but now I see that you are going to die and it's my fault, and I just want to set the record straight that I did, indeed, love you. I wasn't trying to kill you! This comment finally brings consciousness into the eye of the woman in labor.

What did you say?

I said I *love* you! you cry, pulling her arm over your shoulder and dragging her out the door. I love you! I'm sorry I did this to you!

You didn't do this to me, you silly, laughs your wife.

Her contraction must have passed. She is now leaning voluptuously against you, as if there's all the time in the
world. Labor is making her daffy. Her forehead shines with
sweat in the streetlight below your apartment. You fight with
your keys.

We did this to us, she clarifies. And P.S., I love you too. I'm
so glad you came into my life. Do you know that? Do you?

Sometimes I know that, you say.

I am, she says. So glad. I love you quietly all day long. I've
always been—she searches for the word—sort of buttoned-
down. I can be a real wet blanket, I know that. But when I'm
around you, I feel loose. Life feels good and light and swingy.
I feel *inspired*. That's what I feel when I'm with you.

You glance at her, your heart thundering. You believe her.
You wish you could stop and make her say it again into a record-
ing device, but you know you probably have only a moment or
two before you lose her to another contraction, and you need
to keep her *moving*, you need to keep her *focused* because despite
all the useful exercises they taught you in prenatal classes at the
community center, none of them were How to Deliver Your
Own Child in the Backseat of Your Car Using Only a Bottle
Opener, a Flashlight, and a Map of Greater Albany.

Madam, you say, opening the rear door.

And she sits in the hospital for hours washed and waiting
on a bed in the upright position, occasionally saying, Well,
that's the first time I haven't had to wait for hours in an ER.
The night is a rhythm of her anguished screaming followed
by light, casual conversation. In between, you eat ice chips
together. Nurses come in and out and in and out and tectonic
plates shift and stars die and finally the OB comes in and says

let's induce and so the induction begins and the contractions happen faster but alas, no change has been made to the cliff face of the woman's cervical opening. It's like trying to get a bulkhead to dilate. But deadlines have now been set and all sorts of medical fine print has been printed and suddenly the two of you are the honored guests at a medical emergency. You—the father—are given a pair of blue scrubs and thrust into what looks like a broom closet while your wife is wheeled away toward the OR, followed by a tall anesthesiologist who turns out, in a funny twist of fate, to be German.

But you're just glad it's not you who has to operate. (When they gave you the scrubs, you wondered.) You just have to hurry the hell up and change and find the OR, and in the devastating moments in which you are apart from her, changing, you realize that you never, never want to lose this woman, and that the two of you are now connected by some kind of experiential sinew stronger than any cord, any cable, any mooring. Stronger than anything a man could make with his hands. She is lying in the light literally crucified, wrists tied to a T-shaped table, when you arrive and sit in the chair they have placed at her head. And you dry her cheeks because she is crying. And you reassure her. You say, it's OK, baby. You say, I'm right here. And when they cut her belly open you don't even look at her belly. Because you're not talking to her *body* anymore. You are not talking to her body, no. Because a room is created by every love at its apex. And you are talking to her soul in that distant room. It's a room you've never been to before, and a room you may never get to again. You're really not even supposed to know it exists.

In the end, you have never felt this close to anyone in your whole life.

You say to yourself, I will never forget this. I will never betray this. I will live my life to the standard of *this*. And even if I fall short, I will never give up my commitment to believe in and live by this.

But you don't.

That is, you do forget. You become complacent. And one summer evening several years later, while standing on the hill above the College of Saint Rose in the middle of a pickup soccer game, you look out over the balsam green Hudson River Valley and you wonder, Yes, but what was that other thing? What was that dream I was supposed to remember? You're late to get home, but you figure no one will mind if you finish out the half. And right before you jog back onto the field, you observe with perfect sangfroid that you can't even locate what you've forgotten in a category of forgetting. Just like that, you let go of it. You liked the feeling of love, but you weren't interested in the work, so you let go of it. You gave it up because it would have been difficult. You liked it only when it was good, when it made you look good. When it asked more of you, you demurred; in fact, you pretended that no request had been made. You forgot that you owed them anything, that you owed them the effort of love. You hoped they would eventually forget too. You hoped they would forget you and forget themselves and go on worshipfully bearing your icon. It took her years to figure it out. And then she did, somehow. But you. Your understanding lagged behind. You never imagined anything beyond the conquering. And these are the regrets that dog you now, with all this time on your hands.

So. Much. Time.

I let you down.

I let you down.

I let you down.

I let you down.

I let you down.

I let you down.

I let you down.

I let you down.

I let you down.

I let you down.

I let you down.

I let you down.

I let you down.

I let you down.

I let you down.

I let you down.

I let you down.

I let you down.

I let you down.

I let you down. I let you down.

I let you down. I let you down. I let you down. I let you
down. I let you down. I let you down. I let you down. I let
you down. I let you down. I let you down. I let you down. I
let you down. I let you down. I let you down. I let you down.
I let you down. I let you down. I let you down. I let you
down. I let you down. I let you down. I let you down. I let
you down. I let you down. I let you down. I let you down. I
let you down. I let you down. I let you down. I let you down.
I let you down. I let you down. I let you down. I let you
down. I let you down. I let you down. I let you down. I let
you down. I let you down. I let you down. I let you down. I
let you down. I let you down. I let you down. I let you down.
I let you down. I let you down. I let you down. I let you
down. I let you down. I let you down. I let you down. I let
you down. I let you down. I let you down. I let you down. I
let you down. I let you down. I let you down. I let you down.
I let you down. I let you down. I let you down. I let you
down. I let you down. I let you down. I let you down. I let
you down. I let you down. I let you down. I let you down. I
let you down. I let you down. I let you down. I let you down.
I let you down. I let you down. I let you down. I let you
down. I let you down. I let you down. I let you down. I let
you down. I let you down. I let you down. I let you down. I
let you down. I let you down. I let you down. I let you down.
I let you down. I let you down. I let you down. I let you
down. I let you down. I let you down. I let you down. I let
you down. I let you down. I let you down. I let you down. I
let you down. I let you down. I let you down. I let you down.
I let you down. I let you down. I let you down. I let you
down. I let you down. I let you down. I let you down. I let
you down. I let you down. I let you down. I let you down. I

let you down. I let you down.

I let you down. I let you

down. I let you down.

EN FIN

I've been silent a long time now. Twenty-one days by my count. My voice, when I hear it in my sleep, has acquired an odd depth from disuse, a kind of virgin hoarseness. My speech strike has been an interesting experiment, bringing me just about everything except for what I'd hoped. As a tactical method, it's been a clear failure. I've been deemed noncooperative, and despite my polite notes explaining my silence, I've been placed under protective custody and left entirely in my cell for all but an hour of solitary roaming in the gym. I haven't seen my daughter. I haven't heard a word. All I know is that the letter I tried to send against the advice of my lawyer to the old Pine Hills apartment was returned to me unopened, with no forwarding address. I'm left to think that all I've gained from my silence is this document, one I never would have written if I had allowed myself to speak. If I had spoken, I would have jawed all day long in the dayroom with the other guys. I would have sung under my breath at night. I would have made friends with the guards or found my way to the infirmary, or into one of the workshops on

child development offered to those who've acquired an academic interest in how they got here. Instead, I wrote.

I wrote to you, Laura. I wrote for you and because of you and with you in mind, sitting across the kitchen table in your old gray cardigan. I could not have written this document without writing it for you. I could not have written this document if I had thought you weren't listening. But now that I've come to the end of it, pulling up to the present moment, I'm struck by the sudden understanding that I cannot require you to read it. Or maybe I understand that you never will. You just never will. Even if this document passes the vetting of my lawyer, even if he decides that it mitigates instead of aggravates the charges against me, it will be sent to you (at your new address) as an inert pile of papers wrapped in twine. You'll come home one day, see it waiting for you, and you will pause. You'll heft it off your stoop and put it on the table. Meadow will ask you what it is and you'll say *Just some thing.* She'll run away to change out of her school clothes and you will look out the window and sigh. That evening, after she is in bed, her hair damp from the bath, her eyeglasses stored in her sneaker, her face kissed fifty times in all the ritual places, you'll tuck up your legs and attempt to read.

But you'll only get so far. A page or two. It's too much. You'll read it later. You want less and less to do with the proceedings. Your testimony at my hearing will be brief, reluctant. You want to move on. You don't wish me ill anymore, but you've also stopped caring what happens to me. Somewhere in your soul you've disengaged, you've uncoupled, you've let go. You've turned to your daughter, to encouraging her happiness and bracing yourself for her questions. In fact, it occurs to me now, the only reason you would ever read

this document is if you wanted to intercede. If you wanted to save me.

How strange to be quiet here, of all places. I have often wanted to babble just to contribute to the noise. Constant noise, constant light. And me sitting like a poet in the middle of it. It's funny to listen to people talk when you can't respond. People talk *so much*. Gaggingly long monologues on minor personal preferences. Verbatim recitations of pointless conversations. Uninterpreted bits of memory. Take the man in the neighboring cell. A classic recidivist, a real prison grandfather. He almost seems relieved to be back in prison just so he can talk as much as he wants. The whole unblinking day he talks. He arrived about a week after my extradition here to CCI Albany. Having been outside during the heart of my news cycle, he's a fan of my case, and he talks about it through the vents endlessly. He says he knows the prosecuting attorney in my case, and for long hours he parses this woman's trial record with a certain bloodless admiration, and I can't help but listen.

"Don't worry, Kennedy," this man says. "You'll be all right once they realize you're not a monster. And you are *not* a monster. You wouldn't even be in here if it wasn't for your famous name. Ironic, isn't it? If you weren't a Kennedy, no one would have bothered with you."

I rest the side of my head against the wall and massage my scalp with the gritty surface. I'm sitting at my metal desk. My stool is kindergarten short and dented like an old cookie sheet. I've got my yellow legal pad. I've got my dull pencil. An exquisite five minutes go by without commentary. I close my eyes and let my mind dance lightly, remembering. After a moment, I see a familiar shadow approaching, swaying back and forth against the kitchen wainscoting. Someone enters

the kitchen, his face wrapped in gauze. I open my eyes, waiting for pleasanter memories to surface. But they don't come.

"Yeah, you'll be all right, Kennedy. You'll be all right." I hear my friend lean his weight against his cell door, and I marvel at his ability to stand up for the entire day. "But what *is* all right, you know? They won't let you near your kid. They'll try to ship you home to Bavaria or wherever the hell."

I sigh and get up. I lie down on the mattress and put my forearm over my eyes. My legs, the mattress, everything is swathed in the same disposable, gridded material. The sheets are real and you could call them soft.

My friend's voice floats down to me again through the vents. "What I wonder about is this—do you miss it, Kennedy? I mean, your made-up life."

I almost laugh. Do I? Do I miss Twelve Hills? Do I miss my made-up mother and my made-up father? Do I miss even the unsubstantiated connection to a famous family?

I had imagined it so well. It got to the point that I could *see* myself as a child, digging the sugar-fine sand outside our cape, or being read to by my favorite teacher, or walking flanked by the wide asses of my nannies. These visions were so sturdy that if I looked around in my mind, and panned the scene, it would spread itself out for me infinitely—not shallowly, infinitely—and if you had asked me what was beyond, what could be seen, well, I could tell you. To the west were the dunes. To the north, the salt marsh where I gathered sea lettuce. And there, jutting into the ocean, the inoperable lighthouse on whose philanthropic restoration committee my own mother served.

I guess I needed a life that I could revise. If I had just accepted the one life, my first life, I would have honored its

limits. I would have lived quietly, hardly even dreaming. I would have tried to convince myself that a sad and quiet life is adequate. Instead, I dreamt. I decorated entire rooms of my past with the pleasures I salvaged elsewhere. Even falling in love with you, Laura—*especially* falling in love with you, and feeling so changed...Love was my counterargument. Suddenly there were Christmas parties all over Twelve Hills, and well-loved women in silk dresses, and boys nursing crushes on other boys' mothers, and soft rugs for the babies, and brotherhood for the men. My God, it sounds sentimental when I put it that way, but that's what my second life did for me.

And pain. Even pain. It's no good if it's anonymous, monolithic, genocidal. The pain in my made-up life was boy-sized pain. And so it was *better*, because I could *stand* it. I no longer had to be a partial suicide, living only half a life, or less—allowing only the pleasant moments, mild, unthreatening—the small minority. I no longer had to be half alive. A partial suicide like my father.

My eyes shut, he walks blindly into the kitchen again, hands out, searching the air for the door of that little half-fridge that we always kept half-empty. *Vater.* I tell him to go lie down. *I'll bring it to you*, I say.

If we could *know*, if we could be warned, we could claim all our scattered properties before death forecloses. Have I made it sound like I tried? Here's a memory:

1994. A Sunday. I'm driving southeast in a borrowed car. It's a Pontiac Firebird in Collector Yellow with a seriously awesome sound system, and it's just accepted an Aerosmith tape into its deck in a way that feels distinctly sultry to me. I'm twenty-six, beating time to the song on the steering wheel. I've just crossed the Massachusetts border and have taken

the long route across the state via the Mohawk Trail, a road I like for the view atop Mount Greylock and for the knick-knack store that sits there like a Buddhist temple buffeted by crosswinds.

I'm late. I told Dad I'd be in Dorchester days ago. He is to have cataract surgery on both eyes on Monday, and he needs my help settling some affairs. While the delay itself is forgivable—I don't remember the reason for it—driving the scenic route along the Mohawk Trail is not. Yet I drive without hurry. I have not seen my father since the degeneration of his eyesight began, and when I arrive I will be woefully unprepared for his groping debility. I have a girlfriend—not the wife, not The One—but a much less serious girl named Angela. It's Angela's Firebird I'm driving. Angela was my study mate in Spanish, senior year at Mune. She tracked me for several years after graduation until I relented and went to bed with her, and at this stage we are spending a lot of time together, mostly naked. I am thinking about this—about Angela—as I descend into the Pioneer Valley, barely noticing the lurid foliage on either side of Route 91. *Come back soon*, Angela had begged that morning in bed. *Promise you'll come back soon.*

I do not love Angela. I have told her this in an effort to head off future indemnity. She says she's OK with that. She says love is "just a word." In my limited experience, this seems sound. I do not love Angela, but as I drive the Mohawk Trail, I do miss her. She is my main squeeze. She is my working thesis. With her, I associate all that I love about Albany, which is that I have absolutely no familial, cultural, or philosophical connection to it. I'm bound to it only by the exercise of my own free will.

The moment I enter the apartment on Savin Hill Road, Dad sits upright and says, in English, "Thank you for coming." Although he is fully dressed, he seems to have just awoken from a long sleep. As ever, I am not prepared for his civility, how he is calm to the point of frigid, nor am I prepared for how frustrated it makes me that he still sleeps on the couch, instead of in the single bedroom I have long vacated. I feel the need for air, the need to sigh repeatedly, as well as the telltale muscular fatigue I suffer from long after I've finished climbing those three flights of stairs. Just moments ago, I barely survived the foyer of the building, against whose plaster I used to rest my secondhand dirt bike. Why does the foyer hurt me? Why does the memory of the dirt bike hurt me? I don't know. I still don't know. Sliding my key from the lock, I turn and offer Dad an encouraging smile. He stares up from the couch uncertainly. I realize I am smiling at a blind man.

"Ah," he says, and pats the surface of the TV table. He picks up something that looks like a welding visor and places it over his glasses. He finds me through magnified eyes.

"*Now* I see you," he says.

I walk over and clasp his shoulder, suddenly moved. "Hi, Dad. I'm here."

"Sorry for how I look," he says.

"What?" I say. "You look fine."

"I cannot see."

"Well, you can see me."

"I can see you hardly."

"You're going to be *fine*."

He gives my wrist a squeeze. "My son. You came."

My throat constricts. That's right—I remember now—the surgery carries a small risk of permanent blindness. He

is afraid. But instead of offering him reassurance, I feel my stomach drop, and a child's wail begins to climb me from the inside. God no, I think. You cannot cry, you shit. If you start to cry, you will never forgive yourself. You will die of shame. *Trottel. Idiot.* Weakling. That's when I make a deal. I say, Dear God: If you help me make it out of Dorchester without crying, I will never set foot in this place again. I will totally disappear.

The wail stops at the top of my throat and sinks back into silence.

The surgery goes well. At the end of the day, I drive Dad back to the apartment. I lead him up the steps by the elbow. The upper half of his face is bandaged by gauze. I disregard the policies of parking in the shared lot and leave the car closest to the entrance, blocking someone in. I prop Dad on the couch with some extra pillows. He asks for a beer. I go to the old half fridge, get a beer, pop off the bottle cap, and guide the misting nozzle to his mouth. We sit together as he sips, and for a moment, I almost enjoy the familiar sensation of his silence.

"Miscommunication," Dad says, swallowing. "This is the English word."

"What?" I ask. "What did you say?"

"We were crossed stars."

"Who are you talking about, Dad?"

"Your *Mutter.* Your *Mutter* and I."

I slap my knee. "You should rest."

"But it is a simple thing to say. Miscommunication. It was to happen. We had lost the power of speaking. We became as children." He turns his bandaged face toward mine. "I would like to explain it to you."

"Dad. You don't need to explain it to me," I say. "It's ancient history."

"It has long confused me. Love. Opportunity. She said I was unloving. But see where we *were*. See what we lived with. The society we lived with. A false regime, another country's puppet. Artificial. *Paranoid*. Shut. The heart needs inspiration. The heart needs opportunity—"

"Dad, please. Stop."

"You were too *jung* to know. So I tell you now."

"No," I say. "*Nein.*"

"No? Why not?"

"Because. That's why."

"I don't understand."

I laugh, looking for support from the empty room. "By God, you just had surgery. Where in the hospital paperwork does it say that the patient should recount long and painful stories from the distant past? Stories that nobody—that everybody— Besides, you're on like twelve different sedatives and I don't trust you."

"I want to say what happened."

"No."

"You don't want to know what happened to us?"

"No."

"I felt, in surgery, what if something happened to me? And I leave you alone? But I have made it and I will tell you now."

"*Nein!*" I am shaking. "*Ich will es nicht wissen*, Daddy. *Ich will es nicht hören.*"

"Let me tell you. It's all right."

"*Du bist krank. Du bist betrunken.*" I clasp my hand over my mouth, glad he cannot see me. I stand and move to the window. The street below is empty. The top corner of the white

tenement across the street is sheared by the sun like a dog-eared page. Neither of us speaks.

Then my father says, hollowly, "We were given one hour to get to Friedrichstrasse..."

"Enough," I say. I return to the couch and take away his beer. His hands grope the air for it. "You shouldn't be drinking this. You're not making sense." My voice falls to a whisper. "You're not making sense."

He pushes himself upright. "Son. I see you so seldom."

"I know."

A long horn sounds from below. We both turn our heads to look.

"The lot," Dad says. "You must move your auto."

Hey! Hey up there! a female voice cries from outside. *Hey, asshole!*

"She must mean me." I pick up my car keys. "I'll be back."

"No," Dad says wearily. "You go. Go. Live your life. I'm home now. I only want to sleep. Go, go."

I wipe my eyes. "I said I'll be back. Where's parking?"

"Victoria *Strasse*," my father says quietly, pressing the gauze against his eyes. "Monday–Wednesday parking on Victoria *Strasse*."

I descend the stairs. Their uneven risers are embedded in my gait. Out the side door. The slap of the storm door. A woman in a dirty minivan eyes me through her side-view mirror, a clove cigarette tilted at an angle between her fingers. I get into Angela's Firebird and back out.

I am driving fast. Very fast. I'm back on the Expressway, heading north. I did not find parking on Victoria *Strasse*. That is, I did not look for parking on Victoria *Strasse*. I allow the gas pedal to sink to the floor, and veer into the passing lane.

Until then, I've been hewing to the speed limit like I always do, instinctively afraid of police cars, of anything in ambush. Aerosmith sounds all wrong now and instead I just glare at the road, trying to throw myself forward two hours, to those verdant foothills between Stockbridge and Austerlitz, the anticipation of the New York state line, the anticipation of Angela.

Come back soon. Promise you'll come back soon.

I pretend that I am needed, and that's why I weave between the lanes of traffic toward the North Shore. I pretend that I'm impervious, that I have no debts, and no future that will ever have a hold on me. I pretend that I'll never possess anything I can't afford to lose. I pretend that I'm unstoppable, ignorant of the fact that thirteen years later, I will walk into a sheet of glass that I did not know was there and that glass will be my father. That sheet of glass will be my first life. That sheet of glass will be myself. I am covered in shards.

Das Ende

ACKNOWLEDGMENTS

I wish to thank many who supported the writing of this book, including Emily Foreland, Emma Patterson, Libby Burton, Brian McLendon, and editor and believer Cary Goldstein. I honor here Wendy Weil, my beacon and friend, and my mother-in-law, Ellen Arnold Groff; I miss you both. I'm indebted to the Corporation of Yaddo, the MacDowell Colony, and Amherst College. For their expertise, I thank the Scott-Kunkel family, Mira Kautzky, Dan Hart, and Leah Rotenberg. For their insight, I thank Adam Haslett, Nam Le, Sarah Shun-lien Bynum, Jonathan Franzen, Youna Kwak, Sarah Moore, Judith Goldman, Daniel Hall, Catherine Newman, and Ted and Kathy Beery, as well as the works of Adam Jaworski. I also thank my family, Karina Gaige, Norman Cohen, Robert Groff, Ted Watt, my invaluable mother, Austra, my remarkable son, Atis, his baby sister, Freya, and most especially my husband, Timothy Watt, whose love, wonder, and literary spirit inspire every word of this book.

ABOUT THE AUTHOR

AMITY GAIGE is the author of the novels *O My Darling* and *The Folded World*. Her essays, articles, and stories have appeared in various publications, including *The Yale Review*, *The Literary Review*, and the *Los Angeles Times*. She is the recipient of a Fulbright Fellowship, residencies at the MacDowell and Yaddo Colonies, a Baltic Writing Residency Fellowship, and in 2006, she was recognized by the National Book Foundation as one of five outstanding emerging writers under thirty-five. She is currently the Visiting Writer at Amherst College. She lives in Connecticut with her family.

READING GROUP GUIDE

Questions for Discussion

1. Have you ever told a lie that grew beyond your control? What did you decide to do when the lie became more than you could handle?

2. *Schroder* is written as a confessional letter from Eric to his wife, Laura. Have you ever written a confession? About what and to whom?

3. In the novel, Eric tells his first lie when he is five years old. Do you remember your first lie or a time when you witnessed a young child lie? Why do you think you—or the child you witnessed—told this lie?

4. If you could change something about your family history, what would it be?

5. Which famous family might you pretend to be part of? Why?

6. Eric and Laura's marriage began with a lie about Eric's identity. How much of ourselves do we keep from our loved ones? Can omissions ultimately doom a relationship? Or is there room for secrets between spouses and in families?

7. Meadow is often the only voice of reason in the novel. What about a child's mind allows Meadow to trust her father but also to be honest with him at the same time?

8. Were you ever worried for Meadow's safety? If not, why not?

9. How does Eric's immigrant status shape the way he sees the world—and the specific people in his world, such as Laura, Meadow, and Albany?

10. Do you think Eric is mentally ill or just a confused man who doesn't want to lose his daughter? How far would you go to hold on to someone you love?

11. Can someone who has made mistakes or done bad things in one part of his or her life still be a good parent?

12. Are you able to forgive the flaws in your own parents? Do you think Meadow will be able to?

Interview with Amity Gaige

Q: *What events in your own life led you to write this book?*

A: My son was about three years old when I started this book. He wasn't old enough to be as articulate as Meadow, but he said and did a lot of wise things. For some reason, when I realized how much he could actually understand, I started to get nervous. I hoped I was saying or doing the right thing. But no one is entirely "normal," and occasionally I wondered if what I said and did as a mother wasn't a little eccentric—nothing as inappropriate as Eric, but you know, on the playground it seems like either you're doing something questionable as a parent or somebody else is. So I was very interested in exploring what makes a "good parent," how both parent and child get through the crucible of the early years.

During this same time, my parents separated after forty-four years of marriage. This was a profound disorientation for me. Then, my father—who had been the first and most influential reader of my work, to whom this book is dedicated—fell terminally ill. He came to my town to spend the last months of his life in a hospice home up the street from me, and I had to learn how to let him go. Meanwhile, I tried to be cheerful for my son—again, to project a sense of normalcy—but that was getting increasingly harder. Who was I kidding? Anyway,

these things ended up getting absorbed into the writing of *Schroder.* The writing heals. Or, at least, the writing is a vessel to hold the experience.

Q: *What event in the news sparked the particular story you tell in* Schroder?

A: Several years ago, while I was abroad, I read a short AP article about the Clark Rockefeller case, which had just broken. He was the German con man who posed as a Rockefeller. He was also the father of a young girl, whom he attempted to kidnap. His particular case is quite interesting, but I never followed the case nor have I read anything about it since. There was only one thing from his case that really inspired me. This con man was by many accounts a loving father, and he called the days with his daughter "the best days" of his life. The story echoed what I was already wondering about parenthood: can a deeply flawed person be a good (or good enough) parent? What does it take? How would we define that?

Q: *In* Schroder, *the bond between a parent and child dictates a lot of the action. What is it about the nature of this bond that drives Eric? Is there a difference between the bond of a mother and a child and that of a father and a child?*

A: Yes, I think the parental bond is different between genders because men and woman are different. But I firmly believe that a bond between a father and child can be as strong as that between a mother and child. Maybe not in the infant years, but beyond. Personally, I think it's really the primary caregiver who knows the child best, whoever feeds and clothes the child and pries sharp objects out

of his or her hand (what Eric calls "the relentless being-aware" of the child). For at least a year, Eric is a stay-at-home dad. He's not a great one, but for the first time he actually pays attention. Anyone who pays attention to his or her child builds a bond. You can't help but respect their miniature successes and failures.

Q: *Does Eric truly love his daughter or simply the idea of her?*

A: Whoa. I don't know. I think that's a question you could ask of any parent. Eric does think that Meadow is "like him" in certain ways. Parenthood gets just a little bit thornier, I think, when your kid is "like you." Because at moments you might think he *is* you, which is distinctly unhelpful to *him*. There's a moment late in the novel when Eric suddenly realizes that maybe he wanted to test Meadow, to see if she could stand bad things, like he had to stand bad things when he was a kid. It's a disturbing and pivotal moment for Eric, when he realizes his narcissism is harming his own child.

Q: *What is it about the theme of identity—from our formative years through how we present ourselves as adults—that attracted you as a writer?*

A: Someone once said to me, "All your books are about identity." I think so. Who knows why? I had an early and unsettling awareness of the self as a construct. Sadly, I haven't shaken that. I think we all do a lot of "deciding" who we are; we train ourselves to have certain qualities. But who knows—maybe even then, some other god-given self shines through, a self that's better or worse than the one we're projecting.

I guess the same thing gets played out in *Schroder*. Although Erik reinvents himself as Eric, the capable American, he can't *totally* transform, not convincingly. His injured German boyhood self slips through. Even Laura begins to see this. Before she ever discovers he's a fraud, she senses there is something fraudulent about him. So maybe that's my answer. Maybe there *is* a real self that cannot be renamed or repackaged.

Q: *America is a land of opportunity and reinvention. Could* Schroder *have taken place elsewhere? What is it about the nature of America that allows a boy named Erik Schroder to grow into Eric Kennedy?*

A: Yes, this is an *American* story. America has accepted waves of immigrants throughout its history. Sometimes their names were changed by lazy immigration officials and sometimes the immigrants changed their own names. My mother was one of those people. She came to this country from Latvia when she was eleven, was one of the displaced people of World War II. Her childhood was very hard. She didn't want constant reminders of it, nor her ethnic background. Everyone made fun of her name. You see where this is going...

A lot of people come to the United States to reinvent themselves. It's understandable. Of course, Eric does not legalize his name change, and because he's not a citizen, he's actually committing fraud by accepting Pell Grants, etcetera. But for me, the only truly immoral thing he does is lie to Laura. A marriage can't be built upon a phony life history.

Q: *Because* Schroder *is written as a confession, Eric is a somewhat unreliable narrator. Are there parts of the story we are not privy to because of this?*

A: Part of a novel's craft is the hiding and revealing of all the information that the novel touches upon. The order of Eric's confessions is significant. I might point to the very final chapter. He "hides" this information for a long time. In this scene, we see that Eric's father attempted to explain his past to him, but Eric refused this attempt. He's too scared. It's too buried. Eric becomes more reliable as the book goes on, or at least more honest. Let's say he's an unreliable narrator in recovery.

Q: *In many ways, Laura's perspective is absent from the novel. She is a character created out of "negative space." Why did you decide to keep her voice out of the main narrative? Was it hard to exclude her from the central action of the novel?*

A: I identify with Laura. Of course, it's kind of like hamstringing yourself to leave a character you relate to out of a novel. But she's there. I hope the reader might glean what she thinks of Eric, why she left him, etcetera, through the tidbits Eric reveals in the service of other things. But the novel isn't really about why Laura loves or doesn't love Eric. The novel is a love letter—Eric's. It's a long love letter that goes unanswered. I got sad myself writing the end of the letter/novel, when I realized that a "real" Laura probably wouldn't even read it...Meadow will always remain connected to her dad, if only by blood, but Laura can wash her hands of the whole thing. Grown-ups can divorce each other. Kids can't divorce their parents.

Q: *Given his actions as a husband, father, and a man, how sympathetic did you want Eric to seem to the reader?*

A: After the first draft of the novel was done, I did a fair amount of listening to trusted readers and even legal advisers, listening for places where I might have gone a little nuts with my own fictional play. I have a dear friend who's a lawyer, and we went through the draft scene by scene and she pointed out the things Eric does that would "mitigate" the kidnapping charges he's faced with, and which things would "aggravate" those charges. At times, the law matched the moral barometers of my other readers. These were the same places where the readers said, "that's unacceptable." However, I must say that I didn't want to write a book about which there would be consensus. I mean, I'm not trying to create a character about which easy judgments can be made, or upon which we can all agree. I don't want to read such books, either. I'm not saying everything's OK by me when it comes to human behavior. As a reader and a person in the world, I have my own limits for the acceptability or unacceptability of people's actions. But a good book takes me much further into a moral question than I could go by myself.

Q: *Was it challenging for you to write in a male voice?*

A: I don't think Eric is the "typical" male, but his voice came pretty easily to me. I hope he seems convincing as a man. The men in my life have mentioned that he does. I guess it's just years of listening to them talk. My husband—who is a very reliable, law-abiding citizen, by the way—is really honest about men and male psychology. I think he let me into some of the secrets of the brotherhood.

Q: *How did you bring six-year-old Meadow to life, particularly since the reader only sees her through the eyes of her father?*

A: Meadow initially felt like a dream to me, very abstract. But she grew as the book went along. I started to feel her stoicism. She took shape. Also, here and there, I stole lines of dialogue from my son. For example, he once defined "the soul" as the thing that "keeps the body up." I could never have come up with that myself.

Q: *Why did you choose to use footnotes in your novel? Why not reveal these things in the body of the text?*

A: Eric likes to digress, and occasionally show off his esoteric and maybe useless knowledge. For a while, I let him do this whenever he wanted. Then I realized that that's exactly what footnotes *are*, places where the scholarly self can qualify and digress. The footnotes show Eric's second, shadow consciousness as he's writing. At first, that second consciousness tries to be all academic and cool. He uses the footnotes ironically to discuss theories of silence. He's detached from his personal story, or at least he's trying to seem like he is. But gradually, the footnotes turn personal. He stops talking about silence theory in the abstract and begins to talk about himself. The footnotes start to be anti-footnotes. He tries to keep them down, tries to minimize them, but occasionally they are the most honest things he says. The footnotes are just another facet to show Eric's struggle, which is the struggle to tell the truth, the struggle to tell a true story.

Q: *The language in* Schroder *is often beautiful and poetic and sometimes at odds with the story you are telling. What is it about the use of particular language that aids in the telling of a story?*

A: I was just debating with some students about whether the use of a "fancy prose style" makes a narrator seem more or less reliable. I think probably less. But I don't come at writing that way. I write with these poetic lurches that are born out of my writing mind, the mind that's deep in concentration and imagination. John Updike once said that it is the responsibility of every writer to try and convey how the world "hits his or her nerves." I think the poetic language in this book and my previous books is simply that.

Q: *Why did you choose to end* Schroder *when you did? Do you know what is next for Eric and Meadow?*

A: I don't know what's next! I feel sad for them both. When I started writing the book, I had this somewhat unrealistic notion that this confession would give the two of them a clean start. I even thought that Laura would forgive Eric, and maybe she would realize that Meadow needs Eric in her life. I *do* think Meadow needs Eric in her life. Because he's her dad, and you only get one of those. I think total estrangement is bad for the child. It's too confusing. I have spoken to people who were estranged from parents and said they would have preferred some limited contact over total absence. Or silence. I guess I would hope for their family that silence could be avoided. I think that's what Eric would want. That he wouldn't become the new "unspoken" or secret shameful thing for his daughter. He's come clean. And later, if he makes good, I hope they forgive him. I believe in forgiveness.

In her exceptional debut novel, Amity Gaige
explores the quiet joys and staggering mysteries
of love in elegant, magical prose...

Please turn this page
for an excerpt from

O My Darling

BIRTHDAY

T ell me," she said.
      "No," he said.
   "Come on," she was laughing. "Just tell me what it is."
   "No," he said. "You have to guess."
   "Guess? Guess?" She had both hands on her head. "I hate guessing. You know that. Just give it to me."
   "I want you to guess," Clark said evenly, holding the gift behind his back. The young couple, Clark and Charlotte Adair, stood in the middle of their kitchen, which they had yesterday painted yellow. Everything was still in boxes all around the house, for they had just moved in.
   Although he spoke casually enough, Clark was weak with excitement—today was a birthday. Today was a day to honor childhood, which he remembered as something like a galaxy of sweets and coincidences. This was a day to feel as precious and doted upon as one tended to feel as a child, as precious and doted upon as *he* had felt at least, and to forget altogether that one was grown up. Birthdays. He remembered the body heat of his parents behind him as he beckoned the party guests in from the rain. Though Clark was not yet thirty, he would be

soon, and what struck him about adulthood so far was the sheer quantity of issues that arose of their own accord, no matter how pleasantly you behaved. Too many issues to name. Today was a birthday. A day to put all that aside.

"OK," Charlotte said, shrugging. She took two steps backward and looked at her husband, finger in mouth. Suddenly she seemed happy to comply.

"Flowers," she said.

"Nope," said Clark, aware of an immediate look of relief on her face. "Flowers are for normal days. Today is your birthday."

"Well, what did you *get* me?" She was blushing. The sight of her pale face with blooming cheeks transfixed him. They were both very tall and lean, like two halves of the same thing. But where Charlotte was fair, Clark's coloring bore the trace of shadows, with his dark curls and a faintly Arabian nose. Charlotte drew her sucked-pink finger from her mouth.

"Why are you smiling?" she said.

"God damn," he said, almost involuntarily. "You look beautiful. Beautiful like a child. It's amazing. You look like you're about seven. And you've just come in from playing outside."

"I'd never want to be seven again," said Charlotte.

"No no," Clark said, quickly. "Seven in *spirit*."

"I'd never want to be seven again," said Charlotte, "especially in spirit."

"Well, what I meant was," Clark shifted the present behind his back, "you look happy. I like to see you happy."

Charlotte lowered her gaze to Clark's navel. Her face grew serious. With one finger, she drew a tendril of lank blonde hair out of her eyes. She appeared to be trying to see the birthday present through his body.

She looked up. "I hope you didn't get me something too extravagant," she said. "I said no extravagance this year. With the new house..."

Clark's extravagance with money was sometimes an issue, but for him to bring up her bringing it up would have been a whole new, collateral issue. Today was a birthday. (Charlotte's birthday, though did it matter whose in a marriage?) A day to remember the hunger one felt as a child for each new thing, each singular word, and each honest daybreak. He fondled the gift box behind his back.

"It's not extravagant," he said.

"OK," she said, looking up at the ceiling. "It's not flowers, and it's not extravagant."

What is it, Charlotte Adair thought, out of all things? A gift. A birthday gift. Suddenly, she found herself believing that inside this small box was one of the fantastical gifts on some long ago wish list—a harp, a pony, a castle. The thought made her giddy. She felt that she was at the center of everything. She was the birthday girl. The gift was for her. She closed her eyes and felt the rupturing pressure of laughter in her chest. But just then, her eyes snapped open. She was afraid to stand there with her eyes closed, like a child praying to God. She looked around suspiciously at the strange new kitchen. Then she looked at her husband's shadowed face—almond colored, pretty-eyed. What if for some reason he was pulling her leg?

"Let me see it," she said.

"No way," laughed Clark. "You'll guess right away if you see it."

She stepped back. She took a deep breath. Of course he wasn't pulling her leg. He liked giving presents. He liked birthdays.

"Is it . . . ," she said, "another figurine?"

Clark fondled the gift again. It was not a figurine, because the figurine had definitely been an issue last year. He agreed now that the figurine had been a strange gift, something suited better for a child. But it had looked so much *like* her, he still wanted to protest, a porcelain maiden wringing out her long, long hair.

"Nope," he said. "It's absolutely not a figurine."

"Hey," Charlotte said, looking up at him flirtatiously. "Did you get me that necklace I saw at Shand's the other day? Did you sneak back over there and buy that necklace for me?"

It took Clark a moment to remember the necklace they had seen together.

"No," he said. "Listen, I didn't get you jewelry."

"OK," said Charlotte. "Then can I have it now?"

"Come on," said Clark. "Use your imagination."

But as soon as he said the word "imagination" he knew he had chosen the wrong word. Since they'd begun moving in, Charlotte's lack of imagination had become an issue. She would stare at the empty rooms, blinking, unable to envision. Clark felt that she was unable to let go of the expected places and uses for things. She was unable to dream, unable to guess. The week previous, he had gone so far as to call her "boring," and to prove that she was not boring, she took everything back out of the kitchen cabinets and dashed them against the wall. Among other things, such as all of his mother's china, she had broken the birthday figurine, and in that case, thought Clark, the figurine wasn't such a hot thing for her to bring up either.

Charlotte's eyes darkened. She too remembered the incident with the china. She saw the white plates flying like epithets toward the wall. Although they'd had their tussles, they

had never fought like that, never thrown anything, and now their first house was anointed in a shower of porcelain. She felt very bad about it and also implicitly reaccused. She took a deep breath. She tried to remember that today was her birthday, a day to claim one's place at the center of everything before one has to step aside for the next of six billion people, a day to feel cosmically attractive, a day to feel wanted, and she tried to get back to that dreamy, closed-eyed feeling of the birthday girl.

But instead she said, helpless to stop herself, "Is it a rope to hang myself with?"

Suddenly, the issues abounded: Charlotte's rather dark sense of humor, her inability to behave sportingly, and more disastrously, the horribly recent death of Clark's mother, which had been a suicide.

Charlotte's eyes flew open when she realized what she had said.

"Just kidding," she said. "Oh God. It was a joke. I wasn't thinking. It was an innocent joke."

Clark still held the birthday gift behind his back. His eyes flickered momentarily, but his expression did not change.

"Are you going to guess for real or not?" he asked.

Charlotte looked down. Softly she said, "I guessed for real already, Clark."

"Just twice? That's all the guesses you've got in you?"

"Can't I just *have* it?" said Charlotte.

"But this is the best part," he said, "the guessing. Listen," the gift box—covered sloppily in striped wrapping paper—hung now at his side. "You don't enjoy your birthday, Charlotte. You always get sad on your birthday. I thought I'd try to make it fun this year."

They both stood silently for a moment. It was true, about Charlotte and birthdays. She was trying very hard to be the birthday girl but she couldn't stick with it. Outside, the dog gave one of his long, heartbroken howls. They could hear him dragging his chain back and forth across the patio. Clark looked at the floor and Charlotte looked out the window. Outside, the hawthorn tree shook its angry naked branches.

"February," Charlotte sighed. "Why did I have to be born in the sorriest month of the year?"

"See?" said Clark, "There you go, getting sad."

"A lot of times, with adopted children, they just make up the birthday. I mean, sometimes they don't know. So maybe I wasn't even born today. I've never seen my birth certificate. They might have just fudged the papers at the agency. Maybe I was filling their February quota."

"That's it," Clark gestured with his shoulder. "The gift is related to the time of year. Understand? You're getting warm."

"A raincoat?" Charlotte squinted.

"No," said Clark, putting the box behind his back again. It was then he realized that a raincoat was what he should have gotten. A raincoat would have been a lot better than the stupid thing he had gotten. His arms hurt, holding the gift on and on this way. And yet it seemed too late to just give it to her.

"Ohhh," she said. "I know."

A smile arose on Charlotte's face, and for a moment, Clark felt very badly. She guessed that the gift was two tickets to go see the ballet *Giselle* that was being performed in a nearby city, something she had hinted at wanting several times but which was wrong. Then, undeterred, she guessed a scarf, then an umbrella, both of which were wrong but were, in fact, related to the time of year. She guessed a number of reason-

able things, and Clark noticed that each one would have made a better gift than the stupid gift he'd gotten and that all of them were wrong. He had thought long and hard about what present to buy his wife this year, and yet none of those reasonable things had come to mind. He listened, looking at the kitchen walls, which still smelled fresh and wet with paint, his arms aching.

A rabbit bounced out of the hedge into the backyard. Charlotte looked at it.

"Did you get me a rabbit?" she said.

Then she began to guess whatever came to mind and at that point Clark did not stop her: a meat grinder, an egg beater, an anteater, a cheeseburger, a sheepherder, a rectal thermometer, a flower for Algernon, a purple heart, a dark horse, a bird in the hand, a burning bush, a kind word, a million-dollar idea, a guardian angel, immortal life.

"Oh Christ," she said, and began to cry.

Clark went to the pantry and put the gift box on the topmost shelf. They had forgotten to paint the pantry. He looked at the decrepit wallpaper.

"I'll give it to you later," he said aloud in the pantry.

Charlotte sat down at the breakfast table and Clark sat down beside her. He passed her a tissue. They were silent for some time.

"We've been fighting since the day we moved into this house," said Charlotte. "We never used to fight."

"Well, let's not fight anymore then," said Clark. "It's the stress."

"There's been a lot of stress. The funeral. Going through old things. Moving in, all at the same time."

"Packing, unpacking. Painting."

"Breaking plates. So much to do." Charlotte smiled shyly, then she started to cry again.

"Don't cry," Clark said tenderly, grasping her hand.

"Why not?" she said.

"I don't know," he said. "I guess you can go ahead and have a cry."

"A birthday cry," said Charlotte, smiling a little.

"Sure," said Clark. "A birthday cry. You save up enough of those things and someday you'll have yourself a birthday river."

"My own river," said Charlotte.

Clark played with the napkin holder they had just unpacked. He lifted the small bar up and down. He pretended to guillotine the screaming napkins until he finally got her to laugh.

"Well, Charlie," said Clark. "Let me tell you. You certainly used your imagination."

Charlotte laughed again, drying her tears with a napkin. Then they looked out the window together, where the damp winds of February blew like an army of witches over the small yard.

YOU

S he was gone now. But way back, when Clark was a boy, his mother had explained the world. She explained how things functioned, the secrets of things. For example, the passage of time (according to Vera Adair) was overseen by a dwarf who lived in a shack in the desert somewhere outside of Las Vegas. At night, he would hoist the moon up by a rope and pulley. In the morning, of course, he would raise the sun. And the weather? The weather was operated by a series of magical animals that lived in the mountains.

These were stories for children but she did not stop telling them. Even after Clark grew up and realized that his mother had invented everything, that little of what she said was true, even after they told him she was unwell, even after she ended her own life to drive the point home, Clark still thought of the weather in exactly the same way. When it snowed, he thought of the black bear of winter standing on a cliff, tossing the snow out of his satchel. At least once, at the start of every spring, he pictured the little lamb of spring gamboling down from the mountains to deliver the rosebuds.

It was not that Clark still believed these stories were true,

he merely appreciated their familiarity. He knew he was
the son of a madwoman. The years before her death were the
worst. Like his father and sister, he did not cry at her funeral.
And now all of them were behaving as if her death were far
more than three months distant. But in secret, in some sort of
inviolable compact, Clark held onto her crazy and wonderful
stories, much in the same way that aging ladies held onto their
handsome dead fiancés of distant wars. Even now, as the morning was breaking pinkly over his first March in his first house,
paying out the light, there was this sense of magic, of tremen-
dous unpredictability, at which his mother's stories had once
hinted. He missed her. Of course he did. Also, he was relieved.

The wind fell still over the house, and the winter-naked
trees rattled outside the bedroom window. I'll have to take a
look at that window, Clark thought to himself. The thought
made him proud: He would have to take a look at the window. Who else but him, the man of the house? Clark inhaled
and smiled. He raised himself on the pillow, and looked down
into his wife's face.

"Have you ever been in love?" he asked her.

Charlotte grinned sleepily. She drew her forearm across
her brow. Her long hair, which was the color of sugar corn
and without the slightest curl, crisscrossed the pillow. She had
a small mouth and a sudden, snaggle-toothed smile. He could
see the tiny ridges at the bottoms of her teeth.

"I mean," said Clark, "besides with me."

"Who says I'm in love with you?" said Charlotte.

"I don't know. Are you?"

"I'm not that kind of girl."

Clark tickled her just under the arm, and she squirmed.
"Really?"

"I'm asleep," she said. "I'm *asleep*. Shall I hang a sign from my nose?"

"What about that guy who went into the military? The one who proposed to you at a Drive-Thru. Private Downy-ourpants."

"Who, him?" said Charlotte, rolling her eyes. "No, we weren't in love. We just happened to be running from love in the same direction."

Clark smiled. Because it was his first spring-like morning in their new house, and because his pretty young wife had teased him and was warm beside him on the bed, and because he was surviving all that had happened, it felt like the first smile of his life. Everything was wide open. Everything was first. Spring was the most hopeful season, and soon the grounds around the new house would bloom, who knew what buried flowers there were, and maybe Charlotte could finally have a garden. He was proud to own this house. He felt sure that a garden would arise immaculately out of the ground around it. He felt hopeful and young like that.

Marriage, he thought, touching his wife's hair. Marriage, what is it? Why does a person do it? Why does a person grab a girl by the shoulder as she is walking, one summer evening, turn her around and ask her to marry him? Maybe it's simply the most outrageous thing a man can do. A man can jump from buildings, a man can wrestle bulls, but inwardly he will know none of it can compare to swinging a girl round and asking her to marry him. It was irrepressible. It was outrageous. Marriage is the only punishment great enough to fit the crime of love. Clark laughed to himself, fingering Charlotte's hair. Marriage is the only punishment great enough to fit the crime of love, he thought. But of course, marriage

didn't even feel like a punishment. Three years into it, it no longer even felt outrageous. Only on certain mornings, waking up next to her, did he realize what an adventure it was. A billion times it had happened before them, and yet here they were, the first.

Charlotte rolled over and put her cheek on her arm and looked at him. A faintly sweet, confectionery scent arose from her body. Knots of crusted sleep hung in her lashes. Her dark eyes were soft and engorged with dreams. She looked terribly pretty to him.

"You?" she asked him. "I bet you've been in love a million times. Give me a number, if you had to count them."

"Not a million," Clark said. "Three or four."

"Three or four million times?"

"No," said Clark, laughing and leaning back against the headboard. "Three or four times. I have fallen in love with groups of women, but I just count them once."

"Groups? Ethnic groups?"

"No, no. I fell in love with my sister's friends when I was a boy. They used to practice kissing on me. Sometimes more than kissing. I've told you about them. Janine Hoffstead. Kiki Zuckerman. Oh, Kiki," Clark sighed. "I was in love then."

"You were not in love," said Charlotte, clucking her tongue. "You knew nothing about love. You were a boy."

"Then I'm still a boy. Because I still know nothing about love. And I'm still in love."

Charlotte turned her head away, but he could tell she was smiling.

"Who is she?" she asked.

She rolled on her back and yawned, curling up her fists with the thumbs tucked in. She arched her back, her skin vis-

ible through her thin pink rayon nightgown. She stretched one consummately white leg, then she stretched the other. Her skin was so white, almost transparent at the wrists and knees. In the summer, she would carry herself about in the shade like a vial of mercury, wearing a frayed straw hat.

"You," he said.

The bear of winter grunted in his sleep. The dwarf in the desert dropped a grain of sand. The lamb of spring leapt across the clean blue sky. The sky outside was clear and new and first.

"Well," Charlotte said. "I was thinking of making jelly toast. Your father sent us some blackberry jam."

Clark paused. He looked at the walls for a moment, his eyes casting beyond them.

Finally he said, "I won't eat that. Probably his girlfriend made it, the hag."

"You're talking about Mrs. Flanigan," said Charlotte.

"Yes, Mrs. Flanigan," he answered darkly. "The home-wrecker."

"Clark," Charlotte said. "Let's not go into it."

"You asked if I wanted her blackberry jam."

"Yes, but let's not go into it. That home was wrecked long before Mrs. Flanigan came into the picture. You know that."

Clark stared at the ceiling. He wasn't listening anymore. He didn't know that.

"If you want to talk about love," he said. "If you want to talk about two people in love, talk about Mother and Dad. Way back when. Before Mrs. Flanigan. Before me. When they lived together in a chicken coop on the Rio Grande, right after they were married. When they were our age."

Charlotte sat up and reached for her robe.

"I feel a disagreement coming on," she murmured. "I think I'm coming down with a disagreement." She smiled over her shoulder, but Clark was still staring at the ceiling.

Charlotte had heard about the chicken coop half a dozen times by now. Each time it caused her pain. Not only did it pain her that he told the same story over and over with no nod to the fact that she'd already heard it, it pained her to know it was not true. Well, it was a Vera story. It contained *elements* of the truth— one malarial summer spent in Texas with a church group. The truth one had to get from Clark's father in the kitchen over a glass of bourbon. From there, on many a visit, Charlotte had watched her handsome new husband sitting on a tiny footstool in the living room, laughing and hugging his knees, while a woman in a white nightgown spoke in her protracted, actorly way, making large facial motions as if playing to a large room, and Charlotte would think yes, he loves her, but surely he doesn't *believe* her.

"I mean it was unheard of," Clark was saying, "two gringos out there on *La Frontera*. They even had a pet macaw. They called it…"

"Julito," whispered Charlotte, looking at her feet.

"Julito. My father helped the locals build a church at night, by the light of a thousand candles. Afterwards, they'd fall asleep watching the stars through the chicken wire…"

"Clark," said Charlotte. "Do you want some jelly toast? I'll make it for you. I won't use Mrs. Flanigan's jam."

But looking over at him on the bed, she saw that he was far away in his false memories, a place in which he'd been taking refuge more and more often. How *abstract* he'd become lately, she thought, how hard to reach, when what she loved about him before was his nearness, his ready-to-go-ness, how

he would pull a peach out of his pocket, sit down right then and there, and they would make a picnic out of it. He was the most spontaneous person she'd ever met, always alert to some small joy, always jumping up. She had been terribly drawn to this quality, for she herself was reticent, skeptical, often overcome with a great passivity when faced with something lovely she wanted. Now, beside her, he laughed softly to himself. His head was submerged in the pillow like a dark pearl, the black curls flattened against both temples. His large, gray eyes, almost astral in their gray blueness, looked so rapt that she almost turned to see what he was looking at. But of course he was looking at nothing. He was remembering. Remembering things that had never happened.

Charlotte felt her pulse quicken. She felt stranded in the present. She didn't want to be left alone in the present in this new house. Suddenly, the house felt hollow and large and impossible to furnish. She put the robe over her shoulders and looked outside into the small backyard.

"I should work on that garden today," she said. "I should plant things."

"Mom and Dad didn't speak the language," said Clark. "But they learned how to do things sort of anthropologically. Mother learned to make milk from scratch. She learned to make milk the way the Mexicans did."

"Don't Mexicans get milk from *cows*," Charlotte said to the window, "the way everybody else does?"

Clark held up one finger instructively. "She watched, you see. She *listened*. She had the patience of a monk. And in that little schoolhouse by the creek, she would teach the local children to recite William Blake. 'It was many and many a year ago in a kingdom by the sea'…"

"But you weren't there, Clark," said Charlotte. "You don't know what happened between them. You can't tell what somebody else's marriage is really like. That's not even *Blake*, by the way."

And then, out of nowhere, Clark actually proceeded to recite the poem anyway, his long-fingered hands folded over his chest, "'. . . That a maiden there lived who you may know,' and so on and so on and so on."

Charlotte gripped the sheets.

"Jesus, Clark," she said. "If it was all so wonderful, then where was your *dad* when your mother died?"

Clark winced. His eyes refocused. He was back. He stared coldly at the ceiling.

"Yes, why don't you go make jelly toast?" he said. "Use Mrs. Flanigan's jam."

Charlotte lay back down on the bed and hung her head.

"Damn," she said.

She was sorry she had said that, about his mother. She felt better, but she was still sorry she had said it. She watched Clark's chest rise and fall.

"You know I'm just jealous," she said, rolling onto his chest and tickling his nipple. "I'm an orphan. I don't have all sorts of pretty childhood stories like you do. Family legends. Starlight. Candlelight."

Clark said nothing. He continued to stare at the ceiling.

"I'm really sorry," she said. "We promised we wouldn't fight."

When he still didn't answer, she murmured, "Please, Clark. I swear I'll never speak of her that way again. I'll never mention it again."

He blinked slowly and his face seemed to relax. He had

long, dark eyelashes that sprouted delicately like the tines of a fish fork.

"You know, maybe you were right," Charlotte said. "Maybe they *were* in love."

"And maybe you were right," he said, turning away. "Maybe I was just a boy."